DESTINED

ALSO BY
ALI ARCHER

DESOLATION
Sacrifice
Become (book 1)
Desolate (book 2)
Destined (book 3)
Desolation Diaries v. 1-3

MINNIE KIM: VAMPIRE GIRL
First Kisses Suck (book 1)
Deadly Sweethearts (book 2)
Seoul Demon (book 3)
Blood Moon (book 4)
Den of Death (book 5)

THE EDEN PROJECT
Dragon Protocol

DESTINED

ALI ARCHER

Edited and Proofread by Lorie Humpherys

Cover Design by NovakIllustration.com
Formatting: NovelNinjutsu.com

www.aliarcher.com

This story has always been for you—
for the person who never thought
they were good enough,
that there was no coming back from Hell.

It's never too late to choose, so no matter what happens,
don't lose hope—you might just discover
who you are destined to become.

PROLOGUE

DESI

Time is irrelevant as I hang in the dark. My body turns to stone beneath the cold and endless expanse of space. But I can see. And I can think.

I do a lot of both.

I spend the first forever screaming until my voice is raw—a totally pointless exercise considering no one can hear me. I spend the next forever trying to wrench my wrists free of the shackles that bind me to Yggdrasil—another wasted effort.

And then I try to convince the strange, rock-like creatures that live around me to set me free, but they only stare with dark, viscous eyes. Occasionally they bare their teeth and screech, but the sound is muted, almost absent—something for which I am glad. I don't think I want to hear their cries.

They seem to dare each other to get close to me. To touch my fingers. My hair. I close my eyes and imagine myself somewhere else. Anywhere else.

At first, I wish for Asgard, for Michael's embrace, for the perfect place, all sunshine and warmth—the exact opposite of my fate. Then I wish for what I had before all this began—my rooms in Father's fortress in Hell. The constant sameness I hated with a passion seems now like heaven.

I wish to be anything, anywhere, but here.

And yet, moment after moment, for years, centuries, eons, minutes—here is where I am.

ONE

MICHAEL

I have worn down the white stone path beneath my feet from the constant pounding as I trudge along this same route. Every hour, every day.

First to Heimdall. Then to Fiahre. Then to Odin.

Heimdall. Fiahre. Odin.

Always the same.

I stopped in front of the Wheelhouse and breathed deeply. My gaze traveled the height of the column beside me, upward to the lintel above my head. There is a frieze carved there—a depiction of Heimdall, arms outstretched, stars alighting on his fingertips, the nine worlds rotating around him.

Gripping the hilt of the sword that rests at my hip, I stepped across the threshold and into the great god's domain. In the middle of the deepest black of space, the Wheelhouse shone like a beacon, the columns that mark the corners of its octagonal shape a potential doorway to the other eight worlds.

Heimdall stood across from me. Before him a portal glowed with all the colors of light—from where I stood it looked like a prism imbued with the golden glow of a sun. For Heimdall, it was a window into a world. It was knowledge.

I opened my mouth to speak, but his deep voice rumbled through the Wheelhouse before I found my own voice.

"There is nothing." I saw him in profile, saw his downcast eyes, felt his regret. But he didn't look at me. The conversation was over. He knew I would be back and we would repeat what had become a sort of ritual for us both.

In the time immediately following Desi's disappearance, I traveled to all the worlds—all save for Helheimer, to which Odin forbade me go. In every kingdom it was the same. Desi could not be found. I bowed my head, fighting the shame that clawed at my insides. If only . . .

As I turned on my heels to leave, my eyes rose to the lintel again. Heimdall is the greatest of us all. His power allows us to exist, allows the worlds to keep their orbit, allows Gardians to travel to Midgard.

And yet, even he could not help me.

As I marched to Valhalla, I doubted Odin's wisdom, his warning. He foresaw that Hell would claim me, remake me in its image once more—and that I, as Gardian and Demon both—would once again strive to bring Loki's damnation to Midgard. But now I thought, if I could save Desi it would be worth it. She wouldn't allow me to destroy Earth, I felt sure of it. I knew it would cause her pain— endless, torrential pain—but if she lived, if she was well and whole . . . Once she discovered the price I had paid to rescue her, she would never forgive me—never forgive herself. Just as I would never forgive myself if there was something I could do to save her.

Directly across from the Bridge rose the gold-and-white-stone steps of Valhalla, the warriors' eternal rest— though no warrior actually rests there. As I approached I could hear the ring of steel on steel. A large golden door barred the way. Figures in relief on the door's surface shifted and changed, replaying the great warriors' victories. Beyond the door, I heard voices rising with laughter, with friendly taunts that invited the sparring to greater intensity.

I raised my fist to knock, for none could enter without the invitation of a Valkyrie, the guardian warriors, but the door opened before my fist landed on its surface.

Fiahre stood there, ever dressed for war. Her wheat-colored hair coiled at her neck, her golden winged helmet resting in the crook of her gauntleted arm. She smiled sadly, but said nothing. Her eyes said it all.

I clenched my jaw and tightened the grip on my sword hilt.

Her eyes flicked to my weapon, then back to my face, her expression softening. "Would you like to fight?"

Not, *There is no news*. Not, *We have discovered nothing*.

Instead, "Come."

For a moment I hesitated—I hadn't yet spoken with Odin for . . . long enough that there could have been news. He might have heard something.

"Come," Fiahre insisted. She stepped forward and took my elbow in her hand. She led me into the great hall, past the groups that sparred around us and all the way to the far wall that opened into a glorious semi-circular courtyard where roses grew among the trees and sunlight filtered down in gentle fingers. Above the peak of the circular retaining wall that defined the courtyard, Desi's spear, the Spear of Destiny, rotated within a force field of shining light. I tried not to look at it, tried not to remember Desi's fierce beauty when she spun the weapon in her hands.

Fiahre let go of my arm and placed her helm on her head, the golden nose guard slipping down between her eyes, casting her face in shadow. I was ill-prepared for this fight—she wore armor while I wore a kilt, a tunic and my sword. And then I thought, *I have my sword. What need have I for more?*

No sooner had I thought this than my blade was in my hands, the hilt a comfort in my grasp, and we had begun the slow dance of battle.

She was brilliant. Her armor reflected the light of the sun and several times it blinded me, distracting me and giving her openings I couldn't afford to give. Already my thighs and upper arms stung where she struck me with the flat of her blade. But I was not without my cunning. A lock of her hair fell to the stone as proof.

Fiahre laughed when she saw that, where any other woman would be furious. She held up her hand and bent to retrieve my reward. She held it out to me, encouraging a smile and attaining it. "Well fought, my friend."

I bowed my head and closed her fingers around the lock of hair on her palm. "Give it to Longinus with my apologies."

"Apologies?" Her full lips climbed into a half-smile, her eyes still lost to me beneath her helm. She seemed to hold her breath—probably waiting to see how much of their relationship I'd guessed. Their love for one another was as obvious as the sun on a cloudless day to everyone but themselves.

"That he must endure his days without the pleasure of your company."

She laughed, a warm sound that softened her usual stern demeanor—it was not hard to see how any man, but particularly Longinus, would be drawn by such a complex and remarkable woman. Fiahre put her hand on my shoulder and I knew it was time to go. I paused for a moment, feeling myself slip again into what had become my fate. My sorrow fell upon my back like an old and tattered cape.

Fiahre walked with me to the doors, neither of us speaking, both of us remembering. It reminded me that there are myriad ways one can mourn. For Fiahre, losing Desi meant losing a part of her own family—Desi's mother had been more than sister-Valkyrie, more than queen. Mahria had been Fiahre's sister—with Desi's death, Fiahre had no one left to claim as kin.

But Desi is not dead.

I swallowed and raised my chin. I hardened my gaze, focusing on the one thing that mattered most—finding Desi.

"I can sense your restlessness." Fiahre stopped before the golden doors, blocking my exit. "I know what you intend to do." By the set of her jaw, the fire that sparked in her eyes, she truly did know. "You can't go."

I glared at her. "No one can stop me."

"Heimdall can. And you know he will."

I adjusted my belt, the hang of the scabbard at my waist, before looking back at my friend. "I will find a way."

Fiahre's gaze did not waver from mine. I sensed her weighing her argument, considering how best to sway me. "Assuming you found her—and she actually wants to leave—" I opened my mouth to protest, but Fiahre held up her hand, stopping me. "You know what will happen."

"I know I am not as strong as Desi. My return to Helheimer would awaken the demon inside me and the evil of Loki's poison would lay claim to me once more."

"And Desi would be called upon to kill you. You would do that to her?"

This time I didn't need to consider my answer. "Yes." I'd sacrifice her view of me, even her view of herself, it meant she was alive and safe.

Fiahre's lovely face grew dark with disapproval, but I ignored her and stared at the double door behind her. She turned and pulled it open the right door, and I opened the other, so we both stood in the threshold side by side. And saw Heimdall striding toward us, his footsteps thundering into Asgard, lightning flashing in his dark eyes.

The gigantic god strode to Odin's hall, which stood adjacent to Valhalla. He glowered when he saw us and motioned for us to follow. We had to run to do so. As Fiahre and I approached the entryway a pair of youths, clad in white togas with golden spears at their sides and golden leafed circlets on their heads, lowered their eyes as they held the doors open for us.

We slowed our pace, unwilling to disturb Odin's hall with our noise, yet anxious to reach Heimdall and learn what news had drawn the great god out of his Wheelhouse. We could no longer see him, but the boys lining the hall tipped their spears in unison to indicate the way in which we should go. We passed them in silence, the only sound the footfalls of our sandals on the tiled floor, and the occasional clink of Fiahre's sword as it bounced against her armored kilt.

We were directed to the courtyard behind Odin's great reception hall. Heimdall's face looked even more fierce than usual, his irises swirling like restless clouds in a moody sky. When Fiahre and I stepped over the threshold, Odin raised his arm in an arc over his head, erecting a shimmering dome of privacy.

"Tell us; what is your news, my friend?" Odin asked.

I flexed my fingers around my sword, foreknowledge filling my mind with a sense of doom. I both feared and hoped for news of Desi. *Please let her be well. Let her live.*

Heimdall glared at each of us and I felt nothing of the friendship we shared—though we were the best of friends. The man who stood before me now was a god, his status lifting him above our bond for the moment.

"The Muspellarians are mobilizing."

At first none of us responded. His words fell like bombs on my mind and it took me several seconds to process their meaning. Muspellarians—the giants of the fire world Muspelheim. The giants prophesied to play an integral role in Ragnarok—the great war to end all wars, the end of everything as we knew it.

"Does Garin lead them?" Odin's words were smooth, measured, as if he took great care to avoid revealing his emotions.

Heimdall shook his head sharply. "I cannot tell but . . . I think not. There has been much travel the past weeks, Svarts and Giants, but when I turn my eye to them, they retreat to their worlds. I fear there is some greater force at work, a leader beyond Garin's capacity to rouse the other worlds."

"Who do you think leads them? What could be the meaning behind this?" I'd taken a step forward, my blood rushing, urging me into action. A battle would be a welcome distraction. Odin leveled a dark look in my direction while the corner of Heimdall's lips twitched minutely upward. "My apologies." I bowed my head and inwardly berated myself.

Odin placed his hand on my shoulder and squeezed it gently. "I have not replaced you as my general, Michael. In matters of war you have no need to stand on formality." He looked to Heimdall. "This seems to be beyond Loki's reach—have you seen any indication of his involvement?"

Heimdall's mouth resumed its natural frown. "No. I have had my eye on Loki and he remains in Helheimer, playing his usual games." He glanced at me and for a moment his eyes softened. "I'm sorry my friend, but we must consider . . ." He held my gaze until understanding dawned and I swallowed against the growing dryness in my throat.

"I fear it may be Desolation who is at the heart of this turn of events."

"Desolation," Odin said, his eyebrows drawing downward in displeasure. "What indication do you have that she is involved?"

"I have none. Only . . ." Heimdall glanced my way again, then angled his body so he stood slightly before me, and I could not see his face. And he could not see mine. "The source of this new threat, this new leader, is unknown to me. And while I have not been able to locate Desolation, it is still my belief that she lives."

Heimdall had been the only one to encourage my hope that Desi hadn't been killed by the strange black tornado that swept across the battlefield eight months ago. He claimed to have a sense for her spirit, said he could still feel her alive —somewhere. Though the *where* seemed to be the question no one could answer. He could not find her in Helheimer, could not find her on Midgard, nor on any of the other worlds. She seemed to have disappeared, vanished from all the worlds.

I also believed she still lived—when I did not fear she'd been claimed by a soul-eater. If she had been taken by one of the ancient, ravenous creatures, there would be no trace of her. No spirit. No body. No soul. Nothing to hold my love like a sacred vessel.

Odin cleared his throat but did not address Heimdall's statement about Desi. He believed Loki had killed his daughter as punishment for her betrayal, for her constant desire to leave him. Loki had never cared for anything he could not control, and when Desi cut her own finger off in an effort to separate herself from the evil of Solomon's Ring—even with the poison of hellfire racing through her veins—she'd proven once and for all that she was not his tool, not a weapon in his hand.

Desi was herself, something Loki had not predicted but Odin had hoped for. Desi had been a free spirit of the truest kind. *Is*, I told myself. *Because she* lives. *Somewhere, somehow, my beloved lives.*

"We must investigate the war preparations on Muspelheim." Odin's smooth voice shifted from introspective to commanding, its deep resonance striking a gong in my heart. "Fiahre, you and a small contingent—an honor guard, no more—will go to King Garin. Ascertain what his plans are, and remind him of our oath of peace."

Fiahre bowed her head and thumped her fist to her chest plate, her gauntlet causing the metal to ring out like a hammer on an anvil.

13

Odin rested his gaze on me, considering. "My son. Fiahre could use you at her side, but I understand you have not yet completed the mission you have claimed for yourself."

My mission. To find and save Desi.

To find and save a girl even Odin himself believed no longer existed.

I fought the temptation to glance at Heimdall, or even Fiahre. Fought to stay focused on the here and now, on Odin, on the question at hand. Could I set aside my search for Desi in order to help my sister warriors assess a possible threat?

"I will join them." My voice sounded only slightly less firm than I intended.

Odin nodded. "Very well, then. You have my permission to leave immediately."

As he moved, his royal blue robe, adorned with tiny sparkling diamonds, swirled out behind him. It reminded me of the falling night. Of stars in an azure sky. He raised his arm to drop the privacy dome.

"There is one more thing," Heimdall said in his dark, gravelly voice. Odin dropped his arm without dismissing the dome, and all of us turned surprised expressions upon the giant but he refused to acknowledge us. "There is a . . ." He clenched his right fist, the tendons and muscles in his forearm flexing like taught ropes beneath his skin. He seemed to make the decision to move forward, because he released his fist and looked up, meeting Odin's eyes with his usual ferocity.

"There is a dog on the Bifrost."

"A dog."

"Yes."

Odin coughed, then scratched at his temple. He stared at the floor and I saw the corners of his mouth twitch upward. He cleared his throat, fighting laughter, then met Heimdall's gaze. "And how is this relevant, Lord Heimdall?"

"I believe it is a harbinger of some kind. A messenger. Its appearance at the Door to Muspelheim drew my attention to that world."

"Then its message is to warn us of war?" Odin asked.

"I do not believe so. It seems somehow . . . more personal." Heimdall's eyes flicked toward me, the barest movement, but the suggestion was clear—he thought the dog had something to do with me. Something to do with Desi.

"Well, what do you propose we do about this dog?" Odin asked, the slightest hint of frustration cutting into his voice.

"Is the emissary from Alfheim still here?"

"Yes. He is taking his repose. He is to be undisturbed." Odin's tone suggested he was not about to rouse the Alfahr so he could talk to a dog.

Frustration oozed from Heimdall's countenance. He closed his eyes—I knew that look; it was Heimdall counting to ten before speaking, fighting to compose a more diplomatic response than the one he likely wanted to give. "I understand, great king. But perhaps . . ." Heimdall let his words trail away, his eyes fixed on something beyond the dome of light.

I followed his line of sight and watched as a tall, slender man of unrivaled beauty came into view. He nodded once before stepping through the barrier that separated us. A barrier that should have been impenetrable.

"You are in need of me?" the man asked, looking at each of us. His unnaturally pale skin radiated a pearlescent light as if lit from within, and when his gaze met mine, the silvery-blue hue of his large eyes took my breath away.

"My apologies, li'Morl. It was not my intention to disturb you," Odin said.

"Your apologies are unnecessary, Lord Odin, for you did not disturb my repose. But do you mean to say I am mistaken? You do not have need of my gifts?"

Heimdall cleared his throat, but it was Odin who responded in an even tone. "We do have need of you, if you are willing."

li'Morl smiled, a warm, radiant expression that reached into my soul, bathing my senses in warmth. I felt myself relax, my worries ease—and the Alfahr had not even looked directly at me.

"Of course I am willing," li'Morl said. "What is it you would ask of me?"

"There is a dog on the Bifrost, before the Door to Muspelheim," Heimdall said.

"Ah yes, I am familiar with the place." li'Morl straightened the lapel of his pale blue jacket and looked upward, as if seeing a vision above his head. "They make the most remarkable horseshoes there—did you know their shoes are the only ones our sh'lil will wear? You might not imagine that the giant Muspellarians could create anything so fine and delicate as the glass shoes the sh'lil prefer—yet they do. It is the strangest thing." li'Morl chuckled and my ears tingled as though a chime had been rung.

He glanced around at us, making my knees quiver when his gaze fell on me. It seemed he looked for a beat too long, that he peered into my very soul. Something flickered behind his eyes, but the moment passed before I could name what it was I saw.

"But of course you have no interest in the sh'lil's preference for the glass shoes. You say there is a dog on the Bifrost? How interesting. How, exactly, may I be of service?"

Heimdall cleared his throat, the sound like a rock slide grating against my ears, a stark contrast to the Alfahr's musical voice. "It was my hope that you could communicate with this dog, as I feel it is an emissary of some kind."

"An emissary from the lost girl, I presume?"

His words hit me like a physical punch to my gut. "What do you know of Desi—of the lost girl?" I blurted out before I could restrain myself.

li'Morl looked at me once again and I wished he would look somewhere else. His scrutiny was more than I could bear. It felt like he saw right through me and straight into the part of me I wished to keep secret—even from myself. . "Why, I know precious little," he said, though I had the distinct impression he knew more than he let on. "I do know you cherish her. I know she has walked a path no one in all the nine worlds could walk. I know she has defied Loki and his plans to lay waste to Midgard."

I sighed, frustrated with this light elf's circular talking. His charms were beginning to wear thin and my patience was nearly gone.

li'Morl stepped very near to me, so close I could feel the warmth of his body, so close the hairs on my arms rose and reached out to him. I rejected his natural charm—anything that aroused such a response in me without my permission made me uncomfortable.

Even while I raised my arms to gently push him out of such close proximity, I found myself drawn into his eyes. A part of my mind screamed for me to look away—I'd heard stories of Gardians whose minds had been forever captivated by the wonders and beauties of Alfheim and the light elves.

But in the moment I stared into the elf's eyes, I thought I saw Desi, hanging by her wrists, her head flopping forward so her hair hid her face from view. I jerked back, shocked at the vision, then immediately leaned forward to peer into his eyes again. But li'Morl moved away, an indecipherable smile on his face.

"Wait!" I reached out and grabbed the elf by the elbow, tugging him toward me. "What did you do? What did you show me?"

"Michael." Odin's voice held the sting of warning. "Unhand our guest."

But I was powerless to obey my king.

"What is it you think you saw, young warrior?"

"Desi! You showed me Desi. Is she alive? Where is she? Please—" I tightened my grip and stepped as close to him as we had been before, peering into his eyes. "Show her to me. Tell me where she is."

"Michael." Odin repeated, this time not a request but a command. Fiahre put her hand on my arm and applied pressure, pulling me away from li'Morl, forcing me to let go of him and the vision he had given me.

li'Morl only watched, the same infuriating smile on his lips. "I'm afraid I do not know what you saw, Michael. You have my deepest apologies." He ducked his head in a small bow, but it felt insincere. It felt like deception.

Fiahre placed her hand on my chest, her other hand still gripping my arm, and walked me back to the edge of the dome. Odin glowered at me before returning his attention to Heimdall and li'Morl.

"Ah, the fervor of youth." li'Morl chuckled, his laughter like pieces of sunshine sprinkling around us. I grit my teeth and dug my nails into the palms of my hands. How could he be so flippant in the face of my agony?

I shrugged away from Fiahre and she smirked, but her lips stayed shut.

"Shall we go then?" li'Morl asked, gesturing toward the hall. "And Lord Odin, do not fear asking me to serve in this small way. It is the least I can do in thanks for your generosity."

"You are most kind." Odin's voice stretched tight with tension, but the Alfahr did not seem to notice. I realized then that Odin did not trust the Alfahr, or at least this particular one, very much. I had always assumed their relationship with Asgard was an easy one, but I had never before stood this close to a light elf, never had such an extended interaction with one. The way I seemed to lose myself under his scrutiny, even slightly, disturbed me and fueled my discomfort.

Perhaps Odin, like me, disliked anything that aroused so much emotion without his permission.

li'Morl stepped forward and as he passed through the dome Odin had erected, the barrier fell away. I wondered if Odin had removed it, or if li'Morl had done it himself.

The brief glimpse of Desi hung before my mind's eye like a beacon. The elf knew something and I would not stop until I discovered what it was. I made to turn and follow the others from the hall when Odin said my name.

I couldn't recall the expression on his face as one I'd ever seen before—it looked like shame. He tipped his head, as if unwilling to meet my eyes. He put his hand on my arm and leveled his gaze with mine. I read every emotion in them. His love for me and hope for me—and for Desi. His fear for his people, for the children of Midgard.

"There is something you need to know."

"Yes, my lord?"

"You asked once, some time ago, about the Ascended Ones, Aaron and Lucy."

I didn't answer, only watched him. Of course I remembered, and he knew it. I'd wondered if he could contact them, asked if they could find Desi, if they knew of her existence. The Ascended Ones had become friends to the Vanir gods when they took to the great expanse of space. And the Vanir gods were widely accepted as knowing everything—or certainly most things—as they were the creators of the Nine Worlds. If anyone could have detected Desi, dead or alive, it would have been the Ascended Ones and the Vanir gods.

I'd asked Odin, but he had been evasive, claiming he could not call upon an Ascended One, that they had to initiate contact. He had not heard from Aaron nor Lucy since the day we'd gone to battle against Desi and Loki eight months ago.

"I had meant to offer you some hope, but I fear my efforts may have only added to your pain." Though sorrow and regret fought within Odin's eyes, this time he did not look away.

"What is it, King Odin?" Hope and dread clutched me like a tourniquet had been wound around my heart and twisted tight. I swallowed against the bile that rose in my throat. What reason would my king have to lie to me, if not to save my feelings? *She can't be dead.*

"After you asked about Aaron and Lucy, I went in search of an answer for you, but they were already gone."

I listened to his words as if he spoke them from a very deep well. It seemed to take eons for the sound to reach my ears and just as long for my brain to comprehend them.

"It is my understanding that they suspected where she might be, but it was a place where no Ascended One has gone, indeed a place where nothing exists. They put their eternal lives at great risk, and I fear—" he closed his eyes, as if striving to retain his composure. When his eyes finally met mine, he seemed so sad that I felt my own heart break. "I fear they are lost."

"Where—" My voice cracked. I glanced down, cleared my throat, rallied myself to try again. "Where did they believe her to be?"

"At the bottom of everything, my son. Beneath Ygdrasyll."

My world shattered. I felt as if I were falling—off the Bridge, through the vastness of space. Cold. Alone.

Opening my eyes, I swallowed the curse that rose to my tongue and forced myself to clasp Odin's arm. I squeezed, perhaps more firmly than I ought to have done, while he looked at me with surprise. "Thank you my Lord," I choked out. While his gaze met mine a feeling of peace wound its way around my heart. Whatever his reason for keeping this information from me, at least now I knew. I softened my grip as the first genuine smile in so long found its way to my face. "Thank you."

I hurried to the Door, my hope a radiant thing that buoyed my steps and my heart. Now to find a way to reach the end of the worlds—but at least I had a place to look. Surely there would be a way.

I caught up to Fiahre, who cut me a look, but didn't inquire why Odin wanted to speak with me.

"When will you leave?" I finally asked, eager to think about something else, anxious for a distraction from the wild beating of my heart.

"I will see what information this Alfahr is able to glean from the dog. Then I will rouse my sisters and head for Muspelheim. You never said," her eyes flicked to mine, "whether you will join us, or not."

I considered the question as I stared at li'Morl's back.

"I will join you."

TWO

MICHAEL

I stood with the others in the Wheelhouse, the blood in my veins rushing to a faster beat in response to the great power housed there. The white iridescent light of the well of power cast all of us in its shadow—except for li'Morl, who himself shone, his inner light rising to match that of the Well.

I remembered a story I'd heard as a boy when my mother taught me about the nine worlds. How Odin came to be the Great King, ruler of Asgard and Guardian Regent of Midgard. She told me that the Vanir gods had collected material from all across the Great Unknown and created a well of their power and good intentions. With that power they made the worlds and stars, and connected them all to one another with the Bifrost—a bridge made of power and light—because they were family and the gods wished to always have a way to travel between each of their worlds. She said the Svart god's children were among the first to be created and would often play unsupervised on the Bifrost.

One day, one of the children, for they were a wild and unruly bunch, pushed another over the well and directly into the power that lived there. They thought the child lost, but after some time, he returned, though he was never the same. And so the light elves, the Alfahr, were born out of a Svartalfahr, now known as the dark elves, and the magic of eternal light.

Now as I watched li'Morl reflect the Well's light I came to accept what my mother had told me as true. It only helped ease my fears a little—the Svarts were creatures of endless self-satisfaction and mischievousness, after all. I had no promise the Alfahr were any different.

"Let us speak with your dog," li'Morl said.

Heimdall raised his horn to his lips and blew one low, perfect note that reached between my ears and squeezed my eardrums, setting every nerve in my body humming. I closed my eyes against the exquisite pressure—until a moment later the sensation eased and I opened my eyes once more.

Before me, just past li'Morl who knelt on the Bridge, sat a dog. Or rather, a Hound.

My mind looped on all the times I'd scowled at the immobile Hounds as they stood guard over Desi's chambers—the place where Loki imprisoned me. Occasionally I would see the pair of them in dog form, watching me as I walked the corridor to Loki's throne room. Now one Hound stared at me so intently that li'Morl twisted around to look at me as well.

"It seems he wishes to speak with you."

I cleared my throat and rubbed the back of my neck. "What makes you think that? And how can he talk to me?" I knew I was stalling. Knew I wasn't speaking the whole truth. Knew that I'd be forced to live this reality, this pain, the second the words were out of my mouth.

The Hound rose up on its haunches and began to shift from dog to man. His hair slipped beneath his flesh and his legs and body straightened until a golden-skinned youth appeared, dressed in a shendyt, his bare chest adorned with a wide gold and turquoise collar. For a moment he wore the face of Anubis until it, too, faded away. The Bifrost caused his golden adornments to sparkle in its cold, multi-faceted light. Beneath his headdress, warm brown eyes regarded me. I could read nothing in their depths but an endless sorrow.

"We serve the young mistress," the Hound intoned. His voice sounded flat, and somehow less resonant than it had been when I last heard him speak. Then I realized: I was used to hearing the Hounds speak in unison. Not once had I ever heard one of them speak alone. Nor had I ever seen one without the other. I craned my neck to locate his companion, but he was not in sight. Only this one Hound stood before me, his dark eyes fixed on my face.

"The young mistress?" I asked, when my thoughts singled in on what he had said.

"We serve the young mistress," the Hound repeated.

"What about the grand mistress?" I asked. Helena had created the Hounds to be her own personal bodyguards. When Loki had overthrown and imprisoned her at the bottom of Ygdrasyll, she ordered the Hounds to stay with Loki's daughter—the young mistress. Desi. Helena's goal was to have them one day lead Desi to her prison, which was exactly what they did.

The Hound clenched his jaw—a greater show of emotion than I'd ever seen from the creature. "We serve the young mistress," he repeated.

li'Morl smoothed the front of his tunic and smiled ingratiatingly at me. "It seems he serves the young mistress. Does this mean something to you?"

"Where is your companion?" I asked the Hound, stepping past li'Morl, ignoring both his question and his person. I stopped when I stood close to the Hound, when I could look into his black eyes, and see the rise and fall of his chest.

The Hound fisted his hands and the tendons beneath his collarbone flexed. "He is no more," he said at last.

"No more." I shook my head sharply, trying to make sense of the Hound's words—of his very presence here in the Wheelhouse. The Hounds were created by Helena— truly glorified guard dogs. That one spoke to me, seemingly of his own volition, was a marvel.

The Hound met my gaze and nodded his head in the barest of movements.

"And yet you said "we"," I pressed. "'*We* serve the young mistress,' you said."

The Hound did not look away. "I . . . misspoke," he said. "It is only I. Helonius no longer . . . exists."

"What happened to him?" I asked before I could stop myself. I was vaguely aware of Odin joining us, the others shifting to make room for him. Everyone was as intent on the answers as I, but I didn't let myself feel concern for any of them. Hope tingled in my belly, threatening to rise, to sweep me away on its promise of Desi-returned. I swallowed, forcing the hope down, forcing it to remain hidden away until I knew what the appearance of this Hound meant.

"The grand mistress, she . . ." The Hound shuddered and swallowed, his Adam's apple bouncing in his throat. Moisture glistened under his eyes and along his neck. He raised his chin. "She bargained his life in a duel to the death with the pet of the king of the Svarts. Helonius fought valiantly, but in the end the zhaghmar creature overcame him and . . . and devoured him."

The pain in the Hound's eyes radiated in almost palpable waves. "The grand mistress laughed," he added.

And I understood. Helonius had been his brother, his companion through what might have been centuries, eons even. And Helena had treated his life as though it meant nothing.

"We no longer serve the grand mistress. We serve the young mistress only," the Hound intoned. He dropped his head to his chest for a moment before looking up again. "*I* serve the young mistress."

I reached out and placed my hand on the Hound's arm, giving a small squeeze. "I am sorry for your loss, friend."

The Hound tipped his head forward in gratitude.

"It seems you had little need for my translation services after all," li'Morl said from behind me, his voice as cool as glass.

"Yet, it seems your presence is still fortuitous." Odin's deep voice rumbled along the Bifrost. "Come. Let us return to Asgard. It would seem we have much to discuss regarding Helena and the Svarts." Stepping past me, Odin addressed the Hound.

"Horonius."

The Hound considered Odin for the space of two heartbeats. "You are the Great Gardian Odin?"

"I am." Odin bowed his head in acknowledgement. He held his arm out, beckoning to Horonius. "Will you return with us and share what information you have on Helena and Desolation?"

"We—I—serve the young mistress. Yes, I will accompany you."

Odin moved away then, and Horonius fell into step beside him. We returned to Asgard, a journey of mere moments that felt like an eternity to me as every footfall echoed the beating of my heart. Every beat, every step rang with hope. Rang with the name of my beloved.

De-si.

De-si.

De-si.

In Odin's palace, we joined him around a table while white-clad children served us fruit and drink, meats and cheeses. The children giggled when Heimdall glared at them as they tried to dodge him and avoid getting poked by one of his large fingers. He didn't exactly fit at Odin's table, though the enormous god had been a guest often enough to know how to accommodate himself—and how to tease the children.

Horonius refused to sit or take nourishment, electing instead to stand behind my right shoulder. I had to angle my body in order to keep him in my line of sight. Since our encounter on the Bridge he had refused to meet my gaze— or anyone else's it seemed. li'Morl sat across the table, an amused smile on his face and a glint in his eye. When Odin asked Horonius to tell the story of how he came to be standing in Asgard, li'Morl leaned forward, his elbows propped on the table.

I schooled my features, striving to hide the turmoil in my mind and heart. My thoughts swirled through memories of Helheimer, of the soul eaters, of Knowles, of Loki's throne room and his cronies. Memories of Desi, both terrible and glorious. Memories of when she glowed with golden light, memories of when she was mine.

Memories of the black-as-night tendrils that snaked across her skin and the look of death in her eyes when she was under the influence of Loki's dark poison.

Memories of that terrible storm that swept across the battlefield on the day she cut Solomon's Ring from her finger and broke Loki's hold on her.

Memories of the last moment I saw her.

And now Horonius stood at my shoulder, betraying Helena's confidences, claiming allegiance to my love, offering me the first real hope I'd had in so long that Desi might yet live. That she still might come back to me.

For the hundredth time I pushed such speculations aside so I could concentrate on the conversation unfolding around me. It seemed Helena had been rousing the spirits of the inhabitants of both Muspelheim and Svartalheim, making wild promises that mostly involved gifting them each Midgard—a world they could not both possess and was certainly not hers to give.

"You say she coaxed the Svart king from his castle? I've not heard of him stepping beyond its walls since the attacks on his life several eons ago." Odin leaned forward, his hands clasped before him.

"Yes, my Lord. Our mistress lured him with a contest he could not refuse—a battle of wit and strength. My brother and I are known throughout all the worlds for our bravery and single-mindedness in protecting our grand mistress."

"I have heard the claims, yes."

"The grand mistress chained me to a platform far above the arena—though had she only commanded me, I would not have strayed from my perch. Perhaps she saw a weakness in me even I did not know existed." He allowed his eyes to rise from the tabletop but stopped short of reaching Odin's face.

"I am sure she knew you would have rushed to your brother's aide, had you been able," Odin said in a soothing tone.

Horonius nodded once before continuing his story. "The grand mistress made a procession to the center of the arena, Helonius at her shoulder. She wore little clothing and made a great show of demonstrating for the eager crowd that she was unarmed."

"And in the arena—there is no magic. Is that correct?" li'Morl asked.

"Yes, Lord."

li'Morl's eyes twinkled. "Fascinating."

"Helonius is—was—a brave and fierce warrior. I felt certain he would prevail against any foe. But then . . . then the king of the Svarts ordered the great gate be opened. At first there was no sound, even the raucous crowd had quieted. For several long heartbeats I was sure the whole thing would end with laughter and perhaps a few drinks around the old king's table. Not once did I consider that I had embraced my brother for the last time."

Horonius bowed his head and took several deep breaths.

"Take your time, my son," Odin said.

A child appeared at Horonius's elbow and held forward a tray on which sat a cup, its sides glistening with condensation. The Hound at last reached out and drew the cup to his lips, draining its contents in three gulps.

"My thanks," he said quietly, placing the empty cup on the child's tray. She smiled at him before dashing away.

"When finally a trumpeting sound was heard from the shadows of the open cage, the crowd erupted with shouts of delight. My brother stood; unmoving, unconcerned surely, while I craned my neck to see what creature so excited the crowd. I felt certain the grand mistress would not willingly put herself in harm's way, so while I still felt unsure of what was going on I was unwilling to think that things could go badly.

"And of course Helonius was trained—created—to put the grand mistress's life before his own, no matter the cost, no matter the circumstances.

"When his weapons materialized in his hands and I saw his body stiffen, I strained to see what he saw—a creature unlike any I had ever laid eyes on—or dared even imagine." Though his skin had taken on a greenish shade of gray and his hands flexed at his side, Horonius continued. "A zhaghmar appeared, lumbering from the shadows, raising its mammoth trunk, longer than a man, into the air and trumpeting with ear-splitting cries.

"At first it moved slowly, its black eyes rolling to take in the crowd, even to take note of me, lashed to the column above it. It trumpeted again and I wished I could cover my ears with my hands as Helonius did.

"And then the zhaghmar saw the grand mistress. He sniffed the air, pawed with his great clawed feet in the dirt. The mistress laughed and said, 'Come to me, darling. Let's take a look at you.'

"But the creature did not come gently as her tone might have invited. It shook its head, its wild black mane quivering in the strange silver-light of the Svartalheim sun. Helonius stepped in front of our mistress and crossed his weapons, the ankh and scepter, in front of his chest as he had been taught to do when we were boys in Pharaoh's court. But . . ." His words caught in his throat and it took several coughs to clear it so he could continue.

"Helonius fought valiantly, but the top of his head only reached the creature's belly. Enraged by the crowd's taunting and the nearness of our mistress—a tempting treat for him, I'm sure—the zhaghmar made quick work of my brother. It wasn't long before the creature's scales gleamed with his blood."

I glanced at the Hound, but saw his features set and his mouth in a hard line, revealing nothing of the turmoil that must have raged within.

"The creature wrapped its trunk around the mistresses's neck, but stopped when its master called an end. The king stood then, and clapped. Clapped! And my mistress joined him in his laughter. She laughed while my brother lay at her feet, his blood staining the dirt beneath her sandals." Finally his voice revealed his venom and his eyes blazed with fury—he seemed powerless to stop now, the words the only thing holding a flood of emotion at bay.

"He died for her, believing her to be in mortal danger. Though truly, even if he had known it was not but a game, he would have served her however she asked. But in that moment—" He looked upward, allowing himself to peer directly into Odin's eyes for the first time. "Lord, forgive me, but in that moment I vowed I would never again serve her. She did not even stoop to straighten his shendyt or grant him any form of dignity. She stepped on his back as she left the arena to resume her negotiations with the king.

"I hung on the column through the day, while the crowd screamed in morbid delight as the zhaghmar devoured Helonius, and watched my brother's blood dry in the dirt. I was still fettered when the crowd disbursed at last and the zhaghmar was coaxed back into its cave.

"It was not until the next day that I was cut from the ropes and thrown into the chariot that carried my mistress to the Door Between Worlds. She said naught but that I should stand and take my place by her side. That she had need of my services. And I . . . I did as she commanded."

"Then how is it you're here?" I asked. My voice sounded foreign, out of place in the room that seemed to have been filled, shaped and molded by the Hound's tragic tale.

"It wasn't until I saw her beginning the same negotiations with the king of Muspelheim, this time sacrificing a full half of her entourage—the strange rock-like creatures, the genii—to feed the Giants at the king's table, that I understood she cared nothing for us. We were her children; we had served her for so long, doing exactly as she commanded for longer than I dare remember. Yet she is willing to sacrifice every one of us for the pleasure of those whose allegiance she wishes to secure."

The Hound's voice hitched and he choked on the anger that tangled with the sorrow in his throat. His hands curled into fists until he had regained some of his composure.

"When she retired to her chamber that night, I escaped the palace and found the Door Between Worlds. I hoped it would only be a matter of time before the great god, Lord Heimdall, would find me waiting and I hoped he would deign to speak with me. This is all I dared hoped for, and yet you grant me so much more," he added with a gesture to those sitting at the table.

"I am grateful for the chance to tell my story, if only to do my brother the honor of remembering him in such dignified company."

Though he ended formally, Horonius fidgeted with the pleats of his shendyt and shifted his weight from foot to foot.

"Thank you, son," Odin said kindly. "Now, won't you please sit down?"

Horonius hesitated, looking at each of our faces to gauge, I guessed, whether this truly was allowed. When his eyes met mine, I tried to smile, tried to show him that I was sorry for his loss, but when he looked away I was unsure of what had passed between us. The Hound took a seat to the left of me, moving his chair so he would not accidentally brush his body against my own. I scooted away as well, wishing to accommodate him, to give him the space he seemed to need.

"Fascinating," li'Morl said. He steepled his fingers against his lips and regarded Horonius as if Odin had just announced him to be the final course of our meal. I closed my eyes against the rising tide of hatred for the light elf. How could he be so . . . so cold and detached in the face of such agony? "I believe I shall retire to my chamber," he said abruptly. After dabbing the corners of his lips with his napkin, he laid it on top of his plate and stood.

"If you will excuse me, Lord Odin, everyone." He inclined his head in a sort of bow before turning smartly on his heel and striding away.

In the absence of the Alfahr, I felt a weight lift from my heart. Being in his presence reminded me of my time in Helheimer—a time I was most anxious to forget. But there I had experienced a similar sense of oppression and euphoria. A desire to be and do things that were completely unlike me when I was in my right mind. li'Morl was far too beautiful, his presence far too overwhelming, to ever feel like I was my own man while he was near. Judging by the looks on my companions' faces, I was in good company. Fiahre even exhaled loudly, then had to apologize when she realized what she had done.

Odin smiled indulgently at her and I wondered how the Alfahr affected him. He drank from his goblet, and with a wave of his hand he brought our attention back to him. My body tensed, my anticipation rising as I thought, *Now, we will talk of how to rescue Desi.*

"Tell me, Horonius. What is your mistress's purpose in allying with the kings of the other worlds?" By the tone of his voice, the steel in his eyes, I detected my king already had a motive in mind, but my impatience gripped me with a fist of steel. I could not bear these games, these pleasantries for much longer. I shifted in my chair, trying to focus on the Hound sitting next to me while my ears rushed with all the questions that weren't being asked. *Tell me how to reach her. Tell me how to rescue her.*

"My understanding is limited, great king," Horonius said carefully. He examined his hands, his long, lean fingers, as he spread and then curled them on the tabletop in a rhythmic fashion. "I believe she is trying to rally an army—a host with which to come against Helheimer."

"An army—to raise against Loki? To oust him from his throne—excuse me, from her throne?" Odin asked.

Horonius met Odin's stare, his face and lips soft. The Hound seemed to be without guile, an innocent—a far cry from the fierce warrior-protector I'd thought him to be. But even my compassion for him was overshadowed by my need to find Desi.

"My mistress once ruled Helheimer as queen. She was already lord of that place when she spirited my brother and me from our home. At first we were adornments only, pets she took pleasure in shaping into the creatures she dreamed us to be." He glanced at Fiahre, for what purpose I did not know. "And we were glad of it—our mistress was beautiful, kind, and with her we were like sons of the court.

"In those days Helheimer wasn't the dark and evil place it is now. In those days, our lady delighted in a court of pleasure."

Odin sighed. "Yes, I am aware of the type of world Helena created for herself. She always claimed she would create a world where everyone would be welcome, everyone would be loved, and everyone would be happy. I'm afraid, however, that she had much the same idea of happiness as my grandson—a commonality, I believe, that led to her dethronement."

I shifted slightly in my chair. Fiahre caught my eye with a stern expression and looked down at my hands with meaning. My hands were tied into tight fists, the cloth napkin starting to tear in my grip. I dropped my hands to my lap and tried to steady my breathing, to attain a state of peace and patience. But while I could muster peace, for the most part, I'd never been much of a patient man. Right now, it was all I could do not to jump up and shout for the Hound to tell me how to find Desi.

Horonius nodded. "Yes, my king, you are exactly right. Though I am not educated and wouldn't dare speak to the righteous purposes of the gods, it did seem to me as though Loki and Helena shared a great many things in common before he rose up and imprisoned her—and my brother and I were tasked with waiting, then guarding, the young mistress when she arrived. My queen seemed to anticipate it all—though it did little to save her."

"And now that she is free, she wishes to reclaim her throne? Her world?" Fiahre asked.

"Yes, lady."

"Are the Svartalheim and Muspelheim kings with her?" Odin asked, a hard edge to his voice.

"I believe so, my lord."

Odin looked at Heimdall and for a moment the two of them considered one another without speaking. I couldn't bear looking at them, listening to their intelligence-gathering when they were not revealing the only thing that mattered to me. Instead, I stared at the enormous tapestry on the wall across from me.

The weaving depicted the Vanir gods, Freyja, Freyr, Heimdall and others, reaching with outstretched arms. Floating in the starless sky all around their reaching hands were the eight Aesir gods, Odin and Helena among them.

Heimdall startled me from my reverie when he scraped his enormous chair back and rose to his feet. He looked first to Fiahre, and then to me. "I have seen the peoples of Svartalheim and Muspelheim rallying. They have gathered at the Doors, preparing to travel. It is not our concern, should their route take them directly to Helheimer—though I do not hold much faith that their warmongering will stop there."

"Fiahre." Odin placed his hand on hers. "We will not follow them to Helheimer, but we must protect Midgard at all costs. Be ready. The Valkyrie may need to go to battle at a moment's notice. If the Giants turn their gaze on Midgard, it could be the beginning of Ragnarok—my children are not ready for such a thing. And so we must be."

Fiahre slipped from her chair and knelt on one knee. She bowed her head as she placed her fist over her heart. "We will be ready, great king."

She stood and whirled away, the polished metal strips on her kilt clinking.

"Wait," I said, rising quickly to my feet. Fiahre stopped and angled toward me, though I didn't necessarily mean she should stop. Odin and Heimdall looked at me and I felt grateful for their friendship—my speaking out of turn would not be tolerated by most gods, but my question couldn't wait any longer. I cleared my throat.

"Apologies, my lords." I swallowed and attempted to choose my words carefully. "But . . . what of . . ." My words failed me. I dropped my head to my chest and cursed myself for loving someone as special as Desolation. I knew from the start her path would not be an easy one, that she had a journey far more perilous than I could guess. But from that first day, I had promised I would follow her anywhere. That I would always find her. If there was a chance she yet lived, I *must* find her.

"Great King." I took five steps toward Odin, then dropped to my knee as Fiahre had done only moments before. "Forgive me, but I would like your permission to slip into the throng and join them on their path to Helheimer. Perhaps I could . . ." Reason was not with me and my mind grappled to find some argument that would hold sway over my king. "Perhaps you would allow me to enter Helheimer and discover for myself if Desolation yet lives."

Silence fell around me like a wet cape and my heart began to slow as sorrow took the place of the hope that had so recently swelled within me. When Odin's hand fell gently onto my head, I knew. My request would be denied.

"Look at me, my son." I did as Odin commanded.

"You may not go to that place if you ever hope to return. At least, as yourself. Go, and you sacrifice all that you are. Stay. Allow someone to go in your stead, and you may yet see Desolation again."

"I don't care for myself, Lord. It is I that caused her to be there—if that's where she is. It's the only place we haven't searched and now with the forces . . . it would be a perfect opportunity to enter without notice. Great King," I raised my gaze to his as I pressed all my hope, all my need into it. He had to let me go. Had to understand why it must be me.

"It was my weapon that let Loki's poison into her soul. My hand that drove it in. Whatever she has become, whatever has happened to her since that night—it is my burden to bear. It is my responsibility to return her, to make things right, as best I can."

Odin sighed, but then straightened, smoothing the folds of his tunic. He stood tall and when his gaze returned to mine, I knew it was my king who stood before me, King of Asgard and Guardian Regent of Midgard. "I am sorry Michael." His voice held the resolute tone he always adopted when issuing orders or establishing law. "I cannot allow you to sacrifice yourself in this way. Rest assured, as soon as it is possible, an envoy will be sent and every attempt will be made to locate Desolation—but you will remain here." He turned on his heel to leave. "Remember she is my kin. We will find her. Until then, I have need of your expertise as my general while we formulate the best way to respond to Helena's actions." When he reached the doorway, he turned back. "All will be made clear very soon." With that he strode from the room, leaving me reeling and utterly crushed.

Heimdall laid his large hand on my shoulder. Despite its great weight, his hand brought me comfort.

Horonius shook his head. "How can you not know? The young mistress is very much alive and I know exactly where she is."

THREE

DESI

The little creature cocks its head, a sly grin snaking across its sharp features.

"It's okay. It's all right," I croon.

It takes a hesitant step forward. Then another. All the while its black eyes stare, testing me, judging me. We have been getting to know one another for so long now, I'm surprised when it creeps forward and reaches below the ledge to touch the tip of one of my fingers. This is the first time. The first time any one of them has touched me.

And it is the first time I have felt any sensation beyond the metal at my wrists, my hair on my face, my tears on my cheeks.

I laugh out loud and the creature jumps backward, startled. "No, no. It's okay, it's okay." But the little one has dashed to the cairn of rocks that tumble down the side of the doorway on the ledge opposite me—rocks I assume are its family, because that's the same pile the little genii always resolves from.

I am beyond sad that I scared the creature away. I wanted nothing more than to make a friend. To touch . . . anything. I am tired of the few sensations I have. Shedding another tear is as common to me now as the endlessness of space around me.

Unchanging and eternal.

I close my eyes, or they remain open.

I sleep or stay wide awake.

I dream or imagine I live a thousand lifetimes as someone else, as no one else, with Michael or without him. With or without love.

An eternity has passed.

Or no time at all.

All or nothing I can't be sure.

But then there is something else.

A light.

And then two.

FOUR

JAMES

Come on, bright eyes. Talk to me. Tell me what you saw." Mir lay curled in the middle of our bed, her knees pulled tightly to her chest, the sheet soaked with tears where her cheek rested. I stroked her back and willed her to talk to me, to let me help her carry this burden.

She'd gone months without a single dream. Things had seemed so quiet on the demon-front that we even thought we could leave Desert Peak. Thought we could take a break from The Hallowed. Thought all that crazy stuff was behind us.

We'd had three weeks of awesome in Paris. The flat we'd rented was about two feet by two feet but it was right in the heart of the art district—four blocks from the culinary institute and zero blocks from Miri's art teacher. It had been perfect. Better than perfect. It had been heaven.

And now this.

I woke early in the morning to find Miri sitting up in bed, her hands clutched to her throat as if someone were strangling her. Her mouth hung open in a soundless scream. To say I was freaked would be a major understatement.

I shook her, called to her, even shouted at her.

And then all of a sudden she collapsed into my arms. Moments later she wiggled herself free and assumed a fetal position, gently rocking her body while sobs sent tremors through her body.

"Come on, baby. Come on bright eyes. Tell me what it was." Because it had to be a dream—the not-normal kind. Had to be. The cold crawly feeling making the hair on my arms stand up confirmed it. This had *The Hallowed* and *bad guys* and *Desi* written all over it.

I'd known it wouldn't last forever, this little escape of ours. But I had hoped it would last long enough for us to get a summer of happiness out of it.

Miri's dad would pretty much kill her if he knew she and I were living together—even though he'd barely blinked when she told him straight to his face that she was going to Paris for the summer whether he liked it or not. I didn't even think he had her address. Though maybe Connie, her maid, had it. Who knew?

Up until this moment I kind of secretly agreed with her dad. When I told her I'd been accepted into Le Cordon Blue, only the best culinary school in the whole world, she'd insisted she come too. "We can't live together," I told her as she lay on the couch with me, our bodies so close there wasn't a single part of me that didn't feel her. "I'll come back every month. I promise. We'll FaceTime or Skype every day. We'll be okay."

She looked at me with the biggest diamond puppy dog eyes ever and I knew I'd give her whatever she wanted— even if I had already told her the answer was definitely no.

"Do you know what it would do to me to sleep with you every night and not—you know?" Miri and I had danced around this subject at least a million times since the very first days we went out. She knew who I'd been before I met her. Heck, I'd still been that guy. We never talked about it, but she knew. She had to know.

"I'm a guy, Mir. I can't just lie next to you and not touch you."

"Well, you can touch me." She looked at me with that infuriating blend of cute and sexy that drove me wild. Except right then it only pissed me off. I raked my hands through my hair, something I rarely did because I didn't like to mess it up.

"You don't get it." I'd untangled myself from her legs and jumped up from the couch. "Don't come with me, unless you're saying we can have sex."

But she wouldn't say that. And I didn't want her to say it. Miri was saving herself for marriage. She was saving herself for me, but when the time was "right,". as in, after the ceremony. I was determined to let her keep that vow— to be worthy of her. And determined to marry her the second she turned eighteen and could get out of her dad's house. Maybe we should just set a date so I could start a countdown calendar or something.

Yet here she was, curled up beside me, on my—*our*— bed. She'd gotten her way. I probably caved mere minutes after that last conversation, I couldn't remember.

So I took a lot of freezing cold showers. And sometimes I went for a walk while she fell asleep so we wouldn't make out. There was nothing more tempting than those sleepy moments before and after sleep. The mornings were the most difficult—but now, right after this terrifying vision of hers? Well, I was glad she wasn't alone. Glad I'd suffered through all those freezing showers, all those late night walks while I missed out on those precious falling-asleep moments with her.

This was the primo reason for living with her, so she wouldn't have to be alone when something this scary happened.

Except now she wouldn't even let me touch her, hold her. Sensing she wasn't going to talk to me anytime soon, I left the apartment and walked to the café on the corner. A dog sat in the doorway of the building across from ours, and followed me as I walked down the street. It kept ten feet behind me, but stopped whenever I stopped. Sat down whenever I looked over my shoulder. It was weird, but nothing to freak about—until I left the café with a bag of warm bagels with to-die-for cream cheese the shop owner made himself, a coffee for me and an extra-large extra-chocolate *chocolat chaud* for Miri, in my hands. The dog was still sitting there.

It had to be a Doberman or something, even though it seemed like it was twice the regular size. Not that I'm an expert on dogs or anything, but there'd been enough of Daniel's clients who went around with these butch dogs to intimidate any idiots who might try to step into their personal space.

I walked right up to the dog. "What are you staring at?" It looked at me and I could have sworn I saw understanding in its eyes. Totally creeped me out. "Whatever." I moved away from the dog, a vague memory of someone saying you should never turn your back on a wild animal or else it would look like weakness, making its oh-so-helpful way through my mind. At least I remembered not to run.

By the time I reached our building I felt completely on edge, expecting the dog to pounce any second. I refused to look back.

At the outer door, I balanced the cups in my arms, my chin resting on the top cup to keep them upright while I finagled the key in the lock and got it open. As I propped the door open with my foot so I could go inside, the dog dashed past me and ran up the stairs.

"What the—" I looked around, hoping someone else had seen how crazy this dog was, but I was alone. I walked up the three flights to our floor, shaking my head and cursing under my breath the whole way.

When I got to our floor, the dog was there. Waiting.

"I don't know what the hell you're doing here, spooky pooch, but get lost." I stood on the landing, talking loudly and making shooing motions as best I could with my hands full, hoping the dog would take off. No way did I want that thing dashing into the apartment. But the dog didn't budge.

Miri opened the door. "What are you doing out here? We've got—" And of course the dog shot past her, nearly knocking her off her feet. "Whoa!"

"That's what I was doing—trying to get this freaking dog out of here. You will not believe how weird it is." I'd only taken two steps into the apartment before I realized we weren't alone. And I'm not just talking about the crazy dog.

There, standing in front of the window, stood a man—an unnaturally tall and unnaturally beautiful, man. With the crazy-ass dog at his feet.

For a split second I froze, didn't move, didn't breathe, didn't blink.

"James? This is li'Morl—did I say that right?" She smiled one of her world-class smiles and the man returned an equally dazzling one. That got me moving forward, setting the bag of bagels and the drinks down on the coffee table, my hands shaking. I straightened slowly, trying to prepare myself for whatever this visit might mean. Was this a good guy, or a bad guy? A friend of Loki's? Or Michael's? But it was the last thought—*has Desi been found?*—that got me adopting my bad-ass persona.

"What kind of name is li'Morl? And your dog is seriously creepy." I knew I was rude. Could see it in Miri's disappointed expression. But the dog had followed me, looked at me with such intelligence—more brains than any dog ought to have. And here was this guy who reeked of self-confidence and other-worldliness and made me feel weak-in-the-knees as if my heart and mind weren't my own anymore. I'd known people like him—pushers, dealers, controllers. It didn't matter how beautiful he was. How much I wanted him to smile and make me feel all warm and fuzzy. What mattered was he was a strange dude with an even stranger dog and my girlfriend had invited him inside when she was all alone. I stepped up to Miri and put my arm around her shoulders. li'Morl's lips curled into a kind smile, but I still didn't trust him.

I knew my stance looked possessive. Knew I probably looked wary and unwilling to hear what he had to say, but only because I knew whatever it was that brought him here—the morning of Miri's first vision in eight months—couldn't be anything good.

"Spill," Miri said, beating me to it. "You said you'd tell me why you're here when James got back. Please tell me you've found her."

li'Morl reached out and took Miri's hand, giving it a squeeze. "I'm sorry," he said. He motioned to the couch, the only thing to sit on besides the bed and coffee table. "Can we sit?"

Miri and li'Morl sat on the couch, I pushed the bag and drinks aside and sat on the coffee table. I should offer the guy a coffee, knew it was rude not to, but I couldn't/wouldn't take my eyes off of him. "It's all right, James," li'Morl said as he leaned forward and put his hand on my knee. I fought to ignore the spark of electricity, the injection of pure contentment that spread through my veins at his touch. "I don't want a coffee."

Damn. The dude could read minds.

li'Morl leaned back and I took a deep breath. Cleared my throat—and my mind. "Uh, I got enough bagels for everyone, though." I handed Miri her cup and she studied me as she took a sip. She'd rip into me later, I knew. She was a big sucker for good manners. I was just a sucker for keeping her safe.

I opened the bag and saw the dog, now sitting at li'Morl's elbow, staring at me. "What the heck is up with your dog? Did you know it followed me all the way to the café and back? It totally freaked me out."

li'Morl and the dog stared at each other for a freaky let's-talk-with-our-minds second until li'Morl gave an almost imperceptible nod. I might've missed it if I hadn't already been watching him so closely.

When li'Morl looked back at me, he seemed to have decided something and in that moment I thought he looked a little less human than he had a second ago. I narrowed my eyes, trying to get a read on just what kind of man—or not-man—this guy was.

"This hound is why I am here," he said. "He believes we have made the right choice in coming to you."

"The dog's why you're here? 'Cause Mir and I aren't really into dogs."

"I like dogs." Miri acted like it was a crime or something to not like dogs.

li'Morl chuckled softly and looked down at his hands in his lap. "I am here to ask you something James, but it's not to watch over . . . my dog." He glanced at the Doberman.

"But first. You had a dream? Do you have these dreams often?" He angled his body so he could look Miri square in the face. He took one of her hands in both of his. I saw the way she sighed, the way her body relaxed with his touch. He was working some kind of mojo on her.

I reached out, pulled her cup from her other hand and intertwined my fingers through hers. That seemed to snap her out of it. She glanced at me, gave a shaky smile, then took a deep breath. "I used to have them more often—when Desi was around, when I worked with the, uh, The Hallowed."

"Wait a second." I shook my head, trying to get all the pieces to line up better because right now nothing made sense. "Don't say anymore, Mir." To li'Morl I said, "You never did say who you are. And what the hell are you doing in my apartment? Who sent you?"

"James!" Miri pulled her hand from li'Morl and slugged me in the thigh.

li'Morl held up his hands, begging Miri to relax. "My apologies. How rude of me not to introduce myself." He stood, and I stood, each of us invading the other's space as we made room for our bodies in the narrow area between the coffee table and couch. He was taller than me, and way more beautiful. His silver hair stood in awesome spikes and briefly, a split second, I wondered how he got it to look so good. Plus, he didn't look old. *A dye-job?* I wondered.

His flawless skin practically glowed and his silvery-blue eyes peering into mine made it impossible to look away.

In a voice as soft as the downy duvet on our bed, li'Morl spoke. "I am an emissary from the Great King Odin. I am not a Gardian, I am merely lending my assistance. My task is to visit you, and convince you to perform a dangerous duty, one you may not survive. It is a thankless task, as there is never just reward for sacrificing yourself for someone else."

He paused, smiling, as if his words made any freaking sense at all.

"But Desolation's contribution to the world—to all the worlds—is deemed to be of great value. I trust you agree?"

I coughed. Cleared my throat. He expected an answer and oh, I wanted to give him one, but my mind felt numb and sticky, like gummy bears had melted all over it. "Uh . . ."

"You know where Desi is?" Miri's voice sounded like it came from far away, but it pierced through the fuzziness in my head and got me turning away from li'Morl. I sank to the table and took Miri's hand in mine again. I resisted sighing with relief and avoided making eye contact with li'Morl.

He sat back down beside Miri. "We have excellent information that indicates where she might be, yes."

"And you're going to rescue her, right? You have to rescue her."

"Tell me of your dream," li'Morl prompted.

I dreaded the words Miri would say next, but then I realized—there was a weird guy here who claimed to have been sent by Odin. And he had a freaky dog with him. Dream or not, things were about to change and nothing could stop that now. So I took a drink of my coffee to cover up the way my Adam's apple bobbed in my suddenly dry throat, because I felt utterly scared to death of *how* everything would change.

"I dreamt that I was trapped somewhere dark. I couldn't move, couldn't scream. My wrists burned ice cold, and it felt like I was shackled to a wall or something. And there were these . . . these creatures that would kind of break off from the rock walls around me and look at me, bare their teeth and screech. Everything sounded muffled, like there wasn't really any sound at all, like my ears were plugged or something." She dropped her gaze to her lap and I felt her skin grow clammy and her hand tremble.

"It was so dark, but I'd been there for a long time so I guess I could see a little bit, ya know? And it seemed like, after a while, those weird rock-creatures kind of became my friends. But then there was this other . . . presence. At first it felt like creepy crawlies tickling all over my body— as if a million spiders had been set loose on me. But then the sensation began to squeeze me, to tighten all around me like there was a boa constrictor on my chest or something. I couldn't breathe. Couldn't do anything. I was choking and while I died I heard this light tinkling laughter like my death was the funniest thing in the world."

I felt a tear drop onto my hand so I set my cup down, scooted over to sit beside her on the couch. Pulled her against me. "Shh, bright eyes. Shh." I stroked her hair, felt her tears soak through my Offspring T-shirt. "You're okay baby. No one's gonna hurt you." I knew the words were stupid. Knew I couldn't promise her that—not knowing what I did about how evil the world was and just how many bad guys would get their rocks off making any one of us hurt.

Miri shook her head against my chest. "But that's the thing. *I* wasn't *me*." She sniffed and sat up, swiping at the tears on her face. She looked at me, then shifted so she faced li'Morl. "I was Desi."

When I glanced at li'Morl, I saw him gazing at his dog, doing that weird *I-can-read-your-mind* thing. I never knew with these people—none of what I thought about the world was true anymore. In the world of crazy dogs and strange über-tall and über-beautiful men, anything was possible.

"Thank you for telling me." li'Morl peered at Miri with such intensity I wondered how she could stand it. "It is as I expected. Michael will be pleased to hear this."

"You've talked with Michael?" Miri brightened like the sun bursting out of cloud cover and my heart lurched to see the hope and happiness shining in her eyes.

"Of course." li'Morl placed his hand on her knee and Miri's face flushed. "He wanted to go in search of Desolation himself but—he has been detained."

"Detained?" Miri's eyes grew wide and I knew she was picturing all sorts of horrible things because Michael wouldn't ever let anything stand in his way of rescuing Desi.

li'Morl chuckled. "It seems he did not agree with Lord Odin's command that he not return to Helheimer. He is in love, that one! He gave no thought to himself, no thought to what Helheimer might do to him if he should return."

"Oh," Miri said, her countenance darkening. "I hadn't thought of that. It's because of what Lucifer made him do, isn't it? Odin doesn't want him to turn into a Horseman of the Apocalypse again."

"You are most perceptive." li'Morl leaned forward until Miri had no choice but to stare into his eyes. "And exactly right." He waved his hand in a dismissive gesture. "When the love-struck Gardian tried to sneak into the delegation that traveled to Helheimer, Heimdall pulled him right out and set him in a—well, I'm not sure what you might call it. A cell? Certainly, a detention room, if you will."

"Oh no!"

"Oh don't be sad, bright eyes,"

I jabbed my hand forward and punched the guy in the shoulder. "Hey. You don't get to call her that, man."

li'Morl had the good sense to look distraught. "My apologies. I merely—well, you do have stunning eyes." Miri laughed. Laughed!

I tugged her closer to me. "Whatever man, can you just get on with why you're here?"

"Certainly." His tone sounded contrite enough, but I didn't like the sparkle in his eye that told me he wasn't sorry at all. "Your dream *Miri*, convinces me that we are on the right course. Except—" He looked at me and I had to lean away from the expression on his face. Because I knew that look. It was the look of a guy who was about to ask someone to do something really stupid and really scary that the someone could never say no to in a million years. And I think li'Morl saw that I knew something of what he'd be asking and that we both already knew I'd say yes, because he didn't finish his sentence. He didn't come right out and ask me to sacrifice my life for Desi.

Because I already knew that's what he was asking.

And he already knew that I would.

"I guess the first thing, would be to explain my friend, here." li'Morl nodded at the dog.

And then the freakiest thing happened.

The dog sat up on its haunches and, looking at me all the while, began to . . . change. I stood and pulled

Miri after me, putting the coffee table between it and us. I'm no chicken, but come on. *Come. On.* "What the hell?" I said, pointing out the obvious. "Is it like, a werewolf or something?"

li'Morl chuckled. "No."

Miri moved to stand beside me, but she held my hand hard.

The Doberman stretched and thickened, its hair disappearing. I stared, my mouth falling open, and I didn't even care that I looked like an idiot, as the dog became a guy right before my eyes.

"He can't very well go around looking like that—" li'Morl said, indicating the white pleated skirt the dog-dude wore with a fancy "collar" and crown-thing. "And as yet, he has refused to wear anything more . . . modern."

I shot a glance at li'Morl who wore a pale blue shirt. Even though the cut was modern and the tailoring exceptional, sky blue was not the best fashion choice.

"Well, what's his name?" Miri asked. But she didn't wait for li'Morl to answer. In typical Miri fashion, she stepped up to the dog-dude, sticking her hand out in front of her. "Hi. I'm Miri. What's your name?" She added her trademark thousand-watt smile and I knew the guy would be powerless before her. Even with bed-head and ratty sweats, the girl shone like a diamond.

Sure enough, dog-dude bowed his head and muttered, "I am not worthy to take your hand, lady. But my name is Horonius, and I thank you for asking."

"Judging by your clothes, I kinda figured it would be something like that." Miri patted him on the arm. When Horonius looked at her, his eyes bright with something like honor or awe, I realized he was really just a kid. A year younger than Miri, maybe. It was hard to tell because he was basically hairless—I couldn't see a single one on his skin at all. And there was a lot of skin.

Miri seemed to read my mind, because she said, "People really don't go around dressed like that these days. I bet James's clothes would fit you. If I got you some stuff, would you put them on?"

Horonius shook his head the barest bit. "I could not, lady. It would not be right to do so."

Miri crossed her arms and got that look on her face I knew really well. There'd be no denying her. "Well, I don't think I can talk to you while you're dressed like a Vegas cabana boy."

Horonius got this horrified look on his face, like the last thing in the world he wanted to do was offend her. "As you wish, lady."

Miri did this little head nod *humph* thing she did whenever she got her way, which way she was certain was the right way, and walked around the kid. She began raiding my drawers for clothing.

"Not my Grateful Dead shirt, okay?"

Miri looked up and rolled her eyes and my heart did this flip-flop thing it did whenever I got a jolt of love for the girl. She had me wrapped around her finger and I knew I'd strip the T-shirt right off my back and give it to whoever she wanted me to, even if it was my favorite shirt. For Miri, I'd do anything. Even walk through Hell. Even go there on purpose to help save her best friend if she asked me.

But she didn't have to ask because Desi was my best friend, too.

Ten minutes later, a very uncomfortable-looking Horonius sat beside me on the coffee table, dressed in my jeans and my vintage straight-from-their-last-concert Grateful Dead shirt. Miri sat across from us, wearing a very satisfied smile. Her bright eyes gleamed at me and I decided that my Offspring shirt had suddenly become my favorite.

"So what's the deal?" Miri asked. "What are you, Horonius? And what are you guys doing here? And what does it all have to do with my dream?" She delivered her questions rapid-fire style and left Horonius a little stunned. It had no effect on me. Except that I beamed at her like the love-sick idiot I was.

Horonius looked as if he might not ever speak again. Like maybe being a dog was better than wearing weird clothes and answering hard questions. But li'Morl didn't have that problem. He answered all her questions without batting an eye.

"The *deal* is." li'Morl seemed amused at Miri's choice of words, "we're going to rescue Desolation. Horonius is a Hound of Hel—not the "hounds of Hell" you hear about in your pop culture, but a creation of Helena's, the goddess of Helheimer. I think—correct me if I am wrong, Horonius—that he was a human boy in Amenhotep the Third's court who, along with his twin brother Helonius, was captured by Helena and pressed into her service as personal servants-slash-guard-dogs-slash-bodyguards. But a short while ago, Helena had his brother killed in order to charm a potential ally into giving her something she wanted."

"Oh my gosh," Miri said. She reached out and touched Horonius's hand, but he didn't move a muscle and continued to stare straight ahead. I figured he was like one of those guards at the queen's palace in London—those guys tourists try to get a rise out of but are famous for, well, doing exactly what Horonius was doing right now. Which was absolutely nothing.

"We're here," li'Morl said, continuing to answer Mir's questions, "because we need your help—or rather, James's help. And it has everything to do with your dream, Miri, because you answered the biggest question that no one on Asgard, or anywhere else, has been able to answer. Desolation is alive."

Miri threw herself into my arms, spontaneously bursting into tears and leaving all us guys, even li'Morl, looking seriously uncomfortable. As for me, I managed to keep the tears to a minimum and I think I hid most of them in Miri's hair. When Miri leaned back to beam her sunshine smile at us, I noticed Horonius hadn't gotten in on the smile-party.

I slapped Horonius on the shoulder, appreciating the perfect worn-in softness of my T-shirt under my hand. "What's got ya down, man?"

He looked at me and I let my hand fall to my lap. "I do not understand," he said.

"Understand what? How you can look so good in a T-shirt and jeans? It's called style, that's what."

"I believe our friend here is anticipating the rescue. A most arduous task, I would imagine." li'Morl's words fell like a wet blanket on our celebration. "Horonius believes he knows where Desolation is—and now that you have dreamed it, Miri, I feel certain his information is correct."

He flicked an invisible something from his pale blue suit-vest. He wasn't wearing any designer I recognized, but man, I'd like to meet his tailor. When he lifted his gaze, it rested on me. "That is where you come in."

To my credit, I didn't hesitate. I might not have known who this guy was, might not like the way his presence made me feel as if I'd do whatever he asked me to do, but I knew what I'd do for Desi, for Miri. "Whatever you need, I'll do it."

A sad-seeming smile flashed across li'Morl's face. "Michael and Desolation are lucky to have such devoted friends. It's fascinating, really. One day, I'd be most interested in speaking with you." He took a breath and straightened his shoulders while I felt like maybe I'd be sick to my stomach. "You are entitled to say no, young James. You have Miri. I can see what you mean to each other. And you may feel differently about your offer to help once you know what needs to be done."

"Dude, you're making me nervous. Just tell me."

li'Morl read my eyes, maybe read my mind for a second, before he nodded. "Desolation is being held in the darkest, most unreachable and dangerous place in all worlds. No one knows of this place except for a very few people—the Hounds among them. Or, Horonius, rather."

I glanced at Horonius, but his expression—his whole body—remained unmoving, unchanged.

"I suspect she's shackled to the bottom of the rocks upon which Ygdrasyll was built, and that she hangs beneath all the worlds, her body suspended over space."

"Oh my gosh." Miri covered her mouth with a trembling hand. I touched her knee, hoping to share some comfort with her, though my own stomach had flipped over and I'd become less confident about avoiding throwing up.

I took a deep breath to steady my nerves. "Okay. So Horonius knows where this is, right? So why can't you go get her?" Notice how I said *you*? I wasn't stupid. Hell was the last place I wanted to go.

"That is why we're here, I'm afraid," li'Morl said. I so did not like where this was going. "Where Desolation is, I cannot go. I am a being of Light, a creature of Alfheim—my kind cannot exist where there is no Light. I'm sure you understand."

I didn't understand the whole Light creatures and bottom-of-the-worlds bit, but I got the gist of it. I'd be going to Hell. Literally. I always thought I'd go there—before Miri, anyway. Before her, I thought Hell was my inevitable destination. But since Miri, I pretty much figured I'd do everything to avoid going there.

"Heimdall, the god of the Bifrost, can get you into Helheimer, but not to the bottom of Ygdrasyll, not to the roots of the world tree. Horonius could go alone, but he cannot break the shackles around Desolation's wrists. Loki created them to resist the Hounds' abilities—else they would have released Helena when he imprisoned her there.

That is why the goddess remained imprisoned until Desolation released her."

I suddenly felt like an insect trapped beneath glass. My legs and wings pinned aside, my guts exposed. I tore my eyes away from li'Morl to look at Miri. Would she want me to go? And maybe never come back?

But she kept her eyes on her hands in her lap, giving up none of her secret thoughts to me.

"Heimdall will get you in as close as he can. Horonius will be with you every step of the way. I'm sure he knows every nook and cranny of Helheimer, including how to cross the river without the soul eaters getting you."

"Soul eaters? What?" My hands felt as if I'd stuck them in a bucket of ice water.

"Do not fear. He will get you to Desolation. All you have to do is release her, and get her out. As I said, Horonius will be with you."

I glanced at Horonius. His stony expression did not comfort me. "But what if she . . . what if she's, you know, the bad Desi? What if she doesn't want to escape? What if she kills me the second I release her?"

"She's not bad," Miri said at the exact moment li'Morl said,

"She is not *bad*."

"I felt it in my dream, Jamie," Miri said, using her nickname for me that I claimed to hate but secretly loved.

"She was full of remorse. Full of regret. That's partly why the dream was so awful—because I felt so, so sad."

"But what about those rock-creatures you saw? If Desi's scared of them, I sure as heck don't want to run into any."

"They are the genii," li'Morl said. Totally unhelpful. "You probably saw them at the battle in Desert Peak—Odin briefed me on your . . . adventures. The genii are the small dwarf-looking rock creatures you fought. Do you remember?"

My face blanched. "Yeah, I remember." It was possible to kill them—sort of. Mostly it was like knocking their rocks apart. So weird.

"But the genii will cause you no harm," li'Morl said. "At least, I believe they will not. As I understand it, they have become as un-enamored of Desolation as Horonius."

I stared at him. "Well, as you understand it. Great. Let's go then!" I jumped up and grabbed my coat, standing at the door like, *Well, let's get a move on.* I knew I was being childish. I could see myself reflected in each of their faces—even Horonius looked disappointed.

Miri stood and came up to me. She took my jacket from my hand and tossed it at the coat rack near the door. It missed and fell to the floor.

"Look." She wrapped her warm fingers around mine. She took a deep breath and let it out slowly. I copied her.

"I know you're scared. I'm scared too. The last thing I want is to lose you." She stepped closer, our toes touching. "You do know that, right?"

I searched her face, this girl I'd totally changed my life for, and I knew; if I didn't rescue Desi, if I didn't at least try, she would feel it as acutely as if I'd abandoned her. She owed her life to Desi, and I owed my life to Miri. I could see how in Miri's heart, there couldn't be one without the other. Saving Desi would be a way for Miri to know that I got it. That I knew what made her tick. That I knew how hard her challenges had been.

Not that Miri needed me to prove that I loved her, but this would prove it. Seriously prove it.

And the truth was, I loved Desi too. In my heart of hearts I knew I couldn't know where she was, couldn't know I had a chance to save her, and not at least try. And I'd had a run-in with Hell before. Akaros hadn't managed to kill me then and he was the biggest bad Hell had to offer—aside from Loki himself and Desi, of course. If li'Morl said I could do this, and Miri believed it, well, maybe I could.

So I squeezed Miri's hands and then let one of them drop as I faced the dog-dude and li'Morl, the guy I inexplicably loved and hated.

"So what's the plan?"

FIVE

DESI

Through the funhouse sound system that is Hell, I hear singing.

At first I believe it to be my imagination. There are no people here. There are no voices here.

There is no singing.

Is it me? Am I singing?

It's a legitimate question. Maybe I've gone insane. Maybe I've lost my sanity along with my hope, my sorrow, my love.

"He'll reach for me, I'll reach for him. Together we'll make an awful din! He'll reach for me, I'll reach for him, he'll think to give but I will take, I'll take and not give back to him."

I hear the words; hear the music that rambles with such meaninglessness that I know—these are not *my* words. Not my tune. But I do know them.

"Come little one, I'll be your mother, and you will never pine for another. Come little one and reach for me, I'll let you shelter betwixt me!"

With the music, a sharp staccato punctuates my endless sameness. And then a light, bobbing through the darkness. I move my head, hiding my eyes behind my hair. And so I see, through this curtain of strands that fall endlessly before my eyes, the unlikeliest sight of all.

Ophelia bobs and sways onto the ledge, the little creature I tried so hard to make friends with, clinging to her skirt.

"Why look at that and that looks, but why?" Ophelia holds the lantern out in front of her, peering at me—as if the light would be sufficient to reveal what has been hidden so long. She bursts out laughing, and even through the muted sounds of Helheimer, her laughter is like a thousand hammers grinding against metal.

"Lookie, lookie!" She chirps to the creature at her ankle. "It's the Dark Princess. The Princess of Darkness." She sits down on the ledge across from me, her legs dangling over empty space.

"Not a very cozy place you've got for yourself here, Princess. Could do with a little fixin' up, I think." She pets the head of the little genii that has crawled onto her lap. "But you've got lovely friends here, don't ya? So lovely." The little one smiles beneath her hand, showing teeth as sharp as a saw.

Ophelia looks up, peering straight into my eyes as if she can see my face behind my hair. Her lips quirk upward and she drags her tongue over her own sharp canines. Her teeth aren't normally like that, I know. It's a game she's playing—with me or the genii, I don't know.

After a moment of staring, I decide to try the card I've been dealt.

"Ophelia," I croak. "It's so nice to see you."

She throws her head back and laughs some more. Behind her dangling feet I see a light. A light in the darkness. Ophelia doesn't take notice of it and for some reason I feel grateful the light is beyond her line of sight. I don't want her to see it.

"I suppose you'll be wantin' me to let you out, now won't you?"

I remain silent, not sure what the right answer is. Every fiber of my being is screaming *yes*, but what is it Ophelia wants to hear? Has she come as Father's messenger? She is one of his cronies, after all. Or has she come for some other purpose? I can't hope to know, unless she tells me herself.

"Ain't got nuffin to say for yourself, Princess? Or do ya think you're too good to be saved by the likes o' me?" She frowns at the genii on her lap, but continues to pet it. It cuddles against her and she presses its head against her chest. I wonder why the little creature lets her touch it, when it's always been afraid of me.

"I—" Careful. I must be careful. Ophelia is evil, but a little less sane than the rest of Father's generals. There's a huge discrepancy between Ophelia and say, Emperor Xin. I have never known why father granted her such rank. "I am honored to have your company, Ophelia."

"Ah! She's honored, she says!" Ophelia sings to the ceiling. "She's honored to have my comp'ny, she says." This last to the creature in her lap.

"Have you come to release me?"

"I didn't even know you was here—but the Master and his whore don't exactly keep me informed, so. Surprise!" I've said the wrong thing. Suggested she isn't as special as she thinks she is. Opened up the whole nasty line of thought that could uncork her volatile temper.

She stares at the genii, petting, petting, petting.

"I only came this way 'cause my friends live here. They're beautiful ain't they? My little rock babies. My rock-a-babies. That's what I call 'em. My rock-a-babies." She looks at me then, her face hard and dangerous. "She doesn't love 'em, ya know. She's forgotten all about 'em.

She only cares for her fancy worlders—oh I've heard the whispers. They think I don't listen, but I do. She thinks she can just take this place back."

She pets the genii with more vigor, pressing down and down. The creature squirms beneath her grasp.

"And the Master! Well. He thinks he has her wrapped around his little finger, he does. But I know women, and it's her what's got 'im wrapped around her pinky. She pulls him around by his ding-a-ling, she does. The Master thinks she'll be his queen.

"I should be his queen!" she screams. She throws the little genii into the great chasm between us, and it falls to its death in silence. Her words echo off the walls around us and are answered by screaming rocks.

I am shocked. Speechless.

Sorrow for the little genii pools in my heart along with all the other sorrows I keep there. The rocks screech as they fall against one another, crawling toward Ophelia who stands as they encircle her.

"Ahhhhh! Get back!" She screams at them. The sound is mind-numbing. Ophelia is like a detonated bomb, leaving the ground blackened and empty all around her. The genii cling to the mountain. "You will serve me!

"Only I remember you. You think she'll come back? Think she cares anything for you? Only I care. Only I remember!"

And to my horror, the genii detach themselves from the walls and move to her feet. They pile atop one another—not to send her to her death, but to reach out for her hand. She takes the rock-formed hand and does a curtsy as if they're about to dance in some old ballroom. Ophelia giggles and picks up the lantern from the floor. She saunters away, hand in hand with the stacked genii. She never once looks back. She leaves without remembering me at all.

"Wait!" I try to shout. But my voice is raw, hoarse. And the rocks are following her, tumbling away and stealing any sound I've managed to make.

I'm alone again.

Except for the light.

The two tiny pricks of light.

They appear closer now and I don't care if it's my imagination or just hope or the crazy finally setting in.

I love the lights. I cling to them. They are my hope. My reason for breathing another day.

The lights draw nearer.

Nearer and nearer and nearer.

I think; *I will die when they reach me.*

I think; *They are soul eaters.*

And oh, I welcome the death of my soul. The release from this body, from this existence.

"Come on," I say to them.

And they come.

I don't know if soul eaters have light. I don't really care. Maybe there are good and bad soul eaters and the bad ones only eat good souls and the good ones only eat bad ones. Maybe the good ones have Light and they've come to eat me, to eat all my darkness and replace it with Light.

I sleep. Or I don't. And dream of nothingness. My waking and sleeping are the same.

Des, I hear.

D.

Speak to us, baby. You can do it.

Lucy?

I'm here baby.

Aaron?

I'm here, D.

I'm crying. Great, gut-wrenching sobs that threaten to drown me.

I can't breathe.

Can't think.

We're here, baby.

We've got you, D.

And oh.

Oh.

Please let this be death. Please let this be forever.

I'm not alone.

I'm not alone.

Wake up, baby. Come on Desolation, wake up for me now.

Lucy?

That's it baby.

You're here?

Open your eyes.

I thought they were open. Thought the blackness wasn't the blackness of my mind. It was all the same, anyway.

Except—

Except this time when I try to open my eyes, they burn at the light, at the brightness before me.

"Ah" I cry. "It's too—" I'm breathless, my eyes squeeze shut against the burning. Burning, burning, burning.

Try again, baby. Is this better?

It takes me a very long time but I try again.

It's easier this time. Better.

And I see . . .

"Lucy," I cry. "Aaron." I cry and cry and cry.

I want to reach for them, to hold them, touch them, but they are Ascended and I am shackled and there is no way this is real.

"You can't be here," I say to them. I can say whatever I want, because they aren't real. They can't be. My arms are stretched above me, affixed to giant shackles to the underside of a cliff at the end of all the worlds—no one's here. No one but me. Even the genii have left.

We're real, D. Aaron smiles, but he doesn't have his piercing. He doesn't have black hair flopping over his eyes. He looks like a spic-and-span version of Aaron. If he was my dream, I'd remember him the way I loved him. All pierced and tattooed. All lonely and mine.

Aaron laughs.

And oh, it sounds just like him.

There's no time, D. Are you with me?

I feel like I've missed something. A conversation I'm only getting half of. "Did I sleep?" I ask the figments of my imagination—they should know, right?

Something like that, Aaron says. *But I need you to concentrate now. Can you do that, D? Can you concentrate?*

I laugh. "Sure, whatever, Aaron." Anything to keep dreaming this dream.

He reaches one hand toward me, his fingers stretching. I'm fascinated by them. They're long and slender, infused with Light. There are no tattoos. No crosses and knots. No fear against the dark.

I wish I didn't fear the dark.

I wish I could be free. Ascended, like Aaron.

But that will never happen for me.

If you want it, there is something even greater for you, baby, Lucy says. She isn't trying to touch me. She floats in the air behind Aaron, looking like a goddess—not too different from the way she looked in real life. Her black skin is radiant with Light.

"You're beautiful," I tell her.

She smiles and says, *Just like you baby, just like you.* Except I knew she'd say that. Lucy always told me I was beautiful. Figures that my brain would pull on old material.

And then Aaron's finger is touching my forehead and white pain sears through my body and it burns, burns, burns and . . .

Oh

gods.

My body is on fire.

I am a torch.

Fire in the darkness.

"What—" My throat still hurts, my voice still rasps. I think this is still a dream. Because I'm not Ascended, and of course I never will be, so there's no way I could be made of Light. "What did you do to me?" I gasp.

He's sharing his light with you, baby. Can you feel it?

I can feel it. I nod.

Can you feel your own light?

I look at her, at the hope on her face. Why does she look like that? I search inside myself. *Nope.*

I shake my head.

No. No light.

Look harder, Lucy says, and there's a breathless quality to her voice, an urgency I can't make sense of.

I mean, it's my dream, right? Can't she stay forever?

Another burst of fire-light burns through me and as I watch, Aaron's light dims. Just a little. I think it's maybe because I am brighter—maybe he only looks dim because I am bright.

It has to be that.

Look again, Lucy says, reaching out but stopping short of touching me. *Desolation!* The sound of my name on her lips, in a voice that says, *Suck it up. Do it. Now.* startles me into action, and I look.

I close my eyes and think of the spark. Think of Lucy. Of the day she took me shopping in my new car, with my new sunglasses, and shiny new phone—all things Lucy picked out for me, knowing I would love them.

I Remember the sound of her laughter, the way her voice fills my heart with sunshine and honey. I Remember the way she holds me.

She holds me now—not really, but it feels like it. I can feel her arms around me, hear the beat of her heart as surely as if it's happening.

And then I feel it.

There.

Tears jump to my eyes and a sob cuts through the muck in my throat because it's there!

The spark.

The golden piece of Asgard my mother blessed me with.

I wrap my soul around it, squeeze it tight. I hug it and hug it and cry and cry.

I am not lost. At least, when I die, I will know.

Asgard did not leave me.

I have to go now, Lucy says. I look into her eyes, radiating so much light and love—and it's no longer impossible to look into them.

"Why?" is all I can think to ask. "I don't want you to go."

I need to tell Odin. Tell Michael.

"Why?" They can't rescue me. They can't even find me. "Can't you stay with me until I die?"

Lucy laughs, but Aaron doesn't. In fact, he doesn't even smile. His mouth is set in a grim line. He's not shining very much. He's still touching me, but he's drifted lower, his forehead nodding toward my shoulder.

Lucy's gaze flicks to Aaron, then back to me. *Shine, baby. Shine with everything in you. Let the light burn out all the darkness. Let Aaron's gift make you free.*

"Aaron's gift?" I don't want to look at him. His eyes are closed and his skin is pale. "What's wrong with him? Why isn't he shining?"

Lucy smiles at Aaron, places her hand on his arm. Her light flares and so does his. I see him take a big breath. *He's shining for you, baby. Let him do this.*

Wait, I think. *No!*

JAMES

The plan, it turned out, was for me to sneak into Hell, with some dude named Heimdall's help, and follow Horonius-the-dog through the scariest place I could imagine. Find Desi—hopefully in the place Horonius thought she was—release her from her prison, or whatever, and hightail it on out of there.

Without getting caught.

Or killed.

Or worse.

I didn't know there could be a worse, but according to li'Morl there was. Something about soul eaters and complete and utter destruction of your eternal soul. I figured it was better not to think about it.

Miri had pretty much not stopped crying since li'Morl and Horonius left. She tried to convince them to stay, but li'Morl insisted we have some time alone before . . . well, before I went to Hell and maybe never came back.

We lay on our bed, the afternoon sun streaming over us, painting Miri with the pattern of the lace curtains. For a brief second, a flash, I thought maybe we'd have some goodbye sex or something, but one look at Miri's face when she shut the door behind li'Morl and I knew what she needed. So we lay on top of the comforter, while Miri curled against my side, practically lying on top of me in her effort to be held as tightly as possible. In my effort to make her feel as loved as possible.

I held her close, stroked her hair, and prayed my racing heart wouldn't tell her how freaking scared I was.

Sure, I'd said all the brave things while li'Morl and Horonius filled me in on the plan. I hadn't hesitated once I said I would do it. I knew my part. If Miri and the dog-dude were right, there was no way I wouldn't give saving Desi everything I had.

But now, lying here with Miri, I wondered if I'd gone about it the wrong way.

I took a couple deep breaths and tried to get the words straight in my head.

"Mir," I started. Terror squeezed my throat the second I began. "I—Maybe I shouldn't be doing this."

She froze. Held her breath. "What do you mean?"

"I mean, what if I don't come back? What if—well, I don't want to be anywhere, even dead, without you." I moved to the side and slid downward a bit so I could look into her eyes. *Man, she has beautiful eyes.* And right then they were filled with such sadness and fear.

"You have to go," she said in a near-whisper.

"I don't. I could stay." I searched her eyes, wishing I could read her mind, wishing I knew exactly the right thing to do and say. "I don't think it's right to leave you. And maybe someone else could save Desi. Maybe they could send someone else."

I'd had her all the way until the last line. Up until then she looked at me in that way that made me scared to death and proud as all get out at the same time. But then she kind of recoiled, and blinked, and I saw something different in her eyes. Disappointment.

"You don't want to save her?" she asked.

I shut my eyes, let out a long breath and took my hand from her hip so I could rub my forehead. I always said the wrong things at the wrong time. Every time.

"No, bright eyes. I do. I just . . ." How do you tell someone you'd die without them? How even being dead wouldn't be right without them? "I'm selfish, okay? I'm afraid to lose you."

The shadow in her eyes fell away as she squished herself closer and kissed me. I mean, really, really kissed me.

Way before I was ready, she pulled back and tipped her head, so our foreheads touched. I looked at her lashes, at her lips, and pretty much thought nothing but *I love you. Always. Always love you.*

"I don't want you to go either," she said, her words riding on her breath. "But—"

She raised her face and looked at me. I searched her eyes and she searched mine, and I knew. We felt the same.

"You have to go. Don't you?" But it was a rhetorical question. We both knew I did.

I pulled her back to me and held her. I held her until the room fell into shadows and our hearts and tears had pretty much done their thing. When the alarm on my phone—the one I'd set when li'Morl said he'd be back after five—went off, I rolled over and swiped the screen, plunging the room into silence once again. Miri propped her head up on one arm and watched me. I reached over and brushed my knuckles over her cheek. She smiled, a sad and lonely smile that I knew she meant to be brave. And she was brave. She was brave enough for both of us.

She clasped my hand to her cheek and held it there for a second, her eyes closed. I got the feeling she was saying a little prayer and she tugged on another one of my heartstrings. I didn't know who she prayed to, whether it was Odin or Heimdall or even to her Catholic god. I didn't know, but her faith, her belief in help beyond ourselves, was one of the many things I loved about her.

Someone knocked on our door. Miri got up off the bed, never taking her eyes from mine. We walked toward one another, me trying really hard to take a mental picture of her, to get her image so ingrained on my brain that I'd never, ever, forget her no matter what might happen. If I were to be separated from her for an eternity I didn't want to do it with fuzzy memories. I needed her eyes to shine as bright for me every day I remembered them, as they did right this very second.

We left li'Morl and Horonius waiting in the hall while Miri stepped into my arms. She hugged me and I hugged her—except it was less like hugging and more like trying to make our bodies melt together. She kissed my neck and I kissed her hair. She told me she loved me. I told her I loved her. She kissed me with tears on her lips, and she tasted mine. I held nothing back from her—she had all of me, always. Forever. No matter where I was or what I was doing, I'd be doing it with her on my mind. And wherever I was, I would never rest until I was back with her—even if I had to be a shadow clinging to a corner of her room, I'd return to her.

I will return to her.

I walked on wooden legs to the door and opened it in slow motion.

Miri grabbed my leather jacket—the warmest thing I had. It's not like I'd expected to go traipsing through the freezing caves of Hell when I packed for our summer in France. She helped me slip it on while Horonius closed the door behind him. He and li'Morl looked away, to give us our space, but Miri and I had already said our goodbyes.

I squared my shoulders, my hand squeezed tightly around Miri's. "I'm ready."

The sound of my voice had barely faded when a bright, shimmering light cut the air between me and li'Morl. I stepped back, pulling Miri to my side and wrapping my arm around her. I was scared out of my freaking mind.

Right there in front of me, a hole opened up in the room, like a door being cut with a white laser directly through the air. li'Morl and Horonius stepped forward.

"Heimdall will take you as close to the river as possible. Horonius will already be there—but will serve you better as a Hound, so he'll look like the dog you met before."

I tried to swallow in my super-dry throat. I nodded.

"He'll lead you to the Ferryman—I do not know where he is or how to get there, but you must find him. Do not try to cross the river on your own."

I nodded again. Miri squeezed my waist so tight I almost couldn't breathe. I didn't want her to let go of me for anything.

"Once across the river, move as fast as you can. Find Desolation, set her free, then make your way back as quickly as possible. Heimdall will be waiting to open a Door the moment you cross the river. Do you understand?"

I nodded, and then thought I ought to at least say something. I cleared my throat. "Got it."

To my surprise, li'Morl reached out and clasped my forearm like I'd seen Michael do with Longinus a couple times. "I wish Heimdall could take you deeper. However, the bottom of Ygdrasyll does not respond to Heimdall's powers. But he will be waiting. No matter how long."

His eyes bore into mine and I fought the urge to puke. No matter how long? I wanted to believe I'd be back before Miri went to bed tonight, but when li'Morl talked like that I wondered—how long is *no matter how long*, exactly? Like, forever?

"Understood." I didn't understand anything at all.

li'Morl looked at Horonius and without a glance at me, the dog-dude ran through the doorway of light. li'Morl let go of my arm so I took that as my cue that it was time to go. But I couldn't resist one last hug with Miri. One last kiss. One last whispered I love you.

She squeezed me, then stepped back. "I'll wait for you," she said. "No matter how long."

There it was again. *No matter how long.*

Man, I hoped it wouldn't be forever.

"I'll be back," I said. Tonight. Tomorrow.

Not long.

Not forever.

I stepped through the Door and between one step and the next I'd gone into a freaky weird Alice in Wonderland world.

I Remember stepping through the archway into Daniel's garden, looking for the girl he's set me up with. The girl I'll wine and dine—with a heavy emphasis on the wine. Or rather, whiskey. This girl has a thing for the hard stuff.

I don't see her right away, so I look around, already feeling a little off my game.

And then I see her standing there—cute, a couple years younger than me, an easy mark. Until I see her eyes, see the shy and kind of awkward smile, and I'm struck dumb. I never believed in love at first sight. Never believed it would happen to me. Knew it would never happen to me.

But here is this girl, looking at me with the most stunning blue eyes I've ever seen and something changes inside of *me.*

There is such a thing as love at first sight.

I know because it's happening to me.

I have like two seconds to shake my head and breathe, "Whoa," before another memory slugs me in the gut.

I Remember Akaros, the black-skinned man that had come to see Desi. He hits me over the head with something super hard, something that hurts so bad that even when I loose consciousness, I feel the pain.

I'm hanging upside down. Totally naked. But that's not even the worst part.

The worst part is I have cuts all over my body and something wet is dripping into my ears. When it drips into my nose and mouth I taste it and I know. It's blood.

My blood.

Beneath me there's a kiddie pool filling up with it. Each blink of my eyes seems to take longer and longer. The pool beneath me has enough blood in it I can't even see the little fish that decorate the bottom. But I do see a big stick lying there.

Blink.

Wait. It's Desi's staff . . .

Blink.

I fall to my knees on a hard gravel beach, the ground so freezing cold it burns my palms. I lurch to my feet, my stomach squeezing hard enough I have to puke. When I'm empty I stand, sort of hunched, and look around, embarrassed. But though there's thousands of people near me, no one cares. No one's noticed. The people are pushing, pushing their way up and down the stairs-slash-ramp on the side of this mountain. My stomach twists and bucks again.

The stairs themselves are moving. Because maybe they had once been stairs, but now they were people.

People.

And the others are just . . . walking on them. Climbing on them.

A shiver works its way from my feet to the top of my head that has nothing to do with the cold. I feel something wet brush against my hand and I jump away and do a little scream thing like Miri does when she sees a spider in the bathroom. It's only Horonius.

In his totally bad-ass dog form, he barks at me, but I can barely hear him. It feels like I'm under water. I pop my palm against my ears, trying to get them to work properly, but it doesn't help.

Horonius shakes his head and barks again. Like maybe he's trying to tell me something. He takes my hand in his jaw and gently tugs me forward. Well I'm not the sharpest tool in the shed sometimes, but I'm not stupid. The dog's telling me to get a move on. He doesn't have to tell me twice.

I step after him, and when he starts running, I run too.

We run alongside a red river that looks like it's filled with—I don't even want to think about what it's filled with. This is Hell after all; I figure the worst thing I can imagine is probably exactly what I'll find.

As we run, we leave the creepy black mountain with its people-ramp and thousands of people climbing it behind. The gray-stoned beach becomes less gravelly and filled with more rocks and boulders we have to dodge and climb. Horonius runs like a greyhound. He's at least twice as big as any of the biggest dogs I've seen and now his back and ruff seem to be made of metal spikes. Occasionally he looks back at me and barks a muffled warning—to check and see if I'm keeping up, I guess. His red eyes and über-sharp teeth make me glad he's on my side.

Ahead, the river disappears into the darkness of a cave. Relief floods me when Horonius slows to a walk, then sits. He doesn't watch for me to join him though, just focuses on the cave.

I stand beside him, my hands on my thighs as I try to catch my breath. I'll admit I haven't exactly kept up my exercise routine since moving to France. But right about now I'm seriously wishing I hadn't taken my fitness so casually. I'm only nineteen, but I feel like an old man after that hard run.

After a minute I realize Horonius is barking—and not your regular brand of barking, either. He's barking in code.

Bark.

Bark.

Bark-bark-bark.

Bark. Bark. Bark-bark-bark.

And he doesn't stop.

I'm grateful right then that I can't hear very well because his constant barking would have seriously pissed me off. Instead, I can concentrate on catching my breath and psyching myself up for what will come next. I've never been much of a scaredy-cat, I mean, I'd thought I'd seen it all, there at Lucifer's hell-on-earth, aka Daniel's house. But right now I'm about as freaked as I can get.

But what comes next is not at all what I expect.

I'm expecting an old monk-like guy to show up in one of those creepy rowboats. Maybe with a lantern hanging from a staff. Maybe the Ferryman will have bone fingers and no face like I'd seen in the movies.

And for a second, as the boat begins to take shape from the shadows, I think that's what I see. But between one blink and the next, what I see changes.

A glass boat moves toward me, seemingly on its own. Gold pillows fill the bottom, but that's not what floors me. What gets me is the girl.

I love Miri. Man, I love Miri.

But—

This girl in the boat, well . . . I'll admit she's pretty much every definition I have of the perfect woman. She's every wet dream I've ever had brought to life. She has ivory skin—I know because she's wearing a pink silky robe that leaves pretty much zero to the imagination. It's as see-through as her glass boat. She reclines on her pillows, red, red hair arranged around her green-eyed, full-lipped face in perfect waves. In her hand she holds a champagne glass filled with frothy, golden liquid.

Horonius stops barking. I'm aware of his eyes on me, but I wish he'd go away. *Get a life doggy. Let me have a few minutes.* I ignore him, and as far as I'm concerned, he disappears.

Because the boat bumps against the gravel at my feet and the girl is looking at me. Her lips part. She licks them. And I know I lick my own. At that moment all I want, all I care about from my head to my toes, is if she'll let me kiss her.

I grab the front of her boat and pull it up onto the beach. I walk out into the river, reaching a hand to her.

Horonius starts barking again, but it's easy to ignore him with my ears plugged up like they are. Distant alarm bells go off in my head. Something about not going into the water. But I don't care. None of it matters anymore.

Only this.

Only the girl in front of me.

She reaches out, smiling shyly when she has trouble balancing her drink while trying to stand. She laughs and I feel my stomach clench with desire. I want her. I want my hands on her. I want her hands on me. I want to kiss her. To kiss her everywhere.

"Come on," she says, giving up trying to stand and lying back on her pillows. "Join me."

And all I can think is, *Hell, yes.*

If only that damn dog will shut up.

I make to haul myself into the boat, but the girl says, "Wait."

I freeze.

"I really want you to join me. Do you want to? I've been waiting for you for so long."

And oh man. I want to join her. It's the only thing in the world I want.

"Except, there's something I really need. Will you promise to help me?"

I swing my leg back out of the boat, standing in the freezing water that isn't water at all.

"Anything," I think I say. I say it in my head, anyway. I can't hear myself but she seems to.

"Excellent." I hear her perfectly. Like her voice is inside my head. And maybe it is. She sounds like all my favorite sounds. Miri sighing, whispering my name. Miri's laugh when we lie in bed together late at night. The sound of a really great live band. The sound of talking and laughing with Desi and Miri.

Not the sound of Horonius's barking.

Not the rush of warning that swooshes through my mind.

Not my promise to get back to Miri.

I focus on the girl. On her voice. Her lips.

"Where do you need to go?" she asks.

Where do I need to go? I try to think, try to brush away the cobwebs that seem to be everywhere in my mind.

"I . . . I think I just need to get across." That sounds right. "Me and my . . ." I look to the shore and see the dog. *My dog,* I think. "Yeah. My dog."

The girl smiles and reaches for me again. "Come on. I'll take you. Are you sure that's all you need?"

Horonius leaps from the shore into the boat, while I pull myself in. I fall forward, face-planting onto the girl's chest.

"Oh my," she says, laughing. But she doesn't push me away. She holds my head against her. Strokes my hair. I think I hear the dog growling.

"Well, we're across." The boat bumps against the shore. I look up to discover she's right. We're on the other side of the river. Horonius glares at me, his teeth bared.

"Uh, I . . . we . . . might need a ride back. Can you, um, do that?" *Stellar, James. Totally cool.* I hate myself for being anything less than perfect because *perfect* is exactly what this girl deserves. Perfect is what I want to give her.

She bats at my chest playfully, a deliciously sly smile on her lips. I feel myself leaning forward, my whole being intent on kissing her. I feel like I'll die if I don't kiss her.

"I know, baby. I want to kiss you, too. But you promised to do something for me, remember?"

I nod my head so hard I think it might fly right off.

"When you get back. After I return you to the other shore. You'll help me then. Right?"

I nod again. Try to answer but find all I can do is lick my lips. I lean forward. "Please," I whisper.

This time she shoves me kind of hard. Hard enough I fall against the side of the boat and the glass edge cuts into my arm. I hiss as I pull it back. My leather jacket's sliced clear through above the back of my elbow. I wipe my finger across the spot. It comes away slick and red with blood. My blood.

Things start to come into focus. At least enough that when Horonius jumps past me and barks from the shore, I know to follow. I have to go. He's going to lead me to . . .

I look at the girl who raises one eyebrow.

. . . something. Some*one*.

Right.

"Okay, I've um, gotta go. But I'll, um . . . see you later?" I haul myself awkwardly out of the boat, careful of the razor-sharp edges.

"Sure, loverboy. I'll see you later." She raises her glass to her lips and drains the liquid. Her boat moves away from the shore but I don't take my eyes off of her until she disappears into the dark cave. And even then I don't move.

A sharp pain stings me in the fleshy part of my left hand, between the thumb and fingers. I snatch it up to look at it and, for the second time in less than a couple minutes, I see blood on my fingers. The damn dog bit me. "Son of a bitch, Horonius. What'd you do that for?"

He barks at me and moves away, looking for all the world like he's royally pissed. I stare back at the river, the red lava-blood river with the big boulders and no Ferryman in sight. Yet somehow we are across.

"Hey, at least I got us across!" I call after the dog as I break into a run to follow him.

So far, this is a piece of cake.

I hear a sound—like stone against stone. Like nails on a chalkboard. At first I ignore it and concentrate on keeping Horonius in sight. The sound scrapes against my nerves again.

The darkness is so complete that even though I know my eyes are open as wide as they can possibly go, even though I can make out the walls from the floor, the barest outline of my hand before my face, I can't see anything else.

I hurry after Horonius, fear that I'll get forever lost in this place suddenly infusing me with an anxious need to find the dog-dude, rescue Desi and get the hell out of here. A soft, hushing sound from behind has me turning before I give the command to my body, and I find myself face-to-face with a creature I've had nightmares about almost every night for a year. Except, it's not Akaros—he was a lot bigger and a helluva lot scarier than this . . . thing . . . in front of me.

It's a paler shade than the shadows around me, a pallid gray that makes it look sickly. Still, it moves and breathes and looks plenty deadly to me. Anything that reminds me of Akaros can*not* be a good thing. It's missing most of its teeth when it opens wide to breathe out air that smells like the city dump, but the claws on the end of its wings are polished knives that could kill.

The bat-dragon-whatever lunges, aiming for my neck, and I get a sudden image of being vampire-ized by the original Count Dracula, who isn't nearly as sexy and interesting as all the movies make out.

I scream, stumbling backward and falling on my butt because I trip over myself. Nice. At least I don't piss my pants—a distinct possibility given how scared I am.

The creature hiss-screams, though it sounds as if it's screaming through a paper towel roll, which makes it somehow less terrifying. It lunges again, its claws grazing my shoulders as it pins my shirt to the stone on either side of me.

My mind goes blank.

I'm partially aware of my rational brain telling me to kick it, scream, raise a royal ruckus. But the bigger part of my brain has slowed down, taking a leisurely walk through the moment, through my life.

I gaze into the creature's wide black eyes and see myself reflected in their depths. I see the gray, wrinkly skin that looks like it's wearing a flesh-suit ten times too big, drooping all around its eyes and cheeks. I see its elf-like ears, the tendons in its neck as it screams and hisses at me. I see the black, rotted mess of its gums and teeth and think how funny/horrible it will be to be killed by a vampire with only one tooth.

Thinking that makes me laugh out loud. To laugh and laugh. I think of Miri and how funny she'd find this. Think of the things she'd say, the jokes we'd tell each other.

The creature freezes.

It stares at me, tilting its head to the side. Which only makes me laugh louder and harder.

And then something lands on the creature and it's screaming and something else is growling and they're rolling off of me and down the hall. I inch away, pressing myself against a pile of rocks out of the way of the fight going on a few feet in front of me.

In seconds flat, Horonius has his jaw wrapped around the bat-dragon's throat. They stay like that for what seems like minutes, but is probably only seconds, until the creature stops struggling. Horonius gives one last shake of his head before dropping the creature to the ground. He looks at me and a cold shiver wraps itself around my spine.

Horonius looks far more deadly and terrifying than the creature ever had.

But when he takes off down the corridor, I don't hesitate even a second before hurrying to follow.

SEVEN

DESI

Lucy moves closer and reaches out, but stops short of
touching me. *We love you. You know that, right?*
I nod because I know that's what she expects of me.
But do they really? Can anyone love me?

I roll the question around in my mind. Taste it.

And I realize.

They do love me.

And I know it.

I know it.

And so I say, "I love you, too."

And then,

"Thank you."

My whole being flares with warmth. I feel it slip through me like liquid honey until every part of me feels impossibly warm in this wasteland of cold nothingness.

Keep shining, baby, Lucy says, drifting away from me. *I'll send Michael. He'll come for you. But you have to keep shining, okay? Let your Halo become a part of you—of every part of you. Can you do that, baby?*

I look at Aaron. *Can I do that?*

But his eyes are closed again. The light Lucy shared with him is already gone—already found its way into me. Panic rises inside me. Aaron's going to die. He's going to burn himself out for me.

Aaron opens his eyes. *It's my right, D. My gift to give.*

I hear his unspoken question between the words he says.

Will you take it?

I watch Lucy fade to a tiny prick of light.

"Yes," I say to Aaron.

And Lucy's light blinks out.

While I let Aaron's light fill me, fill me, fill me, I watch his own light fade.

I don't know how long we stay there, his hand on my forehead, his light everywhere.

But I am changing.

I try to ignore how he is changing, too.

We talk some. Laugh over the little guilts and sorrows I've kept hidden in my soul. Because he sees all of me now. There are no secrets from him.

Really? You remember that? Even his voice in my mind sounds like it wheezes. He's found regret number three million and thirty two.

I'm sitting in a stall in the girls' bathroom between classes one day. Jasmine Michaels—I know because she always wears this hideous perfume—comes into the bathroom.

"Did you see Freakazoid this morning? He got his lip pierced. What an a-hole. What a freak! I mean, piercings are one thing, but a big ol' pipe or something like that in your lip? I could hear him flicking it against his teeth all during math and it made me sick. I actually had to tell Mr. Johnson I was having female troubles so I could get out of class." She makes a puking sound and the girls she's with laugh as they leave the bathroom.

You didn't do anything wrong, Aaron says.

I feel his light—my light with the help of his—slip over that memory and smooth it out, buffing out all the sharp parts until I can look at it for what it is: the mistake of a child, nothing more.

"I wish I'd said something to them. Wish I'd told them to be kinder to you."

I feel Aaron's love caress me, feel his warmth flare where it feeds into my mind. *Thank you, D.* And then he closes his eyes as his light fades a little more.

I am awake more often than he is, now. I shine so bright I can see all around me and far out into space. I see the empty places in the rock walls, the hollowed-out places. Places where the genii once lived but live no more. They've all followed Ophelia and I wonder what she's going to do with them. I wonder if I can stop whatever it is, and save more of them from dying at her thoughtless hands. My light grows brighter.

Aaron still has his palm on my forehead, but his head now rests against my shoulder. I can't tell if he has any of his own light left, because all I see around us is my own.

I am watching out in space, wondering if Lucy will come back. Wondering how Michael will find me. Wondering if a rescue is even possible. This far beneath Ygdrasyll isn't exactly Odin's territory. And who else is there?

Michael and I rescued Helena and Heimdall and are both children of darkness and light. I trust Odin would never allow Michael to come back because Father would never let him escape the Underworld again. That pretty much left Helena, and she was a god. No matter what she said, she couldn't be trusted to help anyone but herself.

As I watch, a shape takes form. It's black as black, but it moves in the darkness and so I can distinguish it. It moves silently toward me and glides upward—revealing its triangular shape. A soul eater.

I'd seen them fly out of the River Styx and devour the damned who wandered too close to its shores. I'd heard about the ones that live in space; black, where its river relatives were red. Their wants are the same though—to devour souls. To bring death. Complete death. This is the first time I've seen one here, at the bottom of everything. I wonder if I wasn't good enough even for one of them. But that was before.

"Aaron," I say, trying to rouse him. I bend my head down, kiss his cheek. "Aaron! A soul eater!"

Tell me what to do, I ask in my mind, but his mind is closed to me.

Finally he moves and looks at me. "What?" he mumbles out loud and I can barely hear him.

"A soul eater! Tell me what to do!"

He looks at his hands, discovering what I have known for some time—he is no longer feeding me his light. He has no more to give. For a while now I have been trying to send some back into him, to warm him as he has grown progressively colder, but I've been unable to do for him what he has done for me.

The soul eater glides toward us. Up, down, as fluid as a ribbon. Fear clutches my heart. I push out my light, try to throw it around Aaron, to protect him.

I know that soul eaters can't take Ascended Ones unless they fail to protect themselves. I can only guess that their light is what saves them—nothing as dark as a soul eater can exist where there is so much light. So I push mine outward and it slams against the soul eater. It screeches and moves upward, revealing a wide mouth littered with sharp tooth points.

I try to shove it backward with the force of my Halo, and while I do, Aaron is buffeted to the side. The slightest amount, but one hand—one hand!—reaches beyond the grasp of my light.

The soul eater pounces and latches on.

"Aaron!" I scream. The soul eater pulls him away from me, tugging more and more of him beyond my light.

"Shine Aaron! Shine!" He isn't watching the monster on his arm, so he doesn't see when his arm fades and the creature moves to his shoulder, to his neck.

It's your time to shine, D. And—will you remember one thing?

I feel his touch in my mind, feel his breath as if it's on my cheek. His hand against mine. *Remember I always loved you. And . . .*

The soul eater jerks him backward, but Aaron's eyes never leave mine.

I'm crying now. Great gut-wrenching sobs as I be him not to leave me.

And I always wanted to save you, D. Save you from Daniel. From James. From your Father. You are meant to be glorious. Meant to shine bright enough to save the whole world. Let me be a part of that. Let me save you, so you can save everyone.

He is fading.

Shine, D. Shine.

His precious face, the face of my friend, fades.

The last thing I see is his smile before he vanishes into tiny particles of dust in an endless nothing sky.

I can't breathe. Can't think, can't . . . anything.

The soul eater screeches and lunges forward.

All I can do is the one thing he asked of me.

All I can do is honor the gift he gave me.

And so with a scream, I answer the soul eater.

My Halo bursts around me as brilliant as the sun.

And I shine.

EIGHT

JAMES

I slip and skid along icy paths, following the damn dog down and down. If it hadn't been for the sweat I broke to keep up with him I would have frozen my ass off. As it was, I have the wonderful experience of feeling my sweat bead into icicles on my skin. So pleasant.

On one particularly sharp corner I catch myself before I face-plant into some wicked jagged rocks. I push away from them, ignoring the way the sharp stones cut into the bite Horonius gave me. But as I shove off from the wall it feels like it moves beneath my hand. It must be the ice melting from the warmth of my skin or something. Not that I'm very warm at this point.

I feel like we've been running forever until I plow into Horonius, as his human self, standing at the end of the hallway. He is about my height, but way prettier, and with his arms folded I have to admit he pretty much rocks my Grateful Dead shirt.

"You are unwieldy," he says.

"Hey, now." I brace my hands against my thighs to catch my breath. "I'm a little out of my element, ya know."

I look up, but he doesn't reply.

"Are we there?"

He stares at me for a moment more before nodding his head almost reluctantly. His eyes regard me warily.

"Well then get the hell out of my way—let's get her out of here!" I make to shove past him, but he stops me. He holds my arm with a force that would put any heavyweight boxer to shame. There's no getting out of this guy's vice grip unless he wants me to.

"Before you . . . *get her out of there* . . . I must warn you."

I shrug, hoping he'll take the hint and let go, but he doesn't.

"You made a promise to the Ferryman, and that is a price you will have to pay alone. Do you understand?"

I don't, but I nod my head anyway. I don't even remember it, but whatever it is can't be that bad.

"We will try to wait, but will not be able to wait long— we will need to get the young mistress out of here as quickly as possible. We cannot delay."

"I get it" My voice rises with a distinctly *I'm pissed off* tenor. "So I'll do what the old Ferryman dude wants me to do and we'll hightail it on outta here. Got it."

Horonius quirks his head, like he can't make sense of what I've said. "The . . . dude?" He shakes his head. "If you take too long, we will have to leave without you."

"Geez I get it already. Now let's get our girl."

He considers me, weighing me, sizing me up, and I don't like it. In fact, now I really am pissed. Finally he lets go and I can't resist giving my jacket a snap and rolling my shoulders in a show of bravado.

Horonius steps aside and gestures *right this way.*

I step forward only to discover myself standing on the edge of a very steep cliff. I look across from me, left and right. No Desi.

"She's not here, dude. Are you messing with me?"

"She is here."

"And I'm telling you she isn't. Look for yourself." I step to the side and imitate his earlier *take a look for yourself* mojo. I'm tired and scared out of my mind and I so don't have patience for the dog-dude's games.

And then:

What if we can't find her?

Horonius jumps from narrow ledge to narrow ledge, faster and faster, peering into every crevice, every nook and cranny. "She has to be here." His voice slips out of his normal zen-like detachment, rising with a panic I can totally relate to. He even kneels and looks beneath the ledge.

"Well, do you see her?"

He finally stops and stands, pressing himself to the rock wall. "I do not." Now I'm even more scared than before because . . . we're gonna fail. Desi isn't here. Maybe she's dead after all. And if this place can kill someone like Desi—what the hell is it going to do to me?

Horonius pushes away from the wall, jumps to the ledge beside me and brushes past in a hurry. "Perhaps I misstepped. We must have already passed where she is imprisoned." He strides away and I hurry to follow.

He disappears around a corner so I move into a jog to catch up, and plow into his back again. It's like running into a brick wall. "What the hell?"

Horonius holds his hands out to his sides, keeping me back, keeping me behind him. But I can see in front of him—and I see the strangest sight. A woman stands in the corridor, holding a lantern up high.

"Ohhh goodie!" she says. She's as pale as the bat-dragon that attacked me, with hair that splays out around her face like a halo. And she looks crazy. Crazy as all get out. She wears some sort of Victorian gown with a corset and the whole bit, but she is not beautiful. She looks like a vampire. She looks like death.

"You're not dead," she says in this weird snake-like voice. She slithers toward Horonius, sliding around to the side so she's pressed against his arm. She peers at me. Licks her lips. "You're not dead," she says again, this time stretching the words out twice as long as normal and adding a little tune to them.

Holy crap, she really is crazy.

And crazy is a million shades of scary.

"Back away," Horonius growls. "I do not wish to harm you."

The woman doesn't even bother to look at him. She just smiles, all scary teeth and freaky eyes. "Shh," she says, whether to me or Horonius I don't know. Without any warning, everything changes.

The rocks fly off the walls and throw themselves at Horonius. He's forced to spin away, morphing into his razor-backed dog-self. I have a flash of memory and recognize the rock-like creatures that had fought against us that day eight months ago when Desi tried to start the Apocalypse. Genies or something like that. They doggy-pile on Horonius but I lose track of him because I have my own problem to deal with.

The crazy woman presses herself against me, her body waving up and down mine like some ghetto whore at a dance club. She pulls up the cuff of my jacket and licks my wrist.

I thrust outward, "What the hell?" I try to scrabble out of the way, but the rock wall has come alive, wrapping stone fingers around my arms, my legs. She grabs me harder, her nails digging into me. I swear she's drawn blood. And licked it off.

"Get off me, you crazy bitch!" I try to shove and push with what movement I've got, but she won't budge. She puts her hands all over me, and I mean all over me. "Screw this," I finally say.

When she leans in toward my neck, a *holy-hell-this-place-will-stop-at-nothing-to-turn-me-into-a-vampire* fear drives into me and I head-butt her so hard pops of light flash before my eyes. She spins back and hits the wall.

She falls into a heap, her skirts billowing up around her. The rocks let me go and I jump away from them. Standing in the middle of the hall I rake my hands through my hair. A few yards away I spot a dark, shifting mass that has to be Horonius and his attackers.

"Horonius?" I take a few steps forward. I can't tell whose winning and my feet become lead slippers as fear takes hold of me again. What if he's already dead? There's no way I can stop those blasted things.

But I take another step forward anyway. "Horonius!" I hear a growl that has to be his. I take two or three more steps when I feel a sharp pinprick of pain in my side and look down to find the woman's hand wrapped around my waist, her fingernails digging into my skin. I whirl around, trying to pry her hand off of me, but the crazy chick only laughs and wraps herself around me more tightly.

"What are you doing?" I screech-yell.

"Oh, you have no idea pretty boy. But I will show you. You want me to show you, don't you?" She pushes me backward until I crash against the wall again, making me hiss with pain as the sharp points cut into my skin. I hear whispered scrapings as the cold rocky hands take hold of me.

Then I really start to panic. I mean, I *freak out*. I don't know what I say, don't know what I do, but I know I can't stop moving, can't stop screaming until my body is covered in sweat again despite the frigid temperature and my voice can only manage a whisper, it's so hoarse.

And when I don't have anything left, the bitch opens her mouth wide. Wide and wide until it's half her face and I can see every one of her way-too-many sharp-as-needles teeth. For the second time since I've been in this hell-on-crack place, someone wants to eat me.

She drags a razor sharp nail down my neck, whispering weird things like, "Oh so pretty," and, "Tastes so good," and, "So alive, so fresh."

And I just give up.

I will myself to think of Miri. Her laugh. Her kiss. Her bright, beautiful eyes.

When the woman's teeth touch my neck, I close my eyes and let my memories take me somewhere, anywhere, else.

A bomb explodes.

I don't hear it, but I feel it. See it.

A blast of wind blows over us, knocking the woman off of me, making the rock things let go. I feel like I'll never see again, the light's so blinding. It erases everything from my vision, the rocks, the woman, Horonius—everything. All I see is burning white light whether my eyes are open or not.

When I can finally take the brightness, I slowly open my eyes, finding myself curled up on the rocky ground in the fetal position, my forehead tucked against my knees. I uncurl and look around. The light's faded some, but it still fills the corridor like noon at the beach. Horonius–the-dog faces me, dozens of rock creatures littering the floor around him. His eyes shine bright red in the light.

He walks toward me and as he does, he becomes human again. He reaches down and I see his skin riddled with cuts and bruises, yet his grip on my arm is strong when he pulls me to my feet.

"Are you well?" he asks.

I look myself over and see I have plenty of my own cuts. "Yeah. You?"

He nods. "I believe the young mistress has been found."

"Whadd'ya mean?" I look behind me, to peer in the direction that holds Horonius's attention. The end of the corridor—the end that had seemed like a steep drop into black nothingness—is ablaze with light. I walk toward it, feeling like I'm walking toward the light at the end of a tunnel, except I know I won't find Heaven. But I hope I'll find a little piece of it.

The light is so bright I have to shield my eyes, but I step up to the ledge and look down toward its source.

"James?" Her voice is small, broken. A rough and poor imitation of the voice I know so well.

"Des!"

I still can't see her and the bright beacon of light is blinding. She begins to cry and panic shoves at my insides. *Where the hell is she?*

Horonius puts his hand on my shoulder, pressing down in an effort to calm me. When I can I look at him, he gestures downward. I follow the line of where he's pointing and then I see her.

"Des, can you dial it back? I can barely see you."

The light recedes some until I can see that she's hanging *beneath* the cliff—I imagine her wrists are shackled to the underside. She's hanging over complete black nothingness. I understood from Michael's description that this is the bottom of everything. That this isn't even true space, not in the way I understand it. This is nothing. Just . . . nothing. The place where all creation stops.

"James," Desi whispers. "James."

"Follow me," Horonius says. He leaps from one barely-visible ledge to another and I follow without thought because to think about it means looking down and looking down means freaking out and freaking out means plummeting to my death. Or floating around for forever, I don't know. Either way, I am not looking down.

I jump onto the same little ledges Horonius does until I stand beside him on the rock to which Desi is shackled.

I lay down on my stomach and look over the ledge. And there she is.

then slipping down her cheeks. "Thank you," she repeats over and over again. "Thank you."

I reach out and touch her cheek. She leans against me, presses her face into my palm.

"I can't believe you're here," she says in her rough voice.

"I can't believe you're here," I say. I feel like a smiling freak and my cheeks hurt.

"Thank you," she says again.

"Well, don't thank me yet. We've still gotta get you out of here and, according to your doggy, I promised something to the Ferryman that has him kind of freaked out. Tell him to chill, okay? I've got it covered."

I roll onto my side and look up at the dog-dude. "So how do we do this?"

"I cannot," he says. "But you should be able to release the pin and set her free."

"Release the pin," I say, rolling back onto my stomach. "Got it."

"So Des. I'm gonna get you unlatched. Can you, um, fly or something so you don't, you know, go falling to your death?"

She laughs and my chest constricts with how good it sounds. *Desi's alive!* I can't wait to get her back to Michael. And Miri. Best damn gift I could ever give her.

I watch as Desi closes her eyes and mutters some words under her breath. I can't hear what they are and it takes her a really long time but she bursts into tears again and says, "Hurry. Hurry."

So I hurry.

I scoot to her right side and reach out for the shackle. I think it'll be easy, just reach over, find the pin, pull it out and *ta-da* the cuff will come unlatched. But it doesn't. I get to the pin okay, but either I'm not pulling it out far enough or there's something wrong with it.

"Hurry James," Desi cries. It sounds like she's in a boatload of pain. "I can't—" she gasps. "I can't hold on for much longer."

I don't know what she means, but I understand enough.

"Horonius! Help me!"

"I am unable—"

"Just get the hell over here!" I don't care what he can or can't do. Don't care. *Don't care.* When he kneels on the stone beside me I scoot forward. "Grab my feet."

I tip over the ledge at the waist before he even grabs me. Yeah, I'm full of faith like that.

With the dog-dude holding onto my legs, I lean as far into the blackness as I can to get a better view of the shackle. I see Desi more clearly—her tear-stained face, her body trembling with effort, though I don't know what she's struggling against. And anyway, I can't think about how horrible she looks or what may or may not be wrong. I need to concentrate on the damn shackle.

Immediately I see the problem—the pin has rusted in places so it's wider than the hole it's in. I have to shove it up and down and yank it really hard to knock the rust off in order to pull it out of its hole.

I grit my teeth and take a hold of the pin, shimmying it up and down. "Come on, come on, come on." Finally it gives a little and the pin slips upward. "I think I have it!"

I drive it up and down some more. I can feel the pin warming beneath the layers of ice. "Almost have it!"

I feel Horonius's hands on my ankles. Feel them shaking. And ignore it. Ignore the tears that fall anew on Desi's cheeks.

I've barely thrown the pin free and whipped open the latch when I'm scooting over to work on the next one. Desi swings out into space, her wings beating so slowly I wonder if they'll do any good keeping her afloat at all. I bite back a hiss when a sharp edge on the next pin cuts into my finger. I stick it in my mouth for half a second then get back to work.

"Almost there," I whisper. My stomach muscles quiver from the exertion and Horonius has taken to sitting on my calves, which have long since gone numb, to keep me from falling over the ledge.

Desi swings upward and puts one hand on the ledge. I don't stop working on the pin, not even for a second.

At last I say, "I've got it. It's coming out. Get ready!" I shimmy some more, feel the pop as the last of the rust shucks off the side, and yank the pin free.

For a second Desi hangs there, one hand still in the shackle, the other holding onto the ledge. I look at her face; see the momentary elation when she knows she's free. Then see her start to fall. Down and down.

I shout for her. Her right hand slips out of my reach, but I scoot forward again, ignoring Horonius's cries of . . . whatever. Desi wheels her arms as she slowly falls—and I catch two fingers on her left hand. Two fingers, then three.

Three fingers, then four.

I've already started scooting backward. Horonius groans and hollers as he pulls me by my ankles. I ignore the ice and stone digging into my belly and chest as he pulls me, my shirt and jacket riding up.

What I pay attention to are the fingers in my hand. The way her other arm comes up to wrap around my wrist. The weak beat of her wings as she tries, nearly fails, to push herself onto the ledge.

And then she's here. She collapses beside me, and Horonius falls to the stone. We lie there for I don't know how long while we all fight to catch our breath, to stop our tears, to deal with the fact that we've done it.

Desi is free.

NINE

DESI

Are you all right, Mistress?"

I feel a warm and gentle hand on my cheek. Not James. The Hound. I swallow the bitter bile that filled my throat when I thought I was going to die—for real this time—and try to roll onto my side. I have little strength to do even that, so the Hound helps me.

"A Hound?"

"Yes, Mistress," he says.

"You look different." I squint at him.

"James?" With the Hound's support, I sit up and look toward my friend who's lying on the ground, not moving. "James!"

He groans and I sigh with relief.

"I'm alive. I think." He rolls over, grinning like a village idiot. He flings out a hand and I grasp it gratefully, joyfully.

He's alive. I'm alive. I hold his cold, cold hand between mine. I don't ever want to let go. I don't want to see my friends on the brink of death ever again.

I've done a lot of thinking during my long imprisonment. I know what side I want to stand on. I know what I need to do to make sure I never fall so low again. But I know something else now too. Something even bigger than myself.

Love is eternal. It's patient and forgiving, seeing past your faults to the Gardian within. The trick is to love yourself as much as you love others. I'm still working on that one, but I'm getting there.

"Thank you," I say. I lighten my grip on his hand and pull back enough so only my fingertips trace the back of his. "Thank you for saving me."

"It wasn't just me. I couldn't have done it without your dog-dude here." James smiles up at the Hound who rises to his feet and who, impossibly, smiles back.

"The dog-dude, eh?" My face cracks a smile—like putting on an old pair of jeans that feel stiff at first but soon fit like a glove. The Hound bows his head as if in apology. He reaches down and takes my hand, and I let him help me to my feet.

"And you got a makeover. How very ironic of you—a Grateful Dead shirt and all."

The Hound looks at me with confusion at first, but when I gesture to his clothing, his face morphs into a surprisingly soft expression. "Yes. James was kind enough to dress me with his clothes."

"Well, I didn't dress him. Sheesh." James laughs, the sound hollow and muted in the strange acoustics of Hell, but it's good to hear, even like this. He climbs to his feet and puts his hand on my waist. "We'd better get moving. This isn't exactly Club Med here, princess."

TEN

JAMES

Desi walks in front of both of us, radiating like a beacon of hope through the dark tunnels of Hell. I watch the way she moves, the way she knows where she's going, the way she shines, and I wonder just how many ways she's changed.

Once she got over the initial tears—she'd been all kisses and hugs, even for Horonius—she seemed to know, without even asking, that he's alone now and that he's sad.

I guess *alone* is something Desi knows too well. But this kind-hearted, thinking-of-others Desi? I knew she'd existed—beneath all the yuck she covered herself with—but it's something else to see it, to see *her*, like this.

With every step my heart leaps to think how happy she's going to be pretty much right away when she sees Miri again. And Cornelius and Longinus. Especially when she sees Michael.

That'll have Miri crying for days, for sure. She'll be all giddy over the two of them back together. And when Miri gets a load of this new Desi? Well, it'll pretty much push out the last of the shadows clinging to her soul. Miri loves her friends, way more than anyone else I know. She wouldn't ever be truly happy if the ones she loved weren't. I feel my smile stretch from ear to ear as I think about that. About Miri and her happiness. Because everything's going to be okay now.

Desi looks like an angel. An angel with black stringy hair and a cat burglar getup, but still an angel. If I squint I can see the outline of one bright and one dark wing shimmering in the golden glow of her light. She is truly a sight to behold.

When we pass the pile of rubble that had once been a bunch of rock creatures, she stops. She kneels beside them and places her hand on one of them. She closes her eyes and stays like that for a minute. Then she stands and keeps on walking as if nothing happened.

We don't see that crazy woman—who Desi tells me is Ophelia, like the Ophelia Shakespeare created his character after—or anymore of those bat-dragons or rock creatures. Things are eerily quiet.

We step out of the labyrinth of tunnels and onto the wide field of gravel that leads to the river. There are dozens more piles of rocks scattered all around, but it doesn't seem that important, so I don't mention it. It's weird, though. *Someone must be doing a little renovating,* I think with a smirk.

As we near the water, my steps slow and a heavy sense of dread falls over me.

"What's wrong?" Desi asks when she notices I'm not following close behind anymore.

"I—I don't know."

She walks back to me and puts her hand on my wrist. "Are you sure?"

I look to Horonius, but he's busy counting the gravel at his feet or something.

"What is it?" Desi asks the dog-dude, but he won't look at her, either. Desi sighs. "Look, just spit it out, okay?"

I open my mouth to say something, but I have no idea what. Thankfully, Horonius beats me to it.

"It is the Ferryman. She extracted a promise from him in order to take us across. I warned him not to do it, as what she asks is always far too great, but James didn't listen." He looks at me with a totally uncalled-for amount of anger.

"He does not remember yet, but I imagine he is beginning to."

Desi regards me with an expression that's full of both horror and fear. "Is this true?"

I stare at her. I mean, she's an angel or a god or something, right? Shouldn't she just know? Do I really have to spell out my shortcomings?

I shrug. "I guess."

"You guess."

I shrug again.

She looks around, all around, spinning and searching in every possible direction. Then she closes her eyes, her fists clench and she seems to concentrate for a minute. I want to ask what she's up to, but I pretty much feel like I'm in the dog house and don't have the right to interrupt her.

Finally she looks up, and I see tears in her eyes. "I can't cross the river without the Ferryman. Not without risking our lives to the soul eaters and—" Her voice catches when she says that and her eyes glisten. "And we can't do that. We need the Ferryman."

"I know." I didn't think it could be any other way.

"You don't get it," she says, the tears overflowing now. "I can't help you here. I—I don't have any more Shadow or, if I do, I don't know where it is and . . ."

I reach out and take her hand. Step nearer. "Des. It's okay."

"I can't help you," she says in the smallest, saddest voice ever.

Still holding her hand, I lead her toward the shore, with Horonius following behind.

By the time we stop at the water's edge, Horonius has changed into his dog form and has begun to bark like he did before. Bark, bark, bark-bark-bark. Over and over until I see the edge of the gold-trimmed boat.

It moves silently toward us, operating under no engine or oars, leaving no ripples in its wake. The girl comes into view, and all at once I know. I promised her something. Promised I'd do anything she wanted. Her eyes flick to Desi, then settle on me. And when they do . . . I know I'll do anything for her.

The boat bumps against the shore and I find myself wading into the water to pull it further in.

"Helena," Desi says, her voice dripping with ice.

"Desolation."

"You're the Ferryman?"

Helena smiles and gives a half-shrug. "When it suits me."

"And it suited you now—with them?"

Helena glances at Horonius, but dismisses him. "For him," she says. My heart expands three times with pride. For me. *She loves me.*

"I love him," she says.

Desi snorts. I used to think it was cute when she did that, but right now it pisses me off.

"Look, you don't have to like her, okay? But I love her, so show some respect."

Desi spins toward me. "You love her?"

I touch Helena's shoulder and she puts her hand over mine, caressing it. I think I might die of happiness right there. Desi gets an ugly look on her face that kind of undoes all the shining glory of her light. Why does she have to be all high and mighty, anyway? What gives her the right to judge?

"Well, let's get this over with," Helena says. "Come on then."

For a long time Desi stares at me and Helena without moving. Like she's seriously considering not getting in the boat. I feel a sting on my leg and looked down, but I can't see my leg beneath the red lava water.

Desi strides forward, a look of pure anger on her face, and shoves her hand down into the water. My leg burns like a son-of-a-bitch when she pulls her hand out, a red stingray thing in her hand. She throws it onto the beach where it quivers, sizzles, then bursts into flame, leaving nothing behind.

"Let's go." She's about to jump into the boat when a rock goes flying over her head and hits my lady in the shoulder.

"Hey!" The crazy woman—Ophelia—shouts from further down the beach. She has an armful of rocks and she lobs another one at us. "Hey you stupid bitch!"

I snatch a rock from the air before it can hit my red-haired lady on the head. I climb into the boat, pulling Helena down so I can protect her with my body.

"Ophelia," Desi says, striding toward the crazy chick. She holds her hands out, placating, but when she gets too close, Ophelia throws a rock as big as her fist at Desi's face, which Desi dodges.

My lady traces a nail down my neck and over my shoulder. I shiver with pleasure and sink back against her. "Shall we go?" she whispers against my cheek. Her breath smells sweet and I imagine what it would be like to kiss her. I press myself to her, anxious to discover her taste, her feel.

The boat rocks as Horonius, back in his human form, yanks it up the beach and stomps off toward a row of rock-creatures who race toward us. I don't care about the genii, or Desi or the dog-dude. I want to get away from anything that could endanger my woman.

"Son of a bitch." I move away from Helena and jump out of the boat. I'm going to push it back onto the water so we can get out of here. I place my hands on the boat and start to push. When I drag my eyes up to Helena's, she smiles and all I can see are her lips, her red, glistening lips.

Something sharp rips across the back of my knee and I fall to the beach, grabbing at the pain, trying to shove it away. A genii climbs on top of me, baring two rows of razor-sharp teeth as it brings its face close to mine.

"Please don't bite me," I say, because really—haven't I had enough near-misses with vampire-bites today? "All I want is to leave with my lady." Up until that moment I thought maybe I stood a chance with the thing, but at the mention of Helena, its eyes narrow and it hisses, a sound like air leaking from a balloon.

The sound alone isn't that scary, but the creature's black glossy eyes, its rows of teeth, its sharp, angular, polished granite body give a whole new level of scary to everything around me. It sits on my chest, pressing my back into the sharp gravel of the beach. It digs razor-claws into my temples and I arch my back against the pain. It leans down and I squeeze my eyes shut, preferring to picture my lady in my last moments than to see my own reflection in the creature's eyes.

But with an *oomph*, the creature flies off of me.

I rub at my chest, only now realizing how heavy the thing was, how it was crushing the breath out of me. I look to my left and see Desi standing there, watching me, before she whirls around, kicking out like a badass and sending three geniis scrambling across the beach.

I feel gratitude, sure. I'm glad I'm not dead. But I'm still going to get my mistress out of here before anything happens to her, even if it means leaving Desi behind.

I shove the boat out and scramble inside. "It's okay, Lady. It's all right." She looks so trusting as she leans against the back of the boat with a small smile on her face.

I want to be worthy of her trust. But while I have my face turned away from the beach, watching my lady's face for any sign of displeasure—or to hear her speak a word of love to me—something rocks the boat forward, then brutally back.

"What the—"

A line of genii have hooked themselves together and are pulling us back toward the beach. I look in the boat for any kind of weapon, but there are only pillows and champagne glasses. I grab up the bottle and smash it over the head of the genii closest to me, but it only bares its teeth.

"Disgusting creatures," Helena says.

"Disgusting creatures!" I scream.

"Get them! Don't let them get away!" Ophelia's jumping and screeching on the beach, cheering her little freaks on. Desi plows into her side and a great big smile splits my face in half—maybe Desi isn't so bad.

"Let go you little freaks!" I try prying the genii's fingers off the edge of the boat, but they won't budge. Instead the thing snaps and hisses, nicking my hand with its teeth more than a few times.

"Just get us out of here, darling," my lady says, her voice a low, seductive purr.

"I will!" And oh, I will! It's the only thing I want to do. Suddenly I see no other choice but to break the chain of genii that holds us to the shore. Desi's no help—she only cares about Ophelia. She doesn't care enough to save me and my lady even after all I've done.

"Bitch," Helena whispers.

"Bitch," I say.

And Horonius—what good is he? He's just a stupid dog again, plowing through the rock creatures like they're bowling pins. I guess if you want something done, you have to do it yourself.

I throw myself off the boat, landing in the middle of their chain and breaking it in half. Me and about three of the genii roll into the water—the little freaks won't let go of me, and they're going to pull me down.

"Let—" the water-that's-not-water makes me gasp from its frigid iciness, "me go!" I try to scream, but my throat is filling up with the bitter-tasting liquid. My eyes are open, stinging in the red water, but I can't see a thing. I can feel the rock creatures latched onto each wrist and one of my ankles. I thrash and kick, but the things hold fast, dragging me out into deeper water.

My chest burns. I want to breathe. *Need* to breathe. But I'm far beneath the surface now and I suddenly find I'm too tired to fight anymore. I gasp, swallowing down more of the red liquid. Needle-sharp pinpricks blossom over my thigh, but I'm beyond feeling now. After all, what's a little more pain when pain has become your whole existence?

I can't figure out how I got here, why I'm sinking with weights attached to my arms and leg. The last thing I remember is calling for the Ferryman—my eyes fly open as I recall her beauty, gliding forward in her glass boat. Her red, luxurious hair. Her pale skin and the glimmering gown she wears that leaves little to the imagination. I remember how I felt when I saw her, how I only wanted to love and protect her.

But now . . . I can't remember why.

Because it's Miri I love. Her messy blond hair, her to-die-for eyes. I picture her now. My eyes close, my body sinks, and I hold Miri close to my heart.

ELEVEN

DESI

backhand Ophelia across the face, sending her tumbling to the ground. She tries to lift herself, looking around wildly for her little minions—and finds them indisposed. Most have been tossed into the water by Horonius, and those that haven't are busy trying not to be. His fury and speed in dispatching the vicious creatures are a sight to behold.

Not something to laugh at.

And yet Ophelia is rolling with laughter. She flops onto her back, looking up into the red-orange sky while laughter forces tears from her eyes. I stand over her, exasperated and frustrated. I both don't want to know and do want to know what's got her so giggle-happy.

141

She gasps between puffs of laughter. "Your—" more laughter, "human." And she succumbs to more coughing/laughing. But she'd said enough.

I look out to the beach where last I'd seen James and Helena. The boat sits in the middle of the water, Helena reclining against the back of it. She holds a glass of golden liquid in her hand. When she sees me, she raises the glass as if in a toast.

James is not in the boat.

I watch her face, see the moment she knows I've realized I can't see him. With deliberateness she tips her glass and pours it into the river.

The river.

A quick glance around the beach confirms what Helena has suggested. James is not on the beach. He is not on the boat.

James is in the river.

I don't think—there's no time for thought. I dash past Ophelia. She reaches out and grabs at my ankle, but I kick her face, knocking her unconscious. My leg free, I dash for the water. I rush out as far as I can before diving in, forcing my eyes to stay open and my mouth to stay shut. The blood water is colder than cold, as frigid as the vast emptiness of space I've lived in for the past eternity.

At first I see nothing, my vision clouded by the murky red. Something bristly brushes against me and I jerk, only to bump against something else at my other side. As they pass me they take shape and I see them for what they are— soul eaters. Dozens of them. All swimming lazily toward the same destination.

All ignoring me.

I don't have the luxury of questions, besides, I know I won't like the answers. So I dive after the soul eaters, following the creatures down, down, down, hoping they'll lead me to James.

My lungs are burning, my legs and arms growing weak, but I don't stop. I can't stop.

Finally—*there*—I see a large mass resting on the bottom of the river. Soul eaters are everywhere, undulating as if they are one body, one mind. I thrust myself between them, pull them back, throwing them away as best I can with my ever-weakening arms. Flashes of light pop before my eyes. I don't have much time left—but James has none.

I see him then, unmoving, his eyes closed, mouth open, the soul eaters tugging his body to and fro. I grab him by his shirt and start pulling upward, kicking off the genii who still cling to him. At least three soul eaters are suctioned to his body, but I ignore them. There's no time.

Above me, I see the shape of the boat outlined in the water. I can even see Helena's legs through the glass. I thrust James upward, shoving him, kicking with all the strength I have left. To my shock and relief Helena helps pull him out of the water. But when I reach up and grab onto the edge of her boat, she digs her long fingernails into the back of my hand.

"You are not welcome," she hisses. She deepens the dig and though I try to resist, I finally jerk my hand out from under her. She smiles and leans back, smoothing James's hair from his face.

"Don't just let him die!" I scream. Red fluid fills my mouth and I have to spit it out before I can add, "Save him!"

I tread water five feet away from them, feeling helpless, useless. What's the point? What's been the point in any of it?

My legs are so tired. I stop moving and feel myself drifting downward until I kick, kick, kick again. A dog barks behind me—Horonius is perched on a rock that protrudes from the middle of the river. When I look back at her, Helena is pulling a soul eater off of James's body. She grimaces as she tosses it into the water.

Horonius barks again. A splash, then the dog tugs on the back of my shirt.

What's it all been for?

I watch as Helena yanks the last of the soul eaters from James's body. Watch as she pulls him toward her, as he takes a breath and coughs. He's alive! Just knowing that, knowing he's living and breathing, even if he is lying in

Helena's lap, gives me the strength to kick and move my arms in an attempt to help Horonius. Together we make our way to the shore where he continues to drag me until I've scrabbled back from the frigid river water.

"James!" I call. *Let him go!* I scream in my mind.

"Oh, he can't go with you." Even though she's out in the middle of the water, I hear her answer as clearly as if she's standing next to me. Helena wraps her arms around James, one at his waist, one around his chest. I see him roll his head to the side, snuggling himself closer to her.

"Yes, he can. Now let him go!" I'm standing at the edge of the water, screaming, crying. *This can't be happening!*

"I don't want to go with you, Des," James says in a hoarse whisper that rings like a bell in my ears.

I choke on the tears that clog my throat. "Yes, you do. What about Miri?"

"What about her? She'll be okay. She's just a kid— she'll understand that I need to be with a real woman for a change."

Fury burns through me, rapid, all-consuming. Father would be proud.

To Helena I say, "You said you only needed him to do something for you."

"Oh, I do," she says.

"Then tell him what it is so he can do it and we can get out of here."

"I don't want to leave," James says.

Helena looks down on him, her face actually managing a sweet expression of tenderness. "He's happy here for the moment. When I tire of his company, he'll perform his chore. And when he's completed it—*if* he completes it— he can go back to Midgard." She runs her fingers through his hair, teasing it up into spikes. James rolls his head back onto her shoulder and groans with pleasure. "If he even wants to."

I step into the water and point at Helena. "He better want to. Or I will kill you."

Helena laughs and James laughs with her. I stare in horror at the scene, wishing I could erase it from my memory. Wishing I didn't have to tell Miri I'd left him here like this.

"Just get outta here, Des." James closes his eyes as Helena's hands roam all over him.

"Young Mistress," Horonius says from what seems like very far away. "We must go—now."

I back away from the water, fuming, desperately trying to figure out a way to save him. But the boat rocks gently as it glides toward the tunnel and I'm powerless to stop it. Helena is a goddess and I'm just . . . me.

A Door appears, cutting through the murky air and momentarily blinding me. Horonius lunges forward, grabbing my hand and pulling me through and smack into a Remembering that feels like a sucker punch to the gut. I Remember James and my love for him. I Remember how much he had suffered at Akaros's hands. When I step through that memory into another, it's to Remember the way he changed his life to be worthy of Miri. The way he took care of me when Michael had gone to Hell.

To Remember that I'd left James in Helena's clutches with a promise I was sure he'd die trying keep.

I stumbled into way too much brightness and fell to my knees.

Leaving Helheimer, being released from my prison, left me with more worries and doubts than I could name. You'd imagine having an eternity to think, to reason through things or to figure out who I really was, would have left me ready for this new step—my first into a new life.

But now I had different worries.

No matter how much someone else loved me, wasn't there a point at which there was no return? What right did I have to any of their forgiveness?

Like Miri.

Like Michael.

Yeah, I knew James had willingly come for me, knew Michael had something to do with getting the Hound to find me. Knew that Miri had wanted James to go, to risk his life to save mine.

But knowing all that didn't convince my heart to worry any less.

And now I hadn't brought James back home with me.

A hand reached down for me, larger than my own by at least ten sizes, and as black as night. Heimdall. His eyes gleamed and his sharp cheekbones rose high in a broad smile. I took his hand.

He pulled me to my feet and for the space of at least ten seconds I couldn't see, hear or feel anything else other than his arms around me, his huge heart beating beneath my cheek, the comfort of his embrace.

I did not cry.

And for the first time in my very long life, when he released his hold on me and stepped back, I didn't feel inadequate. I didn't feel like there was any ulterior motive behind his retreat. He simply made room for Odin.

Odin stepped forward, a look of such grace and kindness on his face that all of my emotions were immediately laid bare. He reached for me, his smile for me, his eyes alight with love, his arms wide to embrace me. He offered the love of a father, the comfort of a friend. I fell into his arms.

I cried then. Cried for Aaron who was no more. Cried for James. And cried for myself because I still had so much to atone for. I only hoped the people I loved would let me have that chance.

"You know they will, my daughter," Odin whispered in my ear. And I knew he was right. Knew I'd been blessed with people with the biggest hearts the worlds had ever known. They would forgive me. The real question was—

"Can you forgive yourself?"

I shook my head, annoyed that I'd thought of myself—again I was selfish, always selfish. "It doesn't matter—James. Helena has James."

Odin frowned, his brow furrowing, his expression hardening. "I feared as much." He turned away from me for a moment, like he needed to gain control over his emotions before he could talk. "She has ever meddled in my affairs—" He closed his eyes and when he opened them again, he had returned to his normal, kind self. He gave my arms a small squeeze. "James is strong. He has survived much, even before he met you," he added. "I have hope that he will yet be returned."

Odin pushed me out to arm's length and made a show of taking a good look at me. I tried to let his peace soften the edges of my guilt. It didn't really work.

"My daughter, you don't have to carry the weight of the world."

Yeah, 'cause the weight of all my sins is a lot heavier, I thought to myself with a snort.

Odin chuckled and pulled me back into his embrace. I felt his joy radiating outward until it became my joy. He filled me with thoughts of Aaron, helped me remember the light he'd shared with me—and that's when I realized we weren't alone.

Horonius stood outside the Wheelhouse, beside a Valkyrie warrior, her arm in a shield and her other hand on the hilt of her sword. All around us Valkyries and Gardians stood, arm to arm. We were surrounded.

I was surrounded.

My blood ran cold as I straightened and pulled out of Odin's grasp. I tried to convince myself that any punishment he chose to impose upon me was deserved. Even if it meant an eternity in prison, I would deserve it. But the warriors' eyes were fixed to my right, to a swirl of light that grew between a pair of columns.

"The Doorway opens," Heimdall said from near the well. He held his horn to his lips and blew—though I could not hear it.

Everyone tensed. Steel rang out like the sighs of the wind as swords were drawn and arrows notched.

"What's going on?" I asked.

Odin handed me the sword from his waist and pulled another from his Halo. "I fear we may be at war," he said, his eyes trained on the opening Door. "There have been some developments on other worlds that lead us to fear there may be dark days ahead."

Before I could respond, the Door coalesced out of the blackness of space, ripping a brilliant multi-colored portal into the Wheelhouse. Fiahre stormed out. Even though her sword sat in the scabbard at her waist she had the feel of war about her, her face burning with fury. She strode right up to Odin, a dozen or so Valkyries streaming out of the Door behind her.

"My liege." She placed her fist over her heart, but did not kneel. "Our fears have been confirmed."

Odin said nothing, only nodded. He put his arm over my shoulder and when I met his eyes I saw something different than I expected. I saw hope. Compassion. And other tender feelings I didn't dare name.

Fiahre shifted her glare from Odin to me. Her fierce expression faded as she, too, looked at me with expectant hope—like she thought I would do something for her. But I was no savior—I could still feel the cold burning of Soloman's ring on the finger I no longer had. Proof that I'd never be free of the darkness that was a part of me. I opened my mouth to say so, when Fiahre stepped to the side.

Behind her, the Valkyries formed parallel lines, leaving a walkway between me and the Door. And there, stepping out of the rainbow light of the Bifrost, came Michael.

My heart lurched into a new rhythm, my words caught in my throat. Every single cell of my being focused on him. On the way he hung his head. The way he released the hilt of his sword as he swung his arm forward, about to step into a long stride—and the way he looked up and froze.

He saw me.

And I saw him.

And then I was running, flying, diving into his arms.

He caught me into his embrace while laughter, sobs, words of love, all tumbled out at the same time to create a visceral sensation of love.

Between one breath and the next I went from being bereft, to being loved.

Gone was the Wheelhouse, the Valkyries, the Gardians, Odin and Heimdall. Gone was the Bridge. There was only us.

I held him with intention. Kissed him with abandon.

I held nothing back and he took it all, giving so much more in return.

Oh my love, he whispered in my mind over and over again.

I breathed deep the scent I'd been trying to remember for eons—oranges and honey, Lily of the Valley.

I flooded his mind with my love for him. Filled every part of him with *IloveyouIloveyouIloveyou*.

I don't know how long we stayed in the In Between—the realm between the molecules of space, the home for almosts and maybes between one world and the next—but when we finally returned to the Wheelhouse we found ourselves alone but for the Gardians who were stationed there.

I didn't question where everyone had gone, just held tightly to Michael's hand as he led me across the Bridge and through Asgard. I Remembered everything now. Everything that had come before my mortal birth, everything about who I was—before and during. The only mystery to me now was who, or rather, what, I had Become. Though with my hand in Michael's, I had hope.

He led me behind the buildings, off the roads, and through a stand of trees with pristine white bark and shimmering golden leaves. I knew where he was taking me, and oh how I wanted to go there.

Beyond the trees we walked over verdant grass and followed a stream of turquoise water. I laughed when I saw the tiny fish flitting beneath its surface, their scales in all shades of the rainbow. I'd forgotten the glorious beauty of Asgard. Forgotten the feel of its breeze on my skin, like a caress from the sun. Forgotten the smell of hope and love that permeated everything here.

Amidst another copse of trees, Michael held branches back for me as we ventured deeper into the woods. And then we were suddenly there.

A small clearing, the perfect size.

A stone bench, with cherubs carved into the legs. A bench for two.

And all around the perimeter, growing in the shade of the golden-leaved trees, their heads gently bobbing in the subtle breeze, stood hundreds of Lily of the Valley.

Michael held both my hands in his, his right thumb tracing the stub of my ring finger. I closed my eyes, not wanting to think about what I had lost, or to remember that time in my life when I was overcome by Father's dark poison. Instead I angled my face into the warmth of the sunlight, and breathed deeply. I was home. In this moment, in this place, I had everything I'd ever dreamed of. Everything I'd dared hope for.

When Michael pulled me to him, when his hands first cupped my face, then wound their way behind my neck and into my hair, when his forehead rested on mine, and his breath caressed my cheek...

Even when there was too much perfection, too much honesty and love, I didn't run away.

I lifted my face to his.

Parted my lips and fell into his kiss.

Far too soon, we left our garden and Michael took me to Valhalla where Fiahre stood at the gates. "The others will be waiting," Fiahre said with a glare. Michael only smiled and gave me a kiss on the cheek before turning to leave. No way would either of us feel sorry for being a little late.

Fiahre bustled me past the gates and down a long corridor. We hurried through a courtyard where a staff spun suspended in a pocket of shimmering light. "Is that—?"

"Yes." Fiahre ushered me into a small room, one I recognized from so long ago. Mahria's room. My mother's room. "Now you must hurry," Fiahre insisted as she stepped back into the hall.

A thought struck me, like lightning on a sunny day. "Wait, Fiahre."

She paused, looked over her shoulder.

"Mahria—she's Ascended, right? Will I—" I took a deep breath to steady the sudden excitement and hope that made me all jittery. "Will I get to see her?"

At first, Fiahre did nothing. Didn't even blink.

Then she sighed and stepped into the room, folded her arms and leaned against the door she'd pulled closed. "Mahria is not Ascended." Her voice lay low and sad in the room. "You will not see her."

"But Lucy and Aaron . . ."

Fiahre was all business, and when she spoke she did it in a matter-of-fact way, leaving me with the distinct impression she would not be answering any more of my questions. "Your friends were human—Gardians who had completed their quest for Ascension. That you've even been able to see and talk to them is . . . unheard of. I can only suppose that they have not entirely completed their Ascension because once they do, they will no longer have a connection to life as we know it—the concerns of the every day, well . . . Let's just say it won't be in their purview."

I opened my mouth to ask how that can be true if soul eaters can destroy them, but Fiahre hurried on.

"Mahria was not human. She went to Loki as a Valkyrie, as a warrior goes to battle. Valkyrie do not seek Ascension, are not born into a human existence so we can quest for it. We serve our goddess and when we die—I believe we go to Vanaheim, to live with her in peace. But many choose to stay in Valhalla—to train for the day when Ragnarok comes and we are needed once more." She stood out from the wall and opened the door, turning to leave.

"But—if you have to be human, born on Earth and completed your quest, in order to Ascend, and if Valkyrie don't Ascend . . . What about Gardians? What if they die—" Michael filled my mind. Michael with the Spear in his shoulder. Michael, his sword flashing, as Father circled him. I took a deep breath and tried to mimic Fiahre's confidence. "If a Gardian dies in battle or whatever, what happens to him? I mean, them?" I held my breath as I waited for her answer.

She studied her hand on the doorframe for one, two, three heartbeats before she looked back. "He would be reincarnated as a Gardian once more. There is no rest for the soul of a Gardian until he has reached Ascension, or . . . Fallen. That's why Odin created Ascension in the first place—he couldn't bear seeing his children move through one meaningless existence to another. He thought all of them would achieve Ascension, but that was before Loki defied him. Before he learned how to tempt the Gardians-turned-human. Now many more are tempted away from their quest and end up spending eternity with that—that Defiler." Her gaze had drifted inward, but when she spoke of Father it snapped up to meet mine. "My apologies."

I laughed without mirth. "Ha. You don't need to apologize. I know who my father is. What he is."

She nodded, a sharp bob of her chin. "Well, then. I shall return for you shortly. You must hurry."

"Right. Okay. And Fiahre—" She closed the door. "Thank you," I said quietly to the empty room.

Now another question floated to the forefront of my mind. *What will happen to me if I die?*

Clothes had been laid over the narrow bed. I recognized them from my time here in Asgard; they were mine. I tried to be grateful they were clean instead of disappointed they weren't a pair of jeans and a T-shirt. To my left, near the head of the bed, a door stood cracked open—inside I found a rainfall room. Father had tried to duplicate it in Hell, but no matter how hot he made the water, I never felt truly warm. Earth's showers came close, but still . . . I hoped everything could wait for a few minutes of bliss.

I tugged at my kilt while Fiahre dragged me into a dining hall. We found Michael, Heimdall and Odin, sitting around Odin's grand table, a feast spread before them, but no food yet on their plates.

Michael sat on the table edge, turning a dagger round and round, casting glimmers of light onto the wall. When he saw me, he nearly dropped his blade and oh, his expression was priceless. He froze, his eyes the only part of him that moved as he took in the sight of me.

I felt self-conscious, knowing what he saw. For the first time in so long I didn't wear black. No jeans. No heavy combat boots. I did wish I had my Chucks though, the ones with the silver knots—not that I needed their protection here.

Instead, I wore golden laced boots that reached partway up my calf and a tunic the shade of new grass. Over that I wore the white kilt and gold armor of the Valkyries. I'd stared at myself for a long time, trying to come to terms with that. I knew my mother had been a Valkyrie, but it seemed presumptuous to count myself among their number.

"Welcome, my children." Odin stood to greet us. "Come and sit down, we were about to begin." I knew it was a lie. Knew they'd been waiting for us, but I was happy for it. Happy to be wanted, to be included. To feel something close to myself again after so, so long of . . . well, not.

Michael held a chair out for me and I smiled shyly at him when he sat beside me. Heimdall grasped Michael's shoulder and leaned down to him so they could speak quietly together. Michael took my hand under the table and squeezed it. Fiahre smiled at me from across the table and I marveled at the capacity for forgiveness that abounded here. I felt my shoulders relax and my heart and mind give themselves over to the peace of this moment.

Michael released my hand so he could fill my plate with meats, cheeses and glorious fruit I'd long forgotten. My stomach growled at the prospect of eating. Such a mundane act, the smallest of things, really, and yet there was more than taste here—there was life, there was living.

About halfway through the meal, Odin set his goblet down and cleared his throat. It seemed to be a cue of some sort as conversations around the table hushed. Odin turned to Fiahre, but said nothing.

Fiahre's focus did not waver from our king. "My Lord, it is as we feared." She folded her hands together on the table. "The Giants are rallying, and the Svarts are with them. I did not see Helena, but I felt her presence, heard her name in many whispered conversations."

Fiahre let her gaze momentarily settle on each of us. "They are moving on Midgard within days—I am unsure exactly when."

Odin did not seem surprised by this news. "Were you able to ascertain why they would move on Midgard? It was our prior understanding they were being persuaded to move against Helheimer."

Michael leaned forward, his elbows on the table. "It seems they have been led to believe they can conquer—and possess—it. That they can "liberate" it from your grasp." He bent his head and took a breath before continuing. "They express dissatisfaction over you owning two worlds, Asgard and Midgard, and even that Asgard itself is already the largest, the best. They feel that the Vanir gods were misled and cheated by the Aesir gods when they granted you both worlds. They wish to set things right."

For several heartbeats the room remained quiet and though I tried, I couldn't read any of their faces. All I knew was war was threatening Midgard, a world I had come to think of as my own. No way would I sit back and let that happen.

"I see," Odin finally said. And then he sighed. "It has been this way since we were first granted our worlds. Since we first left the home of our fathers. It has always been thus, and I fear it ever shall be."

I watched the people around me, watched them banish fear in favor of courage, watched the determination settle into their features like mirror images of one another. And I thought, *They are heroes. Every one.*

"We must not delay," Heimdall said. "I cannot keep them from travelling the paths that are already lain. I cannot favor the Valkyries over the Svarts, Gardians over Muspellarians. You understand this."

Odin hadn't taken his eyes from Heimdall's face while he spoke. When the large man finished, Odin reached over and placed his hand on his arm. "I understand, brother. I would never ask it of you."

"I can, however, keep you informed of their numbers, the placement of their Doors."

"Thank you."

The two gods stared at one another for a moment, and I had the distinct feeling there was much more going on between them than what we were privy to. While I processed the information we'd been given, and tried to settle into this new life, I thought of my father and how he might be involved.

I felt certain he would never invite the Svarts or the Muspelheim giants to join him in a fight over Midgard. He wanted all of Midgard for himself—he certainly wouldn't want to share it. But Helena—could this be her doing? Would she want Midgard? Or was this just part of her plan to force Father from his throne in Helheimer?

I looked at my hands in my lap, one with Michael's clasped around it. He rubbed his thumb in soft circles over the tender side of my wrist. I remembered him doing that. Before. I studied his face in profile, his chin, his parted lips. They quirked upward when he realized I was staring at them. At the curve of his cheek and the way his eyelashes, darker than his hair, swept over them. At his hair, which had grown since I saw him last and hung in that way I loved, just long enough it curled over his ears.

Michael angled himself so he faced me and cut off my view of the others. "What are you thinking?" he asked in a whisper, his lips barely moving to form the words. I contemplated telling him the truth—that even in the midst of everything all I really wanted to do was run back to our garden. To lie in the grass, with his arms wrapped around me. To watch the sky beyond the flickering golden leaves. To kiss him. To kiss and kiss and kiss him and never think of war again. Never think of Father again. Never Remember all I had done, all that came before.

I wanted to start anew with Michael. To find happiness. To *be* happy. To be free.

Instead I said, "James." Because I could never be wholly free as long as he was not.

He lifted his head and looked squarely into my eyes.

"And . . ." Selfish, so selfish. "I love you. That's all." I felt a momentary stab of discomfort as I became aware that we were still sitting at the table with the others while they discussed war. But I didn't move. I'd spent far too long pushing Michael away.

"That's all?" he asked with a raise of his eyebrow. He tried to don an expression of disapproval, but his lips quirking into a smile gave him away. "Oh my love." He put his free hand around the back of my neck. His fingers separated out the strands of my hair, sending waves of pleasure radiating through me. "My love," he said against my cheek. "I have waited so long to hear you say those words."

A shadow passed over his eyes, but he tilted his head until our foreheads met, his nose resting against mine. When he looked up and regarded me with his lion eyes—golden amber rimmed with darkest brown—the shadow was gone. Flecks of gold swam in the tawny depths of his eyes, reflecting the smile on my face. "I have always loved you."

My breath hitched, my whole being paused. I listened. Not to anyone else, not even to Michael; but to myself. To my heart. But there were no dissenting voices. No more doubts that our love was meant to be.

I felt certain I would live an eternity trying to be worthy of Michael, but I knew—I *knew*—that was okay. I would be with him forever and I would forever try to be the one worthy of his love.

I would never again listen to those voices in my head—the doubts planted there by Father and Akaros—

I would only ever listen to my heart. And my heart had always loved Michael.

"We will find him," Michael said. "If Helen—"

"Ahem." Odin cleared his throat. Michael pulled back and faced our king.

I felt my entire body grow unbearably hot, but Odin only smiled, his eyes dancing with happiness despite the dire topic of discussion.

"We believe we have only days." He was probably repeating himself and my gratitude for such a kind and generous king made my heart swell. "I need you to visit Cornelius, to inform him of what is coming. We will need Longinus in this battle. We will need every good man. Cornelius will know how to activate The Hallowed."

"Yes, Lord," Michael said.

I stopped listening as my thoughts once again turned inward. My stomach flopped as I considered what would happen next. I'd see Miri. And I'd need to tell her about James. When we could set out to rescue him—and how.

And I still needed to tell Odin about Aaron. And . . .

"Where's Lucy?" I blurted out.

"I beg your pardon?" Fiahre asked.

"I'm sorry," I said, acknowledging each of them—Heimdall with his ever-glowering expression, Fiahre, her lovely face as immovable as a Grecian statue, Horonius, obviously uncomfortable in our company, and Odin—my king. "I'm sorry. I should have said something earlier—and I was going to, but . . ."

I glanced at Michael and guilt clogged my veins.

"I thought Lucy would be here. I thought she'd say hello. Maybe she could help—you know, with the war."

Michael stared at our joined hands. Odin watched me, the glow in his eyes darkening.

"That's how you knew where to find me, right? Lucy told you where I was?"

"Desolation," Odin began. "I have not seen Lucy since she met you on the Bridge, so long ago."

"But—"

"She found you?"

"Yes. Isn't that how you knew where to find me?" I shifted, indicating Horonius.

"I led your unruly friend to you, mistress. I suspected you might have been imprisoned in the same place as the grand mistress. And I was right—in a way."

"In a way?" Fiahre asked.

"Yes, she was in the same place but she was . . . I am not sure how to explain it. Hidden behind a spell of some sort. We could not find her until she shone so brightly it undid whatever darkness had hidden her from view."

"Is that true?" Odin asked me.

I lifted my shoulders in a shrug. "I don't know. I only know that Aaron helped me sweep the darkness from my soul. He shared his light with me. Helped me shine. Helped me shine brighter. And he—"

I tore my hands from Michael's and covered my face. Tears, burning and swift, tore through me, through my chest, ripping my heart out, and flying from my eyes like a million thoughts on scissor wings. Michael placed his hand on my back, but it was Odin who spoke.

"When you are ready, tell us what happened, my daughter."

"I-I can't." I fought the sobs that threatened to overcome me as I thought of Aaron and what he had done for me. "I didn't want him to. I didn't want to cause anyone anymore pain ever again."

"Oh, my love," Michael soothed.

I felt Odin's presence in my mind then, felt it fill me like warm honey, like liquid sunshine. Felt him whispering, *It is all right, my daughter. It is all right.*

"He gave everything he had to me." I raised my gaze to Odin's. I felt more exposed in that moment than I could remember ever feeling. Here was my king, my creator, and I was about to tell him I caused the eternal death of one of his sons. An Ascended One—a child of Odin's who had received the highest exultation. And now he was gone. Because of me.

But I forced myself to meet Odin's steady gaze. To open myself and let his blue eyes see more than what was written on my face, but what was written on my heart. "He gave it all until I shone so bright and there was almost nothing of him left. And then—and then—" I choked on the tears that flooded my throat and it took me several heartbeats to push them back down. All the while Michael's hand on mine grounded me, and Odin's focus never wavered.

"A soul eater . . ." I didn't say it. I'm sure I didn't need to. Everyone knew the soul eaters prey on any unprotected living thing.

Though he didn't move, didn't look away, I felt Odin's embrace as surely as if he physically held me in his arms. I squeezed Michael's hand tighter, my whole body trembling with the weight of my emotions. "And what of Lucy?" Pain flickered in Odin's eyes.

"She left—long before the soul eater got there. She went to tell you where I was. To send help. I'm positive she should have found you by now."

We sat in silence while everyone tried to figure out what to say to the girl who caused so much sorrow, so much death.

"Desolation—" Odin's voice was a distant rumble, a coming storm. I snorted. Even after all Aaron and Lucy did for me, I still was no better than my name.

"Lucy's gone, isn't she?" I glared at Odin, at every single one of them, even Michael, daring them to deny it.

Michael flinched when his eyes met mine. "Taken by a soul eater, or lost among the stars—it doesn't matter. Because gone is gone." Even lit up like a star, all golden sunshine, I still knew how to drive in the knife. How to twist it deep.

"I'm sorry." I jumped to my feet so suddenly my chair toppled over. "I'm sorry," I said again, apologizing for the chair, for my cruelty. For Lucy. For causing the death of two of the most beautiful people in all the worlds. Aaron and Lucy died for me. People were always dying for me. My mother. Aaron and Lucy. James.

I took no thought for direction as my feet carried me away. My mind lurched into a constant loop of *Mother, Aaron, Lucy, James. Mother, Aaron, Lucy, James.*

Over and

over and

over and

over.

I found myself in the garden, kneeling with my forehead pressed to the ground while my fingers cramped around fistfuls of grass. I watered the earth with my tears. I cried my sorrow out to it, with the heady fragrance of Lily of the Valley wrapping all around me. *Mother, Aaron, Lucy, James. Mother, Aaron, Lucy, James.*

Mother, Aaron, Lucy, James.

A flash of light, all golden sparks, then Michael said my name.

He sat beside me. After rubbing my back for a moment, he pulled me onto his lap, cradling me like a child. I pressed my face against his chest, gripped his ocean-blue tunic, and cried hollow, dry tears. His consciousness slipped into my mind, gently coiling around my thoughts, my sorrows, embracing all of me, inside and out.

I wanted to reject him. To punish him for being so good like I'd always done in the past. But the truth was I was tired. Tired of being the cause of so much sorrow. Tired of hating myself. Tired of being alone. And so I let him hold me until the darkness around us matched the darkness behind my eyelids. I finally opened my eyes, having cried the last of my tears long ago. Michael's cheek rested on my head and he was so still, so quiet, I thought he must be sleeping.

When I sighed, he stirred. "I'm awake," he said, and despite myself, I smiled. Of course he knew my thoughts. Of course.

"But we should sleep. Odin asked that we gather at the Door tomorrow afternoon—there's time, yet." Time for what, though, I didn't know. Time for us? Time to sleep? Time to forget? He helped me stand, then stood himself. "Your mother's rooms—" he cleared his throat. "The Valkyrie have prepared a room for you—but you're welcome to stay with me."

I waited a beat, trying to discern which he wanted. My heart told me he wanted to be with me, but my mind still denied the love he forever held out to me. He put his hands on my arm, dipped his chin so he could catch my eyes. And in that moment I didn't have to read his thoughts to know what he wanted. It was clear in everything about him, so clear even I couldn't deny it.

"I don't want to be away from you," he said. *Ever, ever again.*

The starlight reflected off the curve of his cheek while he smiled before leading me out of the garden. As we walked, the way became more familiar and I realized I knew this place—all of this place.

I Remembered Mahria and the fierce gleam in her eyes while she taught me to fight with the staff. She was the one to suggest to Odin I'd like one of my own.

I Remembered when she left Asgard, and the mysterious words she'd said. She told me she was going to prepare a place for me, and that I was to never forget she loved me. And never forget who I was.

But even though I Remembered, Remembered all of it, it was still so, so hard to believe I could be the sum of all my experiences and not just a product of Father's evil. How could I believe there was anything good in me when everyone associated with me suffered so much?

Michael stopped and pulled me in front of him. "Desi." His hands gripped my arms tight and when I met his eyes they burned with anger—and love. "You must stop this."

I opened my mouth. *Stop what?* I wanted to ask.

"You wish to punish yourself—still—for the evil you have done. I—" his voice caught and he paused, looked down, "I know some of what you must feel, what you must think." He swallowed against some emotion I recognized but rejected. How could Michael be feeling shame? *What sins has he committed?*

"There was a time when I could only love you, when I didn't understand the darkness in you, but had to hope, had to believe, you were still you. Glorious. Good. I believed it, and I wasn't wrong." When I looked away, he crooked a finger under my chin, pulling my face upward. "I wasn't wrong. But—" Again he dropped his eyes. This was so unlike him, to be unsure, to be lost for words.

"I understand now. The darkness, I mean. The temptation to think the worst of yourself. To expect the worst. To think the ones you love couldn't possibly love you if they knew just how far you've fallen.

"Do you remember we tied the knot—right here, in this place?"

I laughed. "Tied the knot?"

He grinned and took my right hand in his, holding our joined hands up between us. As I stared into his eyes, the Memory came back to me. Odin had bound our hands with the golden cord, tying the knots that would bind us to each other for eternity.

When recognition shone in my eyes, he pulled me to him, clasping me hard against his chest, burying his face in the hair at my neck. When he pulled back, unshed tears shimmered in his eyes. Gently he turned me around, stopping me when my back was to him. He leaned down, putting his face next to mine.

"We have been bound in every way. Even our experiences with Loki and our time in Hell. There is nothing you don't know of me, and I don't know of you."

I felt his cheek against mine. Smelled the sweet, tart smell of him. His hands softened on my arms and he moved so his lips were against my neck. "And now, look. We are in Heaven, love. We are home."

My body stilled against him as I tried to understand.

"Would we be here if we were beyond redemption?"

My eyes opened wide, understanding and hope washing away the fear and doubt so swiftly that it left me weak. I sagged against him. He whispered against my neck, my ear, my cheeks until his words turned to kisses. He swept me up into his arms and carried me to his house.

He lived in a small, single-story cottage made of stones I knew he had laid himself. At the green door I held out my hand, stopping us from passing through the doorway. I traced the knotted heart carved into the lintel and raised a questioning brow.

"Always," he said.

He'd always remembered, while I hadn't. He'd stayed faithful when I had forgotten him. He had fought for me, long after I'd given up. *Always.*

He opened the door and I wrapped my arms more tightly around his neck. As we crossed the threshold I wondered, can we really let go of the past? Let go of our mistakes? Because whatever had come before, we were here now. No matter how much I'd forgotten, I remembered now. No matter how lost I'd become, how lost we had both been, we were found now. That had to count for something.

In the morning I woke to golden light dappled over the bedcovers. Michael had slept on the couch, tucking me into his own bed late last night—I didn't even remember saying goodnight, I'd been that tired. Now I stretched and drew a deep breath through my nose, relishing the scent of him everywhere. I closed my eyes and drank in the happiness, the peace that whispered through me, in sync with the shimmering light all around.

After a time I heard Michael moving about in the other room, and smelled the unmistakable scent of coffee—though I knew it wasn't a drink normally found on Asgard.

That simple thing made my heart rush with love for this man who knew me so well and would do even the smallest of things to ensure my comfort.

I dressed quickly, and for half a second thought about doing my hair as Fiahre wore hers—in a sort of braided knot that sat low at her neck. But in the end I opted for a ponytail. I couldn't change everything at once. Before I left the room, I stared at my skin—no longer as pale white as I'd been for so, so long, and my eyes were no longer the endless ebony black of a demon. Now flecks of gold swam in their dark depths making me a hundred shades of relieved.

It didn't mean I'd forgotten what I was—what I still was. No amount of sunshine skin or flecks of gold could undo the half of my DNA that belonged to my father. But I also knew I had been through a refiner's fire. With Aaron's help and love, most of the darkness had been burned out of me, the bad changed for good, the evil cast aside to make room for the golden spark that no longer resided in my heart alone, but permeated every single cell of my being.

I knew what I was. And what I was, was glorious.

I am glorious.

So when Michael reached for me, every hope and all his love laid bare on his face; when his eyes hungrily devoured me and searched my eyes . . .

I knew what he saw in me.

He saw what I wanted to be.

My father's desolation. The end to his reign. The end to the evil he constantly levied on the innocent Gardians on Midgard. I no longer despised my name, but embraced it. I would be the weapon my mother hoped I would be.

TWELVE

DESI

"What am I going to tell Miri?" We walked hand-in-hand down the street, smiling at the people we passed. They greeted me happily, their faces reflecting their joy, their hands reaching to touch me. I had a brief flash to the wanters and needers in Hell and all the many times I plowed through them as though I were a rock and they the stream that rushed past. I had despised their touch, their need to take something, anything, from me. But in Asgard everything was different; the people gave, asking nothing in return. They gave their blessings. Told me how glad they were to see me. How much they loved me.

I felt like two separate persons walking among them—there was this part of me, the part they remembered, the part that remembered them. This was the part of me Aaron had sacrificed himself for. But there was another part—the part I knew best. The girl who let her friends down. The girl who had abandoned a most brave and generous guy to the clutches of an evil goddess. The girl who had to tell her best friend that she'd left the love of her life behind. What could I possibly say to make it okay?

"What do you remember? Of this place?" Michael gave my hand a gentle squeeze, pulling me out of my reverie and grounding me in the moment.

Small shops, their colored signs hanging over the doors, lined the quiet street. A statue of an Aesir god—Odin's father—rose tall and glorious from the square opposite Odin's palace. The figure reminded me of Heimdall—larger than life with a wavy beard and hair. He held his right hand high, a lightning bolt clutched in his fist.

We'd stopped walking as I stared up at the giant statue. I suddenly had the feeling of déjà vu—standing there with Michael reminded me of the times we'd stood like this beneath the stony gaze of a cherubic statue in St. Mary's cemetery. Of all the times I'd wished for an answer, for some indication there was more in the universe—some hope or guidance beyond the usual.

What if there is? a voice, like a forgotten part of myself, whispered in my mind. *What if we aren't really alone? What if the gods do still care? Odin and Heimdall certainly do.*

"Desi?" Michael squeezed my hand again.

I shook my head to dislodge the strange line of thought that had taken up residence in my foggy brain. "I think I remember most of it." We stood in a little park with green grass, stone benches, and flowers of all variety and color. When I tipped my face upward to see Michael, I found him smiling at me expectantly. "I remember all of it."

His lion eyes lit up, all golden sunshine and dark chocolate, and his lips quirked into a delicious smile that made me want to cover it with kisses.

And so I did.

He stumbled a little in surprise as I leaned into him, pressing my lips to his. I felt him Become, felt him wrap his arms around me, and then his wings. Felt nothing but joy and exquisite release as he transported us from the public square to the quiet, fragrant sanctuary of our garden.

And still we kissed, his lips both soft and demanding, pulling out the best of me, claiming every wild beat of my heart.

It had been so long since we'd been together like this. No more tender kisses full of hope and fear. No more fleeting moments of love. No more restraint. And absolutely no more doubt.

Michael felt alive with fire beneath my hands, beneath my lips. He held me so close I could hardly breathe. I wanted to breathe with him, be one with him. I pulled myself closer and felt his body respond to mine. Our kisses grew more insistent, until all I could think about was Michael.

His taste.

His touch.

His love.

Oh, love. Glorious. Everlasting. Complete.

Sometime later I lay snuggled in the crook of Michael's arm, gazing up at the blue sky above us.

"I wish we could stay here forever." I closed my eyes and tried to push the world away, tried to concentrate on this moment, on right now.

"I do, too." He propped himself up on one elbow and traced his fingers over the golden whorls on my arm, following their course from fingertip to shoulder. I shivered beneath his feather touch. "So much is the same and yet—nothing will ever be the same again."

He brushed the hair back from my neck and let his hand rest there. I opened my eyes and found him gazing at me. "I knew, even before we actually met, that you were destined for great things. Did you know it? Back then?"

I closed my eyes again and willed myself to Remember. To truly examine what I knew and not just what I dreamed or imagined. "I suppose there were clues all around, weren't there? The way Mahria trained me harder than any of the other Valkyrie. The staff Odin gave me from the Tree of Knowledge."

I tugged myself tighter to Michael's side and breathed in the smell of him. "Mahria came to see me before she left. I was warming up in the courtyard, waiting for her to spar with me. I'd been planning a new move to try on her. But she refused my invitation.

"I think she tried to explain, tried to tell me what she was doing, but words failed her. Instead she hugged me— only for a second—but enough to leave me reeling as she left." I smoothed my hand down Michael's strong chest. Felt the warmth and life of him, even my fingertips thrummed with love. "I think I knew, then, that I'd never see her again, even though I felt pretty sure our paths would somehow cross.

"I think I knew all that and maybe even more—but I never once thought I would be any kind of hero. I thought I was a good soldier—and maybe I was. That's what Father and Akaros used against me for so long, anyway. Wasn't it?"

Michael lay back down and didn't say anything for a long time. Only the steady beating of his heart, the rhythm of his breath, told me he wasn't asleep. When I glanced at his face, I saw him staring up at the sky.

"Loving you hasn't been easy," he said. Everything in me stilled, as if each cell of my body held its breath. "All of us—we knew from the moment we laid eyes on you that loving you would be a journey fraught with danger. Lucy,

Aaron, me and Mahria. Even Longinus, Cornelius, Miri and James—all of us. We all knew you. Before. The way you shone, the way you glowed with love and life—you were always bound for greatness.

"And like most great things, we knew your climb wouldn't be a golden staircase. We knew there'd be a cost to loving you, a price to pay."

"I'm sorry," I whispered, the words skimming across his chest. He squeezed me to him.

"Oh, my love. I am positive not one of us would change a thing. It's only that you are unlike us. You are like a lioness, beautiful and glorious, but fierce. And just as a lion loves his mate, he also knows she is greater than he."

I breathed with him as I counted his heartbeats. "I don't want to be greater than you. I don't feel greater. I want to be loved and cared for, doted on and spoiled. I don't want to be running into danger every five minutes, seeing the people I love die, feeling them ripped away by my enemies."

"Love, you know Loki is not *your* enemy only." He twisted toward me, making certain our eyes met. He radiated sureness, his words ringing with confidence. "You do know this, don't you?"

Tears filled my eyes so I ducked under his chin and snuggled close. "All I know is that I've done a lot of bad things because of Loki. But *I* did them—not him. If I'm so great and glorious, wouldn't I have known better? What of all the people who've lost so much because of me?

"Like you—how can you love me after spending an eternity in Hell? You won't tell me what Father made you do, and I think it's because it's so awful you're afraid to add to my burden. But I know what Hell is like. I know what Father is like. Whether you tell me or not, it is my burden. Everything Father has done is because of me." I sat up, scooting away from Michael, and wishing for a longer skirt or jeans so I could wrap my arms around my knees.

"If it hadn't been for me, you would never have done what you did to Heimdall. James and Lucy wouldn't be missing, Knowles wouldn't be dead—Aaron wouldn't be dead." My voice broke and I buried my face in my hands, but managed to force the tears back down, my chest like a forest fire. I thrust my thoughts out through my burning throat, each word scarring me with its truth. "If only I'd done what Mahria and Odin wanted me to—if only I'd Remembered and finished Loki off right away—none of this would have happened. Midgard would be free. The people I love wouldn't be gone."

Michael knelt on the grass in front of me and cupped my face in his hands. He speared me with his gaze. He opened his mouth to say something, then closed it again.

I knew I shouldn't dwell on all the bad that happened. Knew I should be glad to be here now—in Asgard, with

Michael—but I also couldn't pretend to be this awesome warrior hero that the others seemed to think I was—that even Michael seemed to expect me to be.

He pulled me to my knees and brought my face to his. He pressed his forehead against mine. Breathed my breath.

"Love. We have both suffered at Loki's hand. I know something of the burden you bear. But I promise you, I will gladly live the rest of my eternal life dedicated to the task of proving to you that you are, ever have been, and always will be, worth any sacrifice I could make. And I know—" I tried to drop my eyes, but he held my face firm between his hands and pulled back so I had no choice but to meet his gaze. "I *know*, that everyone who has ever loved you feels the same."

"But—"

He swallowed any argument I might have given with his kiss. His hands slipped into my hair, pulled out the elastic that held it back and deepened his embrace.

I tasted honey on his lips. I tasted hope.

I tasted love.

Do you forgive me? Can you?

I leaned back from him, searched his eyes, but he pulled me close again.

Can you? he pressed.

There is nothing to forgive.

For a moment, an image filled his mind before he pushed it aside, forced it away. But I'd seen it, I knew the fear he still harbored. He remembered lying in Cornelius's bed, recovering from his time in Hell. He felt the warmth of the whale-tail charm I'd given him, the one that protected him and left me vulnerable in its absence. He remembered watching the darkness infiltrate my body, understood it was in me because of him. Because of what he'd done while under Father's influence.

You need to forgive yourself too, because I already have.

Michael groaned, a sound of infinite need and hope. He wrapped his arms more tightly around me.

And will you? Forgive yourself?

I will if you will. The words sounded so much more confident than I felt. But I remembered Aaron's last words to me—that I should take what he had given me, his very essence, all his light, and use it to shine. For him. For love.

And in that moment, with Michael's hands in my hair and his kiss on my lips, I thought, *Maybe I can let go of all the guilt I've clung to.*

Let go of Father, and his claim on me.

Let go of Aaron, with thanks for his gift and for the chance he gave me at a life far brighter than the one I'd created for myself.

Let go of Knowles and acknowledge the sacrifice he made—a grand and righteous act befitting any Gardian.

In Michael's arms I let myself reclaim who I had been and remake her into who I should be. *Who I want to be. Who I will be.*

I would find out what happened to Lucy.

And I would find James and free him from Helena's grasp. I would return him to Miri and make sure they had the happy ending they deserved.

In Michael's arms, I embraced the Desi he believed me to be. I allowed myself to be the girl he loved—part demon, part Valkyrie, all Desolation. All his.

In the early afternoon we left our garden and I knew I wouldn't be coming back. I didn't belong in Asgard and Valhalla anymore. And maybe Michael didn't either. He plucked a tiny stem of Lily of the Valley and held it between us. I drank in the fragrance and closed my eyes. I would always remember this smell, and remember this moment, this day. The day I chose who I would be. And who I wouldn't.

Michael tucked the flower behind my ear, pressing it there with a kiss.

I bent down and plucked up a handful of the little blossoms and tucked them into the baldric that crossed his chest.

"Really?" He looked down and shook his head.

"It'll help you remember me."

He picked me up and swung me around, kissing my cheek when he set me back on my feet. "My love, I have never, ever forgotten." That shadow crossed his eyes again, just before he bent down, kissed my lips, his hands on my face, his lashes brushing against my cheek.

I pushed gently on his chest. "Michael."

He kept his eyes closed a moment but when he looked at me, he let me see all that troubled him. "I know you think you forgot. I know, even when Father poisoned you against me, against . . . everything . . . a part of you—the real part of you—never forgot."

I placed my hands on his cheeks, let my heart fill with all the love I had for him, my love, my forever love. "Just like the real part of me never forgot you."

With a whoosh of air Michael grabbed me to him and pressed his lips against mine. I lost myself in his touch, in his kiss. Gave everything I was—the good and the bad—in exchange for all that he was.

When we finally pulled apart, we took one last look at our garden, then walked through the shimmering trees to the city and wherever our path would take us.

Odin, Horonius and Fiahre stood outside Odin's palace. When we came near them, their conversation stopped as they turned to watch us. Fiahre smiled and I had a flash of Memory. I Remembered her and Mahria laughing, teasing me about Michael. Laughing that I was the only maiden he had ever laid eyes on—that after seeing me he'd been ruined for any of them.

She was my mother's near-sister, the Valkyrie version of family. When our eyes met, I could tell she knew I Remembered. She bowed her head in an act of recognition. Of acceptance.

"Your sisters?" Michael asked Fiahre without any preamble.

She nodded. "Ready."

"Good. Then let us go."

"Hold," Odin said. "I thought perhaps you would like to say goodbye to your friend. He has served well, I believe."

I tried to reason out Odin's words, when it finally dawned on me. Horonius, the Hound. "You won't be coming with us?" I asked. "What of your companion? Surely you want to find him." I hadn't asked where he was, I'd only assumed Helena had separated them. I saw my mistake the moment a shadow darkened the boy's eyes.

"My brother is no more. And I have been so long removed from Midgard that I feel I would be of little use."

"Midgard?" I asked, confused. I thought the Hounds were Helena's creation. That's what she had told me, what she had shown me.

Odin placed a hand on Horonius's shoulder. "Horonius and his twin brother were children in Pharaoh's court when Helena discovered them. They were boys of great beauty, and so innocent, sharing such love between them, that Helena became jealous. She took them into her own court and tried to make them hers, but their love for one another kept them pure. When she could not change their hearts, she changed their bodies and forever changed their future."

He smiled at Horonius, but I wondered if it wasn't cruel of Odin to remind the boy of all he had lost. Horonius examined the ground at his feet.

"Or so she believed. What the goddess forgot, was that as children of Midgard, Helonius and Horonius are mine."

My chin snapped upward, my eyes searching Odin's. Horonius did not understand, but I did—and so did the others. Smiles passed between us like a warm cup on a cold night.

"Horonius, my son, I believe someone has come to see you."

Horonius searched Odin's face, at first unbelieving, hope being such a rare and unlikely commodity in his life. Oh, I knew that truth. I knew what it felt like to hope even when you knew you had no right to.

"Brother?" a boy's soft voice asked from behind us. We all turned, stepping back, clearing the path, so none of us stood in the way of their reunion.

While I watched, brother fell upon brother. Their arms reached, hugged, pushed back the pain and sorrow they'd lived with for so very long. My heart broke for them, then sang with joy.

They thought they'd fallen so far. Thought there was no place of rest for them. No place of peace and happiness. And now here they were. Smiling into each other's eyes, discovering a life after the hell Helena had subjected them to. Here, there was redemption, and hope.

The boys smiled unabashedly, each with a hand on the other's shoulder. Horonius bowed his head. "Thank you, Lord."

Odin stepped forward and placed a hand on each of their shoulders, so they made a circle between them and I thought it fitting. Perfect. They had been renewed, remade. And it was Odin who joined them together again.

"I am saddened by all you were made to endure, my sons. But I am so glad you are home." He kissed each of them on the cheek, which they accepted gladly. He stepped back and gestured behind us. When we turned we saw two Valkyrie striding down the street, the golden-winged glory of their Halos spread wide behind them. "You have earned Ascension, if you wish it. Or," he nodded at the Valkyrie, "You can join the brave and victorious in Valhalla, as you have been ever faithful warriors."

The young men looked at each other for just a moment before breaking into wide grins. "We are grateful for the invitation to retire to Valhalla. To fight again if it is asked of us," Horonius said. "We will always—" he started, then his brother joined him. "Serve the young mistress."

Horonius smiled shyly at Odin. "May I?" he asked, gesturing toward me.

"Certainly."

"My lady." Horonius and Helonius both stood before me, their fists over their hearts. "If you ever have need of us, only call for us and we will obey."

"I don't ever wish to command you," I said.

"Lady," Helonius said in a quiet, shy voice. "It would be our honor."

I didn't know what to say, so I just smiled and inclined my head. They bowed in unison, then Helonius stepped toward one of the Valkyrie and took her hand, Horonius following.

With peace in my heart, I watched them walk through the gates of Valhalla and disappear behind the golden aura of the Valkyries' Halos.

Between the gates of Valhalla and the Bridge to Heimdall's Wheelhouse, the street was crowded with the most magnificent creatures I'd ever seen. Valkyries, dressed in their golden armor and crisp white tunics and kilts, sat atop pristine white-winged horses with silver manes.

"Beautiful," I breathed as we walked past one of the magnificent creatures.

"They are shi'lil, a gift from the Alfahr. They are glorious, fierce warriors," Michael told me.

As we passed, the shi'lils bent one knee and leaned down low, their noses nearly touching the golden stones of the street, their riders holding a fist over their hearts. I kept moving forward, focused on the street ahead of me. It felt wrong to be walking beside Fiahre and Michael—their people loved them so much. I wished I could take to the sky, skip on ahead to the Wheelhouse, and not detract from the respect and adoration poured out upon them.

Michael's fingers brushed against my elbow and he gently pulled me to a stop. "Desi." His eyes burned when I faced him. "They are showing reverence to *you*."

When I glanced at Fiahre, she smiled briefly before lowering herself to one knee. In slow motion I turned all around, and found each and every person, including Michael, bowing low.

At first I felt nothing but my usual feelings.

Confusion. Fear. Doubt. *They don't know me*, I thought. *If they did, they'd know I'm not worthy of their respect.*

Gradually, hope and love filled my heart, I realized in a sudden burst of Truth that they knew exactly who I was. And it's because of that—because of what I'd overcome, that they were here, giving me this honor.

I remembered what Michael had told me that I owed it to Aaron and Lucy to shine with all the light and love they had given me.

Michael was the only one who met my gaze from his spot on the ground, his eyes watching my face, waiting for the moment I'd finally accept my place at the head of this army. I searched his smiling, love-filled face, and while he watched, I let myself Become.

Not the dark demon Father and Akaros had fashioned me to be.

But my own creation of darkness and light.

My father was the son of a god. My mother a Valkyrie queen. I had been loved and blessed by Ascended Ones, eternal friends, and humans as generous as any Vanir gods. I was what they had made me, and more.

I radiated with the light of a sun, my body a pearlescent glow that was all my own. My wings stretched to twice my height, golden feathers reflecting the faces around me, but for once I didn't begrudge the black ones that covered my left wing. The darkness was a part of me, but it would never again *own* me.

I held my hands out in front of me and watched as ribbons of black swirled up my left arm, while golden threads wound their way up my right. I was black and gold, dark and light. I was Desolation. The gathered crowd erupted in cheers.

Beyond the mounted warriors stood thousands more Gardians and Valkyries. They made room for us to pass as we strode straight to the Wheelhouse and joined Odin and Heimdall there. The god of the Bifrost held out his hand, a swirling mass of energy and light suspended above it.

Odin greeted us with a nod.

"Helena is not taking her forces to Helheimer—she is rallying them to Midgard, as suspected. I have diverted their paths to a vast expanse of barren land in Earth's northern continent. I believe this to be in the interest of all the worlds, and not a breach of my contracts with them." Heimdall glared at us, daring any to deny him. "They have already begun arriving."

"What about The Hallowed?" Michael asked.

"They have received their instructions," Odin replied. "And they are on their way." His focus shifted to me. "Cornelius and his branch have arrived—they will tend to the injured and keep me informed of the state of battle."

The Hallowed. That would mean Cornelius, Longinus and maybe even Miri. But not James. My stomach clenched as I tried to think of how I could break the news to Miri.

Odin reached for my hand. "She expects to find him there—with the two of you." And before I formed the question in my mind, he said, "There has been no word of him."

No word of James.

The darkness no longer owned me, but all the light in Asgard couldn't stop the stab of remorse and guilt I felt that James was suffering because of me. But I'd spent my life running from my destiny, trying to avoid taking responsibility. I wouldn't do that any more. I took Michael's hand, taking strength from his firm grasp. I owed Miri the truth.

THIRTEEN

DESI

We shot to Earth like comets falling from the sky. I landed beside Michael, throwing a hand out to the dry, packed ground to stop myself from landing on my face. I watched as a thousand gold and silver comets plunged to Earth or circled the sky above us. I saw more lights falling all around—and not all of them the Gardians and Valkyries we had brought with us.

Fireballs of red and orange plummeted earthward, materializing into men the size of Heimdall with skin that glowed like red hot embers. Fire burned in their hair and beards. They marched toward us, swinging flaming hammers in each of their fists as they approached.

I took a step backward, suddenly unsure if I could survive this fight, if I could do enough to save the Gardians and Valkyries I stood with. On my left, a flash of white-blue caught my eye as flashes of blue and black fell to the earth, materializing into elves that shifted and moved like living ice.

We're all going to die, I thought.

Michael slipped behind me, his shoulders a reassuring strength while we stood back-to-back. *Don't be so quick to underestimate our power, my love*, Michael said in my mind. *I am here. You are here. And together, we are fearsome.*

He sent me an image, a Memory. My subconscious dusted off my own long-hidden memories of the day we'd fought Father—Loki, as I knew him then—and all his many millions of followers. We'd stood like this—faced an innumerable host, impossible odds.

And we had won.

Michael and I spun around so he was facing the Giants and I faced the dark elves—the creatures of Svartalheim. I hefted the staff in my hand— it wasn't the treasured one from the Tree of Life Odin gave me so long ago, but I was glad for that. This weapon would never reek of the darkness and temptation the Spear of Destiny had. At my hip rested a Valkyrie's blade, with daggers tucked into each of my boots. I curled my fingers around the smooth wood of my staff and felt Michael tense behind me.

There was no more time to fear what approached, because in front of me a host of dark elves drew their bows and raised gleaming kukris, oddly curved blades that flashed with cold light.

Fiahre fell into place beside me. She had a wild glint in her eye and a broad smile on her face.

"Welcome to your proper place, Sister," she said. "We shall make quick work of this fight." And without looking away, she Became . . . a creature too glorious to name.

Become, she said in my mind.

Before closing my eyes I saw the sky alight with bright streams as Valkyrie and shi'lil rained arrows down on the enemies surrounding us. When I Became I let the good and the bad fill every part of me, embracing all that I was. All I was created to be.

A Svart dove for me, his mouth opening in a screeching cry, revealing sharpened, jagged teeth. He raised his weapon above his head, its blade gleaming in my golden light. I thrust my staff forward and blocked his arm, spinning three-hundred-and-sixty degrees around to my left, catching him on the side of the head with my boot. He fell to the ground and I kicked his sword out of the way before slamming the butt of my staff against his head.

I had barely lifted my weapon before another Svart dove low and tried to thrust his blade upward into my stomach. I shoved my knee into his sternum at the same time as I slammed each side of his head with my fists.

I spun again, slicing the edge of my right wing through the chest of a Svart attacking Fiahre. As I rotated I saw the scene behind me—the press of fiery Giants and Michael shining glorious in their midst, wielding his sword like a whirling dervish.

But my sisters and I were pressed on all sides by the icy Svarts and there was little time to consider my love and how he fared. I had to trust we hadn't come this far to be torn apart now.

Gods, let it be so, I thought.

Three Svarts fell upon me, one digging his blade deep into my left wing. I bit back a cry—no time for pain. My concentration narrowed down to one singular thought: *Survive*.

Only movement existed. Only thrust, parry, strike. Kick, feint, block.

My fists were frozen where they fell time and again on the icy skin of the Svarts.

The staff in my hand slipped in my palm from their blood that painted it a pale blue.

My throat grew raw from screaming.

I barely moved from my spot as the enemy came to me. It seemed they meant to bury me alive in their bodies, as the pile of their dead surrounded me on all sides—yet still they came.

My arms grew weak, but I forced myself to fight on.

The sound of battle deafened me, gradually taking on the muted tone of Helheimer, as if it came through a long tube. Exhaustion teased me, made me long to lie down. Made me consider giving up.

Yet still I pressed on.

And then . . . the attack stopped.

It took me a moment to recognize the change. To realize the air no longer rang with steel.

I climbed over the bodies to survey the barren landscape. The bodies of Svarts littered the hard-packed ground all the way to the rocky mesas that dotted the horizon. A few Valkyrie sat or crouched on the ground, but I didn't see any lying among the dead. I could not see Fiahre.

I whirled around, seeking Michael—but I couldn't see him anywhere, either. There were far fewer Giants dead upon the ground, and more than a handful of Gardians that I could see. The Svarts and Giants had retreated, no doubt calling for reinforcements—for though their number had surpassed ours by far, they had suffered badly in battle.

Where the hell is Michael?

An alarm went off in my mind. A persistent driving sound of need.

I ran toward the Giants, then flew, excruciating pain accompanying every beat of my injured wing. Everything fell into my peripheral vision, everything beyond the singular focus of my need. I darted from one fallen Gardian to another, but could not find my love.

"Michael!" His name tore from my throat, burning with fear, again and again.

Someone flew into me, plummeting me back down to Earth, holding me in her arms.

"Shh," Fiahre said, pressing my head to her shoulder. "Shh."

I grabbed the shoulder straps of her armor, and wrapped my fists around them as I fell against her. I felt myself die. I could not exist without Michael. I didn't want to.

"What's it all been for?" I asked over and over. "Without him, what's the point?"

Fiahre made no reply, but continued to hold me. I wanted to die. I willed myself to die. My Halo faded. My knees gave way. Fiahre held me upright by her strength alone.

And then . . .

as quiet as a whispered breeze

rustling the golden leaves of our garden

as gentle as the nodding bells of the Lily of the Valley . . .

I am here, love.

I am here.

I didn't know if Fiahre heard him, or if she knew intuitively, but she threw her arms back and I burst away from her, Becoming and taking to the sky in a flash of golden light and black shadow. I followed my heart across the battlefield, where the survivors crouched together, tending to their wounded and dead. I flew to the rocky outcropping and the soul of the person I would never again forget and would always find.

Landing near the rocks, I let my spirit recede into Halo and Shadow, unwilling to entirely let go of the strength and comfort they brought me. Fiahre landed beside me. I glanced at her, then stepped into the cool darkness of a maze of rocks, my staff held ready.

A dark form separated itself from the shadows.

"Longinus!" Fiahre cried and took two fast steps forward before stopping abruptly. She glanced back at me, and for a moment I saw her as a young woman in love, and not the fierce warrior she usually portrayed. While I watched, she assumed that mask and instead of leaping into Longinus's arms like I knew she wanted, she reached out and they clasped forearms. They didn't say anything, but I understood it all.

This was relief at finding the other unharmed. This was joy in being in another's company again.

This was love.

I hadn't known they loved each other, but it sat on my heart with the easiness of inevitability. They were perfect together.

Longinus stepped past Fiahre, but I didn't miss the way his fingers trailed up her arm as he let go of her. He took my right hand in his. "Lady," he said, bowing his head. The respect and care that radiated from him made me uncomfortable, but I tried not to show it. It would take time to get used to this new me. This warrior girl. This responsible girl.

"Come with me." A stone settled in my heart as he led me behind the outcropping and into a small sunlit chamber between the rocks. Fear of what I would find slowed my steps and filled my throat with unshed tears.

The first thing I saw was Cornelius sitting on the ground, his head bowed. And then . . . Michael.

His back was to me, but as soon as I stepped into view he stood. In a flash he had me in his arms, lifted me from the ground, buried his face against my neck. *Oh, love*, he said in my mind.

Something was wrong. Very wrong.

"What is it?" I asked when he set me on my feet.

"Come." He took my hand and led me forward to where Miri lay on the ground, her head in Cornelius's lap.

"Miri!" I fell to my knees beside her, stroked her hair and searched for how she might be injured.

"What's wrong with her?" I asked when I couldn't see any sign of injury.

Cornelius's blue eyes sparkled with a brief smile. He reached out and touched my cheek. "I am so glad to see you, Desolation."

I put my hand on his, pressing his palm to my skin. "And I'm glad to see you."

Our focus returned to Miri, and Cornelius brushed back the damp hair on her forehead. "We stood together near the rocks, watching the battle unfold," he said. "She saw you return, saw Michael—and oh, she was happy." He glanced at me and I caught his eyes.

"She asked where James was, and I didn't know what to say. I put my arm around her shoulder, to offer what comfort I could, but her body began trembling, then convulsing, with great force. At first I thought it was sorrow or fear, but once I helped her to the ground I realized she was not responsive. Longinus helped me bring her here, where she is out of harm's way." His eyes met mine, as he added, "I believe she's had a vision. A terrible premonition that has sent her mind into a state of shock."

He poured a bit of water from a bottle onto a piece of torn cloth and dabbed it on Miri's forehead. "She stopped seizing shortly afterward, but has since lain still, not waking, not stirring. Her breathing has remained even, which I take as a hopeful sign." He looked at me, an expression of expectation on his face, though I had no idea how to offer him, or anyone, comfort.

My mind spun, the usual war raging within me. If only we hadn't needed to release Helena in order to rescue Heimdall. If only I'd chosen Michael over Miri—maybe an eternity in Hell would be better than all that I'd put her through since then.

I felt Michael's hand on my shoulder; warm, steady. "You made the right choice, love. This is Miri's gift and her burden. She'll come out of this, I'm sure of it."

"I fear she is dreaming, and what she sees has her heart and mind strangled with terror." Cornelius's tone was as soft as the touch he used on Miri's brow, but it didn't do anything to diminish the weight of his words.

"But what could she be dreaming about? How could there be anything more than—" I waved my hand to indicate all the hell we'd endured on the desert. "How could there be anything worse?"

Michael said, "Odin believes this may be Ragnarok— Midgard's Apocalypse. This fight is not over, my love. The enemies are merely regrouping, taking time to tend their wounds and replenish their numbers."

I noted how haggard, sad, and resigned he seemed. "We can't win a second time," I said, fear coloring my words like mold on bread.

Michael stroked my hair, a constant soothing rhythm. "But we must."

And I realized—it needed to be as simple as that. We could not afford to fail. Midgard might be a small planet, but it was the bridge to Asgard and should Midgard fall, then Asgard would fall. And without Asgard, there could be no order among the worlds and chaos would invade all creation.

The scrape of a boot against stone came from behind me and I turned in time to see Fiahre, followed closely by Longinus, run from the rock enclosure. I focused on Miri, willing her to wake, whispering words of encouragement. A moment later, Longinus returned.

"Excuse me, Lady." He leaned down, took my hand and pulled me to my feet. "It has begun again."

My eyes grew wide while my mind looped on, *Again?* My mouth said, "What?"

"The Svarts and Giants have joined forces and call us to battle. Fiahre and her sisters have already been forced to engage them."

Michael jumped to his feet, placing a hand on Cornelius's shoulder. "Keep her safe. Call for me should she wake or . . . if anything changes." Cornelius nodded in reply.

"Go safely, my son." To me, he said, "Desolation. The story of your mother's courage and strength has been passed down through eons of time. What she did for you, and the potential of what you could do for our cause—for the victory of light over dark—has been the foundation upon which we have built all our efforts for millennia."

He gently moved Miri so he could stand. He took my hands in his own and pierced me with the intensity of his gaze. "You are not only her daughter, not only Loki's—but all of ours. You are the best of all of us—though you have a great capacity for evil, you must never think yourself unworthy because of it. We all have sins to bear and darkness to overcome." He held my left hand, palm down, tracing his thumb over the swirls of black that covered my skin. "Your darkness and light give you a strength unlike any other. It enlivens your soul with a richness and depth no one in all the worlds possesses. You, unlike anyone else, have the power to push back the darkness in the worlds— just as you did in your own soul."

"But—" My mind reeled with the implications of his words. "I didn't do it alone. Aaron helped me." And had died doing it.

To my surprise, Cornelius smiled. "As you're not alone now." His face lit up as if what he'd said made sense, then he released my hands and shooed me away. "Now go. Make haste and return to us swiftly. Miri will need you when she wakes."

I searched his eyes and didn't see even a shred of doubt there. Not a hint of worry that I would fail to do as he asked, as hope demanded. At stake was the fate of all the worlds, and all that stood between life and death was me— a broken, confused half-breed with a handful of the best friends in all the worlds. I nodded, hoping Cornelius knew I'd do my best. Because I might not feel like the sharpest blade or strongest fist, but I'd be damned if I'd let my friends down.

Michael grabbed my hand and pulled me away from Miri and Cornelius before I had a chance to say any of the things that rose like buoys in my mind. *Thank you. Thank you for believing in me. Thank you for being there for Miri. Just . . . thank you.*

We ran out to the desert and beheld the battle in full swing once more. We saw Fiahre, her sisters and Gardians, as well as some Hallowed warriors, fanned out in front of us on all sides—it wasn't until Michael and I took to the sky that I got a clear view of the enemy. And an understanding of how dire our situation had become.

The tall, pale, blue-skinned Svarts stood atop the rocks that rose out of the sand, lobbing volleys of arrows like rain upon the Gardians that stood against them. On the desert beneath them, the Giants spread outward, their numbers so vast I couldn't see the end of them. They seemed to be as numerous as the grains of sand beneath our feet.

I felt a wave of love pass from Michael to me—no words, only love. Only a reassurance that, whatever happened, he loved me, and knew I loved him. I tried to push my love for him through the muck of fear and doubt crowding my heart, but I was out of time. I followed him to the ground, to join my sisters and brothers, the Valkyrie and Gardians, the children of Asgard, in a fight for all that was good.

I swung my staff in wide arcs, spinning, spinning, spinning. I fought with every ounce of my being, fought with all that I had, all that I was. I fought with staff and sword, wing, elbow, knee and foot. I used all my body to take down enemy after enemy, and still they came.

My breath grew ragged in my throat; burning as if I were swallowing searing hot coals, yet still I fought on. From time to time, I was aware of Michael, Fiahre or Longinus fighting near me, but my attention was always drawn away so I had no idea how they fared, or the state of the battle in general. I only knew what was right in front of me—the never ending press of bodies and killing weapons.

With a blast of heat that blew over me like a fiery furnace, a Giant stepped in my path, rocking the earth beneath my feet and making me lose my balance. I fell forward, reaching out to steady myself, and landed against him. The heat of his skin burned my hand and his breath singed my eyebrows. He grasped me by my shoulders and proceeded to squeeze, lifting me from the ground, a visceral scream building in his gut and pouring out in a barrage of burning air.

I felt helpless in his hands, trapped, and so, so tired.

But beyond him I saw something that fueled my weary body, breathing fury into my weakening heart. I saw James.

A canopied litter sat atop a rocky outcropping some twenty yards away. The curtains were pulled back to allow the occupant a clear view of the battle. Helena reclined on a throne of red and gold cushions, wearing a sheath of pale pink, her red hair cascading down her shoulders. She smiled as she caught my eye and glanced downward, inviting my line of sight to follow hers.

In her hand she held a fine gold chain which led to the collar around the neck of a young man wearing only a white loincloth. There, on hands and knees, providing a footstool for Helena, knelt James.

I sunk my teeth into the inside of the giant's wrist. He howled and let go of my left arm. I swung wildly in his one hand, my feet unable to touch the ground. I reached for my boot and the small golden blade I'd tucked there. Grabbing the dagger, I kicked my feet and brought myself around, thrusting the knife under the giant's chin. He screamed, feral and vicious, baring his teeth and lunging forward, but now I was on my feet and he was falling forward, trying to staunch the flow of blood that gushed down his neck.

He fell face-first into the dirt, soaking the baked clay with his sizzling blood. I jumped onto his back and grabbed my sword with my free hand. With a blade in both fists, I ran toward the litter, a battle cry on my lips while my brain shouted, *Kill Helena. Save James. Kill Helena. Save James.*

But before I reached them, a blast of frigid air threw me backward, twisting, sending me skittering several feet chest-down across the dirt. People—Valkyrie, Giant, Svart, Gardian—fell to the ground all around me. Only Helena remained untouched within her canopied sanctuary.

Only seconds after I'd recognized my father's power, did his booming voice cry, "This is my world, and you will not possess it, Witch."

I tried to stand, but found myself pinned to the ground beneath the force of Father's will. To my left and right I saw others struggling against the weight of his presence. He flew slowly forward, coming to hover above the ground in front of me, blocking my view of Helena and James. Father was glorious—his ebony bat-like wings towered far above him, blocking out the sun, blocking much of the sky from my view. He radiated power like an armed missile prepared for launch.

Helena laughed.

"This is not your world, Loki," Helena replied in a sultry, lazy voice. "It is merely Odin's playground. But I say it's time for others to enjoy its bounty."

Father stepped to the ground, sending shockwaves like small earthquakes trembling through the dirt. "This is no place for Svarts or Giants," he said. "This world was never meant for them."

Helena laughed and the ground trembled beneath me. "And it was never meant for you. One of your birth has no claim on *any* of the worlds."

"Thor is my father and Odin my grandfather. I lead a third of his Gardians. I have every right to this land." His voice trembled with fury and his wings stretched and snapped in the frigid wind he conjured around him.

Fear clouded my vision until I saw only black. I feared he would take me up in another of his dark tornadoes and leave me imprisoned once again. Imprisoned or worse. My friends were here, and James on his knees between the two combatants. Thoughts of what Father could do to those I loved plagued me. I called out to Michael in my mind— but he was as trapped and helpless as I.

"Testy, testy," Helena teased. "You may be right, Loki. And perhaps you do have more claim to this world than my friends here, but I don't think it's me you have to worry about convincing—I think it's all of them."

A burst of power shot outward from Helena's litter, sending Father flying backward and releasing me, and everyone else, from his control. As soon as I was free I was on my feet, running through the black wind, diving for the litter out of instinct—and finding it gone. I spun around.

"Helena!" I screamed. "Where are you?" All around me, Giants and Svarts fell on my people. I took to the sky, searching for Helena, for James, but all I saw was the battle. Then, beyond the line of Odin's warriors, I saw a sight that made my blood run cold.

Father alighted on the ground, and held out his hand. A woman stepped forward, placing her hand in his. Even from where I hovered, I could tell who it was—her wild hair and pale skin could only be one person. Ophelia.

Father held his left hand out, and Ophelia mirrored him on his other side. And there—ripping through the fabric of space, came an army of dark, sharp-edged creatures as black as Father's granite mountain. Ophelia and my father commanded Helena's own creations, the genii, and they fell upon everyone before them, on Valkyrie, Gardian and human, on Svart and Giant, trapping my people between them and Helena's pawns.

My heart cried out for James. With every ounce of my being I longed to follow Helena—wherever she might have gone—and find him. But carnage roiled across the battlefield with such ferocity that I had no choice but to join the fray. I saw Michael, his golden light shining brighter than any of the others, and fell to the ground beside him.

I am here, I told him, my hand brushing against his arm. I reached for the staff within my Halo, but it was gone—probably lost when I'd been thrown to the ground, and there was no time to search for it now. I tossed my sword into my right hand and thrust it at a genii crowding in on the left.

I will not leave you, Michael said.

And then there were no words, no thought.

There was only the sword in my hands, the sweat on my palms, and on the desperate need to prevail.

FOURTEEN

JAMES

I watch my hands, willing my wrists to stay strong, to stop trembling. I've been in this position for as long as I can remember. My knees and wrists have long since gone numb, but it wouldn't do to lose my strength beneath my lady's feet, to embarrass her in such a way. No, I will not fail her.

But then . . .

I hear a name.

James.

My head jerks up when I hear it, though I can't exactly say why. The reaction is as sudden and automatic as if my lady has yanked on the chain she keeps coiled around my neck.

She pulls upon it when I move, a hiss of disapproval escaping her perfect lips. It's not right for me to act on my own volition. I'm my lady's pet and I'm a good one. I don't disobey her.

But before I return my attention to my trembling hands, I see a face. Hear that name again. And both make my heart race with something new, a mystery that slips into my brain and makes me wonder.

Do I know that face? That name?

My lady tugs on my leash once more and I push the traitorous thoughts away, focusing on what's important—my lady, and only her.

FIFTEEN

DESI

Our forces were divided, fighting against the genii on the south, and the Svarts and Giants on the north. Father and Ophelia viewed the scene from atop one of the great rocks that bordered the desert. I remembered the last time I had been with him and had commanded the genii as Ophelia did now. I wondered if she knew she would be just one in a constantly changing retinue of Father's favorites. If she knew how quickly she would fall. Or if she even cared.

The Gardians had reduced the Giants to a handful of groups, all on the run. One climbed the rocks west of us, and while I ran forward, I was aware of the mounted

Valkyrie flying downward, picking off the giants as they climbed. I was the first to reach those climbing onto the mesa. My sword flashed in the fading sunlight as I sent another giant to his death. I jumped over the enormous man at my feet and lunged forward, only to be caught at my ankle by the one I'd thought dead. He pulled me to the ground, wrapping his fist tightly around my hair. He produced a blade, no more than a dagger for him, but it was as long as my arm.

He yanked on my hair, forcing my head back and I felt his blade—icy cold and red hot—slice through the skin at my neck.

My eyes flew open, but I saw nothing but the blue sky, colored with the warm reds and oranges of the setting sun streaked across it. Everything seemed to slow. I felt the Giant expel a long breath. Felt his hands begin to loosen around me. Felt the warm flow of blood as it sluiced from my neck and down onto my shoulder.

I couldn't breathe. Couldn't call out.

I closed my eyes as blood filled my lungs.

I hadn't seen the end of the battle. Hadn't experienced the pleasure of seeing the last of the Giants and Svarts escape through the portals to their worlds. Hadn't seen what Father did with his genii. I tried to send my thoughts to him.

Go, I said. *Leave them alone.* I tried to fill my words with the tang of commandment, but I heard no reply.

I opened my eyes. Noted how my vision had narrowed to a pinpoint. I saw a tiny patch of blue. Saw a fingertip's pink-tinged sky.

Closed my eyes.

Odin, I thought. *Protect them. Miri. Cornelius. Longinus. Fiahre. All the Gardians who had to pass through the mortal challenge of Midgard.*

Please protect Michael.

The Giant's great fist fell from around my hair and I slipped down until I lay mostly on the dirt, my head cradled on the bend of the big man's elbow. I tried to lift my head but . . . it was so much easier to just lie still.

My heart found a new rhythm. One that lulled me into a peaceful rest.

Thump. I opened my eyes, stretching them wide.

Michael. Promise you'll find James.

Thump.

Promise you'll save him.

Thump.

I love you.

Sleep beckoned me and oh, I was so tired.

I'm coming! he replied.

I opened my eyes. *Where are you?*

Thump.

I'm coming, love.

But I couldn't wait. Darkness descended on me from the inside out and I closed my eyes again.

SIXTEEN

MICHAEL

I hadn't seen her fall. Didn't even know I was about to lose her, until she called my name.

In the moment her voice dropped into my thoughts like rain, I knew something was terribly wrong.

I'm coming!

With her words came the impression of all we hadn't said, all the hopes for a future we wouldn't have.

Where are you?

Without thought, I shoved a Svart into the portal, and spun around—seeking Desi. Searching for her. I shouted her name. Screamed for her.

I'm coming, love.

But there was no answer, and that silence terrified me more than anything else. I couldn't lose her. Not now. Not like this.

I ran from one cluster of fighters to the next, though there were precious few left. I found her nowhere.

My eyes sought out Loki, standing on the rocks above us. "Where is she?" I screamed, letting my cry echo through my thoughts while it tore like thunder through the air, hoping someone—anyone—would find her.

Loki Became, his Shadow bursting outward and sending a shockwave over the last of the skirmishes. Everyone, including myself, fell to the ground, but I was the first to rise. And that's when I saw her.

Lying several hundred yards north of me, I saw her pale green tunic, her black hair.

I ran for her, jumping over and skirting past anyone and anything that stood between us. I cursed the injuries I'd taken to my wings that robbed me of their use. My feet were too slow and with every step I saw the truth of the situation, saw it and dismissed it. *She isn't dead*, I told myself.

But she did not move.

She can't be dead.

A shadow passed overhead, but I did not look up. Loki hovered above her. "Don't you touch her!" I screamed as I ran with all my strength. As I came to her, saw her lying on the arm of a Giant, saw her hand outstretched, palm open, her sword on the ground just out of reach, Loki disappeared.

Blood on her neck.

Blood everywhere.

"No! Desi!" *Love, love. Don't leave me.*

I tore the Giant's shirt and pressed the cloth to her neck, telling myself all the while that her heart still beat. Told myself she hadn't lost too much blood.

My knees were soaked in it.

I tied the cloth around her neck, fearing if I tied it too tight she wouldn't be able to breathe, but anxious to stop as much of the alarming flow of blood as possible. With great care I extricated her from the Giant's dead limbs, laid her upon the blood-soaked ground, pressed my ear to her chest. Willed myself to stop breathing, to stop the beating of my own heart so I could listen for the only sound that mattered. The only thing.

Please.

Thump.

"Longinus!" I pulled Desi to me, cradled her in my arms as I jumped to my feet. "Fiahre!" I ran—ran, I didn't know where. After stumbling several steps I suddenly stopped, fear finally overriding the adrenaline.

I pressed my ear to her chest.

. . .

. . .

Then, oh so quietly, almost imperceptible—

thump.

I threw my head back to scream for help, just as a portal opened and Heimdall was there. I burst onto the Bridge, running, calling to them—calling for anyone who could save her.

While I ran, she lay motionless in my arms, her breath a mere whisper against my wrist, her heartbeat indecipherable from my own. *No, my love. Don't go.*

Don't go.

My mind ran through the options, raising questions to which I had no answers. Odin had already denied her Valhalla—he'd told me of her choice to go back to Midgard when she'd died at Akaros's hand. And of course she'd chosen to fight for her friends. She always doubted her worth, but oh, she was the most valiant of us all. But if she couldn't seek the eternal rest of Valhalla, would she go to Vanaheim and be with her sisters there? Could she, as only part Valkyrie? As Loki's child?

Because she was not human, Ascension was also denied her. Where then, could her spirit go? There was only one place I knew for sure that would take her. Loki would croon with pleasure if Desi returned to him. And oh, it would be an eternity of misery for her. And for me.

Don't go.

Heimdall convinced me to put her onto the lap of a mounted Valkyrie. No stranger to the battle-wounded, the warrior cradled Desi's head in the crook of her arm, careful to keep her as stationary as possible. She turned the shi'lil who flew as smooth as the wind toward Valhalla. Heimdall clasped onto me, holding me upright while we watched the warrior carry Desi away.

I traveled onward, toward Asgard, and when Odin met me on the Bridge I fell into his arms and cried the sorrow of the battle weary, the sorrow of a general over so many lost soldiers, the agony of one with a broken heart.

"It is well, my son," Odin said, his deep voice rumbling through my ears and heart as if they came from both inside and outside of myself. "She yet lives."

"I must go to her." I moved to step past Odin, but he restrained me with a hand on my arm.

"She has been taken into the heart of Valhalla, to be tended by her sisters."

Though my face must have revealed the thoughts of my heart, I still pressed him. "But—"

Odin waved his hand as if to dismiss my concerns. "In this moment, all that can be done, is being done. She will be well. You have my word."

All the adrenaline that had fueled me until this moment left and I all but dropped, all but fell against my Lord. *She will be well.*

Odin placed his hand on my shoulder, pressing down a little until I turned my face to his.

"You must return my son. The battle yet lingers and you are needed."

Beyond us rose the shining city of Asgard and the golden spires of Valhalla. Could I go back? Could I fight a war while my love fought for her life?

"You will give meaning to the sacrifice of your brothers and sisters who have already lost their lives." My king did not spare my feelings or his own. I would return and fight or else deny my fallen comrades the worth of their souls.

I nodded and turned sharply.

"Michael," Odin said, his tone softer, kinder.

I looked over my shoulder.

"I will send word."

SEVENTEEN

DESI

I sat up, gasping for air, hungry for life. My hands clutched at my throat as memory flooded back—my throat had been slit, hadn't it? I thought I was dead.

And yet . . .

Here I sat in a narrow bed of white, blankets trimmed with gold. On the side table, beside a golden goblet with droplets of condensation on its side, lay my sword and dagger, polished to a mirror-like shine. I grabbed the sword and held it before me, stretching my neck this way and that—no scar. No indication that anything had happened to me at all.

My thoughts clasped onto the only possible explanation—*I am dead.*

The door opened and Fiahre strode in. I saw other women at the door, but they stayed in the hall. Fiahre closed her eyes and exhaled a long breath.

"I am glad you are awake." Standing by the foot of the bed, she clasped her hands behind her back. Her white tunic was splattered with dirt and blood, her face smudged and her hair radiated around her face like a halo. Even battle-worn she was beautiful.

"I'm not dead?"

She quirked a smile and bowed her head. "No, you are not dead."

"But how? I felt him slice my throat. I felt my heart stop."

"Well, you were wrong. He did cut your throat, but you did not die."

I traced my neck with my fingers, searching for a raised scar, for anything to prove my memory true.

"I don't understand."

Fiahre plucked the goblet from the nightstand and held it out to me. "Drink," she said. There was something about her—a hardness or impatience that made me feel like she was angry with me.

I took the cup. I was so very thirsty.

I took a sip of the cool liquid and realized as it passed my lips that it wasn't water. I sighed and licked my lips. "What is that? It's the most delicious thing ever."

Now Fiahre's expression softened and she gave me a small smile. "It is ambrosia. It is what gave you your life back, and healed the wound at your neck."

Ambrosia.

I knew what it was in an abstract form—knew in some of the books I'd read they called it the nectar of the gods. "It gives gods their eternal life—right?"

"In a manner of speaking," Fiahre said. "Yes." She sat on the edge of the bed, seeming about as uncomfortable as one could get. She fiddled with one of the leather flaps that hung from her belt.

Even though my mouth and throat craved more of the refreshing liquid, I set the cup on the table. "I'm not a god," I said. "I shouldn't be drinking that."

Surprise danced on Fiahre's face. "Yes you are."

"What?" I frowned at her dumbfounded expression.

"You are Loki's child in both your lives. He is Odin's grandson. You *are* a god."

Her expression grew in intensity as she stared into my eyes. "Desolation, you must listen to me. I do not know who your original mother was, but you are my sister's child—my sister who was the greatest Valkyrie I have ever known. There was no greater warrior—in war or in love. You are like her in all respects." She shook her head sharply when I opened my mouth to protest.

"I know you don't believe it. Maybe it makes it easier for you to be less than you can be, maybe it's easier to excuse yourself because of the dark that's a part of you—I don't know. But what I do know is that my sister died giving you life. Ensuring that you would be greater than her—greater than all of us. Whatever Loki has decided to do with his life, he is still the son of a god. Because he is your father, you have inherited his gifts—his strengths and abilities. You don't have to adopt his darkness, that is not a given."

She pierced me with her direct gaze and I was powerless to respond.

"Do you know how the Valkyries came to be?" she suddenly asked.

I found my memories fuzzy—so I kept my mouth shut and twitched my head in response.

"The gods created us—the Vanir gods. When the Aesir gods were forced to flee from their old home, the Vanir gods allowed them to rule the worlds they created for them—Odin, Helena, and the others. The Vanir gods created the Valkyrie to be Odin's justice, as he, being the leader of the Aesir gods, would, in essence, rule the rulers—though through the passage of time the other gods have come to deny that fact. The Valkyrie have no leader except the woman we appoint to guide us. Mahria was our queen from the beginning, the only one we've ever known. In her absence, I have led—but it is not my strength, not my gift. I am seeking a warrior who will take her place."

Dread dropped like a stone in my stomach.

"But I—"

"No." Fiahre's voice was surprisingly soft. "No, I know it will not be you. I remember when Odin invited you to Valhalla and you refused—and I know you made the right decision. The bravest choice." She looked at her hands in her lap, though she kept them quiet.

"Perhaps I will have a daughter one day." A small smile wisped across her face then disappeared. "Or perhaps another of my sisters will reveal her gift for leadership. Anyway." She straightened her back and focused on me, her expression somewhere between fierce and tender. "That is not what I meant to talk to you about, and my sisters tell me I am needed on the battlefield—I'd only wanted to speak with you because Michael is my friend and there is something I need to say."

She leaned toward me, her face fierce and alight with passion.

"What I want is for you to realize the greatness that lives within you. You are, in part, great because of the people who have come into your life—every good general knows she is only as good as the warriors she commands. But you are not only great because of them. Recognize the gifts your parents have given you, and claim them for your own. Be great because they were. But don't be only what they were. Be yourself."

She trailed the back of her hand over my forehead and down my cheek, brushing aside my hair.

"Be great, Desolation. Be glorious."

She rose and left the room, leaving me alone with a million questions and a nugget of warmth that vibrated with the truth of her words.

EIGHTEEN

MICHAEL

Sheathing my sword, I fought to slow my breathing while I surveyed the battlefield. The scattered forces had regrouped, and though their numbers were small, they were still a fierce and deadly opponent. The Svarts had fallen back to the Door, but the Giants still pressed the Valkyrie. The way the Svarts had lined up, though, with the lethal, curved blades of their kukris held across their chests, I feared they drew their courage from a new wave of reinforcements about to cross the Bridge.

I glanced up the ridge to where Cornelius had his makeshift hospital, caring for the wounded. It was then that I saw him struggling with a body in his arms. I cursed under my breath; fear that Miri had taken a turn for the worse forcing me to the sky toward the pair. My injured wings had already begun to mend, but flight still made them burn.

"Cornelius?" I landed with an awkward thump, just behind the man. He startled and turned, but thankfully did not drop Miri. "Is she well?"

"I'm sure she will be, my friend. But she hasn't woken, and her trembling has not stopped. Taige, my newest acolyte, has come to retrieve her—I thought perhaps, if she was away from the battle, her heart and mind could be put at ease."

I nodded, then stepped forward to take Miri into my arms. "I will carry her to the car."

"Thank you."

"Perhaps you should return with her." I looked to my left, willing Cornelius to meet my eyes, but he kept his focus on the rocky terrain in front of his feet. "I desire your safety as well."

Cornelius waved his hand in the air as he stepped off the rocks. When I caught up to him he said, "I feel my place is here. That this is where I should be." He glanced back and I saw that he felt the same dread as I that the battle was not yet finished, but that he would not be moved from his decided course of action.

"You are not a warrior." I couldn't stop myself from stating the obvious, from trying to convince him, even while I knew he wouldn't likely change his mind.

Out of the corner of my eye I saw him shrug, saw him focus on the ground once again while we walked. "I am needed here. The injured—with my help they can return to the battle sooner. Perhaps, with my small skill, some may not have to die."

I found myself without words to express how much his life meant to me, how much I worried.

Sensing my thoughts, Cornelius slowed and placed a hand on my arm, drawing me to a stop. "I will be fine, my friend. I am staying close to the rocks. The battle hasn't come that far, as you and your people are doing a fine job holding off stray attackers. The fighting will be over soon, I'm sure of it. We will share a cup of tea when we are through."

His clear blue eyes sparkled in the lowering light. He'd been my friend since he first joined The Hallowed some fifty-five years ago. He'd grown from eager acolyte to seasoned patriarch but he'd always been my friend. He turned and we continued toward the small convertible that had just arrived, kicking up dust in its wake.

I lay Miri on the backseat, her skin cool and her breathing even. I felt certain she only rested, that soon she would wake and be well once again. I stepped back and Cornelius leaned in to kiss Miri on the forehead.

"I'll come straight away." Cornelius put his hand on the driver's shoulder—a girl with black hair and pale skin who I remembered from Desi's dark days. When she glanced my way and I shared a smile with her, it pleased me to see the darkness no longer held her captive.

Cornelius patted the car's roof and we stepped back while Taige pulled away. We watched the car move across the hard-packed desert ground toward the road that lay far out of sight. Before long the dust obscured it from view, so Cornelius and I strode toward the battlefield. My heart lifted to see a fresh wave of Asgardian warriors leaping from the Bifrost to join us—just as the Svarts also received reinforcements. Taking a deep breath, I squared my shoulders and roused my waning energy.

"We will yet win this war." I quickened my pace. "Stay safe." I put my hand on Cornelius's shoulder.

He nodded. "I will. And as soon as you can, bring me word of Desolation."

Not, *Please beat Loki.* Not, *Please save us.* No, Cornelius was a man of great faith. We would beat Loki and send him away from this world—if not Helheimer, then somewhere. And when we had defeated him, Cornelius expected me to visit and report. And so I would. He and his brothers and sisters of The Hallowed had long been Midgard's defense against Loki's evil, and deserved to kept in the loop.

"Of course," I said.

"God be with you, my son." I looked at him quizzically—he knew as well as I, there were many gods. But then I realized that this was Odin's world, as surely as if he were its god. He might not possess the omniscient, omnipotent power of the world's religious icons, or that of the Vanir gods who more closely resembled the human concept of god, but he would be the world's savior—he and the warriors who were the extension of his hand.

Desi. Me. And the other Gardians. Fiahre, and the Valkyries.

"And with you also." I clasped his forearm, then ran toward the Giants and the Bifrost that shot like a pillar of fire into the sky. I called upon my memories of the good in this world and my hopes for Desi to fuel my speed and lend strength to my arm. There was a war yet to be won.

As I ran on the hard-packed earth, taking notice of the shape of the battle around me until I found myself in enemy territory. Nearest to me the Giants swung their cudgels while swarms of genii attacked from all sides, outnumbering the Giants by at least five to one. Across the battlefield I saw other pockets of these pairings, and knew the giants would soon admit defeat. The genii were minute in size compared to the Giants, but they worked together as if of one mind and they were remarkably nimble, avoiding the hammer-falls that crashed onto the ground all around them.

Near the rocky outcroppings where Cornelius had his makeshift hospital, two dozen humans fought against the cruel and vicious Svarts who took far too much pleasure in the most painful forms of death.

I embraced my Halo, sending sparks of golden sunshine falling on those beneath me—some of the genii cried out as my Halo sent them reeling back. I hurried downward, toward the Svarts and the humans and Valkyries who fought them. I saw Longinus there, Fiahre by his side, and as well as a few members from other Hallowed watchtowers.

"When did they arrive?" I shouted at Longinus as I released my Halo and reached for my sword.

"Only just—but we are hard put. I fear their sacrifice will be in vain." We fell into step together, back-to-back, our swords whirling around like great shining wheels.

We fought through the largest pocket of Svarts, dividing their attention. A Svart taller than the rest, with regal bearing and a slow, almost casual spin of his curved silver blade, drew me away from the others.

"I have long desired the chance to try my hand against one of Odin's notorious Gardians," he said. His voice had a silver, sparkling tone to it, all sharp edges and brilliance. I ignored its lure and dove forward, thrusting my sword into the air where, until that moment, his chest had been. I spun away, seeking him, and found him standing behind me, leaning on the hilt of his sword as if it were a walking stick.

"Not as impressive as I'd hoped." He whirled, a flash of silver, and I felt a stripe of blood bloom across the skin on my shoulder. "And you're Michael, are you not? Odin's own general? The greatest of them all?"

I stood still, trying to make sense of him, to gauge his next move, to determine how I could best him.

"Oh, but then again." He removed a white cloth from his pocket and ran it along the length of his blade. He held up the cloth and wrinkled his nose at the blood on it. Between one blink and the next the cloth was gone. "I forgot. Your darling love is the greatest of you all. And yet, where is she?"

He made a show of looking all around and while he faced away from me, I struck.

I claimed my Halo and used my wings to thrust me forward, bringing my blade downward to his neck. It was a cowardly move, but I had no time for word games. I would not miss this time, I would not fail. I could see it in his eyes when he spun back around.

When he lay on the ground, my knee on his chest, his blood on my sword, he laughed.

"You think this is all there is, Gardian? You think if you win here, you can live happily ever after with your beloved half-breed?" He coughed and blood flecked his lips, coloring them an unnatural red against his pale, icy skin. "Look around you. The battle has changed, has it not?" He waited, but I resisted the urge to obey him.

"Hurry up and die, already," I said through gritted teeth. I did not enjoy death, but I wished for her to come claim this creature before I was forced to kill him twice.

"This has—" he coughed again and my heart lurched. What was I doing? *End him!* Yet a part of me held a sick fascination with his words. I felt like I had to know his message—needed to know. "Only been a ruse, Gardian. Only a game." He laughed then, which drew his coughing to such a state that the two became one until he finally fell silent.

I stayed with him longer than I had to, fearing what he said might be true. I heard the familiar clang of steel against steel. Heard the sound of flesh hitting the hard-packed earth. Heard the cries of anguish and courage that rang out on all sides.

Slowly I stood and turned.

All around me, humans lay. Warriors of The Hallowed, bleeding into the barren land.

The Svarts and Giants cowered from my wrath. Fiahre and her sisters, and the few humans that remained, still contended with the genii, and the fight was not fair. The humans were exhausted, almost to the point of being utterly useless. The Valkyrie fought with valiant, fierce determination. They fought as if they had only begun—but I knew the truth. They would pay the price—just not now. Not yet.

For now they were all that saved this place from the genii's crush.

I signaled to my Lieutenants to spare who they could and join with the Valkyrie against the small-but-lethal genii.

I made my way toward Fiahre, crushing to dust those genii who fell upon me.

"What is happening?" I shouted at Fiahre between grunts of exertion.

She thrust forward, knocking the midsection of a genii backward, causing it to fall to the ground in a useless pile. With the momentum of her arms she moved them sideways, whipping her leg around to knock the head off another stone creature on her right. "The battle has changed," she said.

"I can see that!" Frustration oozed out of every pore. I punched and kicked at the genii with an unnatural ruthlessness.

"Loki has been exiled from Helheimer," Fiahre shouted as she pressed her back to mine. I reached backward, grabbing the knife she kept in her boot, and brought it up to stick it into the chin of a genii who had grabbed Fiahre's hair and was about to take a bite out of her neck.

"Helena used this war to distract him, to leave Helheimer unguarded—and now Loki has been cast out."

I used the dagger to hold the genii's head in place while I thrust my knee against its midsection, dismembering it. My gut twisted, but I pushed down the revulsion that threatened to rise at thoughts of how Loki would seek vengeance.

Fiahre and I worked seamlessly together, like a creature with eight limbs, as we thrust and kicked at the unceasing genii. I don't know how many we killed. How many fell under my hand or hers. As the creatures fell, they disintegrated into dirt and blew away on the breeze like so much dust.

All I knew was, as the sun sank beyond the horizon, my limbs were slowing. The cool desert air settled in around me, luring me to rest. Fiahre separated from me and I'd only just turned, only begun the walk back to the rocks where The Hallowed were treating their wounded, when I heard it.

A cry of grief and pain—a man's. I had never before heard that voice cry out in such sorrow and so I walked faster. Then broke into a run.

"Longinus!" Fiahre cried. I saw her huddled form, saw she held Longinus in her arms. And even from a distance, I could see the blood that colored the ground where he lay.

I fell to my knees by her side, horror making my stomach sour.

"He will be revived." I spoke with haste, not realizing that it wasn't Longinus's wounds that were deadly, but the man's behind him.

Fiahre helped Longinus sit up, the wound on his neck already healing. But Longinus took no care for his own body, which should have been mortal but instead could never die. He spun as soon as he was able, to reveal Cornelius on the hard dirt beside him.

"Father," Longinus cried. But I could tell, and surely Longinus could see as well, that the man was already gone. "He shouldn't have been on the field. He was supposed to remain on the rocks, tend the wounded." Longinus crossed the father's arms on his chest, his calloused hands trembling. "I tried to protect him, but the Giant's thrust was too great, his reach beyond my ability to deflect."

"You did what you could." Fiahre hesitated only a moment before placing her hand on Longinus's arm. He looked away from Cornelius and locked eyes with Fiahre.

"I am tired of this death. I am tired of losing the ones I love."

"I know," Fiahre said.

I focused my attention on the ridge where Loki stood with Ophelia. Before I could move, Fiahre touched the back of her hand to my arm.

"Here." Her fingers held a small golden vial. I looked at it, then at her. She nodded.

I took the vial, popped the cork with my thumb and drank the teaspoonful of liquid left. Ambrosia. It would not heal all my wounds, but it was enough.

Without a word to Longinus or Fiahre, I grasped my sword and flew toward Loki.

In a flash of light, a scream already tearing through my throat, I landed on the mesa and backhanded Ophelia. She fell to the rocky surface a few feet behind me. I circled my prey like a lion hunts the zebra.

"Michael, my old friend." Loki, dressed in black slacks and a white silk shirt that fluttered in the breeze stirred up by my wings, spread his arms in something like a warm greeting.

"We haven't been friends since before civilization began on this planet."

"Ah, but I still care about you. I still want the best for you." His words were sweet but I saw the way his chin dipped and his eyes darkened with bitter poison.

"*My* friends are tired. It is time to end this."

"By all means." Loki stopped clocking me, and stood still as I crossed behind him. "But I won't be as easy to defeat as you once found me."

I stepped to his front. He smiled like the snake he was—slow and deceptive.

"Hey!" Ophelia screeched. "What about—"

Loki raised his hand, a flick of his wrist and Ophelia was thrown backward again, this time down to the desert floor far below us.

For a moment we considered each other. My former friend, my one time master. I understood him better than ever before, his evil still tainted my memories. I had no idea how much of him still remained inside my heart, inside my mind, but I intended to exorcise him—and any lingering connection to him—thoroughly and without prejudice.

Loki would be defeated and I would banish him from this world.

I drew my blade from its sheath, its voice ringing, revealing my intentions in the way it sliced through the air, thirsting for blood. My focus narrowed to Loki's eyes, gauging the moment when he would Become, and I would be Odin's fierce hand against the dark.

Loki burst forth with black lightning, his wings beating a maelstrom around me, but I held my ground, swung my blade and pressed forward.

In his hands appeared two dark blades, each double-edged, their surface gleaming as if already drenched in blood. With a roar I raised my sword and fell upon him, our weapons clanging, ringing, our voices echoing around us. Rocks skittered beneath my feet, wind beat around me, until I drew my focus inward, lasered it on the face of the man before me. The face of my enemy.

I watched him, watched his eyes, the curl of his lip, the sweat that dripped on his brow. I watched him as we danced, our blades beating to the rhythm of our steps, our breath. He lashed out with his wings, but I blocked him, matched him blow for blow.

Odin, I prayed. *Grant me strength.* Then there was no more time for thought, there was only action, only now. I allowed my mind to conjure an image of Desi, the golden light of Asgard flickering on her face while she smiled, the sunlight bringing out the freckles on her nose. *For you.*

And I was no longer Michael, no longer a Gardian, no longer a soldier. I was my blade. *I am the blade.*

NINETEEN

JAMES

I lie curled up like a baby on the cold granite floor, trying really hard not to shiver overly much because my lady doesn't like it. My butt and back sting from where she kicked me with her stilettos when my shivering annoyed her. I am so cold I think maybe I will freeze to death—and the idea seems like a great one. I'd be glad for death right now.

I don't remember feeling this way before. Never until I'd been with my lady at the battlefront and I'd seen that girl and heard that name.

James.

Until then, I think I was happy. I think I enjoyed being my lady's pet.

But not now.

Now all I can think of is that face—the pale skin and dark hair. The wild eyes that seemed to see right through me, that seemed to see *me*. I can't remember a time when anyone had even taken notice of me. And why would they? I'm just a dog. My lady said so.

But that name. *James.*

James.

I like the sound of it. Like how it feels in my mouth when I whisper it quietly to myself. *James.*

With the name and with the face of the girl. Feelings bombarded me. Regret. Shame. Forgiveness. Hope. I'm not even sure what those words mean, what those feelings are, but they rise up inside me like leaves floating on a river.

And there are other faces, other feelings.

A pair of crystal blue eyes, brimming with tears. Those eyes feel like a stab to my heart. The first time I saw them in my mind, I gasped—my lady lashed out and dug the heel of her shoe into my calf. I learned to control my reactions after that. To let the tears fall without notice.

The eyes, those shining diamond blue eyes, make me feel strong. Powerful. They fill me with a need to do something—what, I can't say. To be something for the owner of those eyes. To protect her.

Her.

A girl with messy blonde hair, a small face, with lips that I . . .

Another gasp, another reprimand immediately followed by a stabbing pain in my back . . .

. . . like to kiss.

I kissed this girl. This blue-eyed, blonde-haired girl.

I loved her.

I love her still.

Her name haunts me, whispers at me from the corners of my memory but I can't quite grasp it. All I can remember is the name on her lips.

Her whispering my name to me.

James.

My name.

This time I keep my reaction to myself to avoid my lady's displeasure, but inwardly, my whole self shouts with joy and amazement. I know my name.

I am James.

TWENTY

MICHAEL

I'd grown weary, the leather wrapped around the hilt of my sword soaked with my sweat and blood. Still Loki came. The edge of my wing sliced through his cheek, a small victory. Loki thrust his hands upward. I'd stripped him of one of his terrible blades, but the other flashed before me, narrowly missing my chin as I threw myself into the air, flipping backwards and landing on my feet two yards away.

He rushed me, left me with no time to think.

He jumped into the air, and I watched his weapon, not his face—a deadly mistake.

Loki fell upon me, knocking me to the ground. My right wing bent painfully beneath me until I forced him to the left, rolled onto my knees with Loki's chest heaving below me.

And my sword stuck through his gut.

Everything suddenly came to a stop. I heard my breath wheezing through my throat, my blood rushing in my ears. Saw Loki's Shadow recede, leaving him a vulnerable man, blood spreading a crimson stain across his white shirt. His mouth moved. He coughed. A bubble of blood popped on his lip. I couldn't hear him over the rushing in my ears.

I'd done it.

I'd finally done it.

Empty laughter rose out of my throat and I looked to my right, then my left, in that strange way of one who has momentarily lost their mind. It took a second for my eyes to register the scene on the dark desert floor below me. Svarts poured from the Door, Giants converged on the dwindling contingent of Gardians and Valkyrie who were pressed together, the enemy surrounding them.

"Finish it," Loki hissed, his hand clasping onto mine where I gripped the hilt of my sword.

"My friends have greater need of me than I have need to put you out of your misery." Without ceremony I pulled my sword free and wiped the blade on his white shirt. I grabbed his arm and picked him up, throwing him over my shoulder. My wings would not fly me, damaged as they were, but I jumped off the mesa anyway, landing painfully on the ground—hoping it was more painful for Loki who's wound lay directly against my shoulder.

I forced my way through the throng; Svarts and Giants both ignoring me as I kept my course for the Door. When I reached it, a pair of Svarts lunged at me, their blades flashing, but I sliced one in half with my good wing and knocked the other down with Loki's feet.

And then, as I completed my spin, I threw Loki into the Doorway. *Let the Svarts deal with him.*

TWENTY-ONE

DESI

The sun cast long shadows across the room when I swung my legs out from under the blanket. The room was small, simple, but not as nondescript as I'd thought earlier. I dressed in my mother's clothes—a warrior queen's attire: a tunic and cape the color of cranberries, the gold and silver armor of a Valkyrie.

Across from the window, a portrait of a shi'lil hung above a dresser. The animal was drawn with colored pencils, with so many swirls between air and sky, horse and wing, that it gave the image a dream-like quality. Something about it drew me nearer, so I walked the few steps from the bed across the warm tiles beneath my feet.

I stared at the drawing for a long time before my eyes wandered downward where I noticed the name scrawled into the corner of the canvas. *Mahria.*

I reached out and touched her name. Felt the minute dip in the paper where she'd pressed her pencil. For a moment I thought I could feel her, but as I closed my eyes I realized it wasn't her presence I felt, but her Memory. Memory was everywhere in this room, like whispers from Mahria's spirit called to me from every corner. If I didn't know she was dead—gone to Vanaheim, if Fiahre was right—I'd expect her to appear. Instead, I sought more Memories, more connections with my mother.

I caught my reflection in the mirror above a small vanity. I sat down at the bench and started to pull my hair up into a ponytail, but for a second I thought I saw Mahria there and my hands dropped to my lap.

I looked the same as her, with only slight differences where I took after my father. My hair was black, where Mahria's had been more golden brown. My eyes a deep brown-black where hers were more chestnut with many flecks of gold. And where she had golden skin, mine was pale and marred by the swirls of black on my left arm and ribbons of gold on my right. Yet we were built the same. The shape of my face, my nose and lips, were so similar to hers.

A flash of Memory hit me then—an image of Mahria, head thrown back while she laughed from her belly at something Fiahre had said. I couldn't remember what it was, but I remembered how beautiful she had been. How full of life. I leaned closer to the mirror and slowly, feeling more than a little stupid, I tried a smile on my face, the face that was so much like Mahria's. My friend. My mother. I remembered what it felt like to stand with my warrior sisters and listen to Mahria teach us. She was like a brilliant star from which we all drew our light.

I smiled, and my smile looked like hers. Natural. I made a laughing sound, let it seep into my stomach, let it slowly find its way out. I closed my eyes and laughed. I laughed and laughed as memory after memory rolled in—most were of my time in Valhalla before I was sent on my quest, but some memories of my life as Desi crept in. Painting with Miri. Teasing James over his love for her. Tears squeezed out between my eyelids, but still I didn't stop. I let the laughter come and come, wanting to lose myself in it. To just be. To be happy.

"You were always so beautiful when you laughed," Father said. My eyes flew open and I saw his image in the mirror before me. I watched while he brought up his hands as if he would touch me, but he dropped them again as though it wasn't the mirror, the barrier of Asgard and Valhalla that kept him from me. "It's been far too long since I've seen such happiness on your face."

Because I haven't had anything to be happy about in forever.

"What are you doing here?" I shaped my words, every part of me, to be as cold and sharp as he. I fought to control my fear, to stomp it down and give him no satisfaction. I focused on breathing, on calming the fire within, just as Akaros had taught me. I did learn a few useful things from him, after all.

"I heard you'd been injured. Of course, as your father, I was concerned for your well-being. I wanted to check on you myself. Make sure you were being well taken care of."

"So you've seen me. I'm fine." *Now get the hell outta here.*

"That's the welcome I get?" He leaned to the side, peering around me to examine the few possessions Mahria had collected on the dresser top. "She never was terribly sentimental, your mother. All business, all the time."

Not all the time, I thought, remembering the laughter.

"I suppose that's why she chose to be my bride—she figured she couldn't be converted to my point of view so easily. She had so few weaknesses. So few vices." He pinioned me with his gaze, as directly as if there were an invisible bridge between us. "But I've always been adept at using people's wants and desires against them. Odin knew it was because of my ability to give people what they desired that I was such a threat. Even Mahria was glad for what I could give her, in the end."

I felt his Shadow press against my mind, so I sealed myself shut against him and didn't say a word, though it took all my concentration to keep from lashing out with every bit of ice in my veins.

"But you asked me a question—two questions, actually." He crossed his arms over his chest, his white silk shirt, utterly pristine, making him seem so normal, so human. "It seems the locks to my home have been changed and I am in need of some assistance." My brain wanted to relinquish itself to him, but I fought it, digging my nails into my palms—anything keep my focus. "Naturally I thought of my dear daughter."

"I would never willingly help you."

He shrugged as he inspected the small room, ignoring my remark. "I was hoping you would be more generous, of course, but I did not come unprepared."

"I'm not going anywhere with you." I moved to put my right hand on the scabbard at my side, only to realize I hadn't armed myself. My sword and dagger still lay on the table beside the bed.

He smirked, no doubt inferring my thoughts even though I knew I held my mind tight against him. "Helena has mutinied against me. Even my generals have joined with her. She may have shut the Door against me, but I suspect she wouldn't refuse you."

I sighed. "You expect me to believe that? You're Lucifer. Hell is your territory. All those dead bad people? They're yours." I crossed my arms. "When will you ever figure out that you can't keep lying? When will you get it through your head that you lost? Give up already."

In an instant, his demeanor changed. His countenance lost its benign expression and his eyes, even his skin, grew darker. The whole room dimmed as his Shadow-self stretched beyond the mirror.

"You think I will be content to run away to Svartalheim like your lover expects? I will never give up. I will never stop." He thrust his hand, like a claw, forward. Though he remained within the mirror, his fist gripped my throat. His Shadow-hands were ice cold, burning against my skin, reaching into my mind like lasers, breaking past all my barriers.

I grasped for his hand to pry his fingers from my throat, but I found nothing—only my own skin beneath my hands. My eyes grew wide as I tried, unsuccessfully, to demand what the hell was going on.

Father laughed. "You forget I am a god, little daughter. Odin might have closed Asgard to me, but as my offspring I will always find you. And you *will* do what I ask."

I tried to speak, but only gurgles escaped my mouth.

"Shh, shh. Don't talk." He leaned toward me, his presence suffocating. "Odin's worthless barriers keep my physical form from entering his beloved Asgard, but nothing he can do will stop my Shadow from finding you—even here." His face twisted into an ugly mask of hatred. "You will help me get my kingdom back."

I tried to shake my head, willing my countenance to match his, hatred for hatred.

"You will help me, or I will destroy all that you love." He filled my mind with images: Michael on the battlefield, his blood staining the desert sand a deep maroon. Miri, huddled in the corner of the school, a bottle in her hand and Shadows pressing in on all sides. James, walking into the river as soul eaters converge on him. On and on the images flashed, showing me the desperate end of each of my friends, each of the people I loved. Longinus, Cornelius, Fiahre. All dead. All prey to Father's vicious retaliation.

Stop! I screamed in my mind. *Please.*

Father laughed, his lips curled in a brutal sneer. He squeezed my throat tighter.

I'll do it. I'll help you.

Suddenly, the pressure at my neck was gone.

Come to the Door. He gave me a glimpse of the Door at St. Mary's, then disappeared as if he'd never been there at all.

I slipped from the stool and fell to my knees, clutching my neck, fighting to breathe. With effort, I pushed the fear away, pushed all thought away. I grabbed my weapons and stormed toward the Wheelhouse. "Take me to St. Mary's," I demanded of Heimdall as I entered his domain.

He whirled toward me, towering, ready to defy me.

"Michael," I choked out, my mind spinning with possible excuses. "He needs me to meet him there."

Heimdall's eyes softened and he nodded. He spread his fingers wide and drew them across the beam of light that was his power. A pathway opened before me. I nodded toward the great god, then ran onto the Bridge between the worlds, hoping he would be too busy to track my progress.

I stumbled over the rubble on the floor of the old crypt, but wasted no time reaching the Door, pressing my hand to it and willing it to open. Father stepped from the Bridge seconds before the Door opened. Before I could think, before I could hesitate, I was falling through the Door and into the Remembering.

The Memories come fast and furious.

James on his knees beneath Helena. Michael clasping me to his chest as he ran for Asgard, desperate to save me. Miri collapsing beneath the visions that tore at her mind.

Father pushes forward and I trip and fall onto the polished granite floor of the throne room. When I realize I've stumbled over the dead body of a zabaniyah, I jump up, taking a step backward and smacking against Father.

And then all hell breaks loose.

Father Becomes and lunges toward Helena who rises from the throne, her long gown shimmering pink in the torchlight. I make to leave, not wanting to be any part of what's happening here, hoping they wipe each other out of existence, when I catch a glimpse of a pale human form curled beside Father's throne.

"James?" I whisper. Of course my words are lost in the sudden explosion of sound as Helena and Father fall on one another. I take a step forward.

Father roars and bends to dig his teeth into Helena's neck, but then he is flying past me, smashing against the granite wall. His impact shudders the stone and he falls to the ground. Helena marches up to him, her strappy gold sandals crunching the dust on the floor.

I inch past her, willing myself to blend into the wall, to go unnoticed. I wish with all my heart that I had my weapons. Instead I feel like a dorky Halloween cast-off in a stupid Roman centurion costume.

I cover my ears and lean into a run as Father and Helena's battle escalates. To my left I see Father's generals slip out of the throne room. *Cowards.* But I don't care. The fewer people I have to contend with, the better. I look forward and focus on the body curled so small you can't tell who it is. But I know.

Another blast and I cringe, waiting for the fallout to lessen, willing the throne room to stand long enough for me to get to James. *Please let him be okay.* He isn't moving and it suddenly worries me that maybe he isn't even alive. *Please, please let him be okay.*

"You won't fool me again," Helena screams before Father flies through the air and lands with a resounding crash on the stairs to the dais. "Do you know how long it took me to get my nails fixed? Do you know how many baths I needed to take before I felt clean again? How many conditioning treatments before my hair felt silky smooth?" She stomps toward him, somehow managing to appear elegant and lovely despite the fury burning along her skin in licks of red-blue flame.

Father climbs to his feet and roars with pure hatred. He thrusts out his hand, his fingers shaped into claws, and twists. Helena stops in her tracks and reaches for her throat. She rises off the floor, her feet kicking, her eyes bugging out. Father steps down the stairs and slowly advances toward her.

I dart up the steps and dive for James.

"James. James." I whisper his name over and over, touch his forehead, smooth his dirty, matted hair.

"James." He sighs, and relief rushes through me because I know he's alive, even if his eyes are still tightly shut, even though his body is riddled with sores.

I rip the cape from my shoulders and lay it over him. He grabs it and pulls it around his shivering body.

"James, it's Desi."

"Desi," he repeats.

"I'm here."

He finally opens his eyes, looking first at the stone floor against which his cheek is pressed, then slowly shifting his gaze until he finds mine.

"We've gotta go," I say. I want to reach for him, to pull him to his feet but he seems so much like a wounded bird, a scared little creature—I worry he might bolt or scream if I rush him, if I force him to move. The last thing we need is to draw attention to ourselves.

Helena is hurled through the air this time, crashing into the throne that had once been mine. I throw myself over James, trying to protect him from the explosion of bone. A skull, half of it smashed, rolls toward us and James yells, batting it away.

"It's okay, it's okay," I croon, unsure if anything will ever be okay again.

I help James sit up while Helena stands and shakes herself free of debris. She growls when she sees the strap over her right shoulder is torn. When she looks up, her face is dark with fury. Before I can react she grabs the back of my tunic and pulls me to my feet.

"Leave, or I destroy her." Her voice rebounds off the walls, as if she's speaking through a bull horn. I cringe against the sound of it, squeezing my eyes shut.

"You will not harm her," Father says. I hear him take a step forward and I open my eyes.

"James!" I shout. I need to warn him to get away, to run for the Door—but he isn't there. I see a void in the debris at my feet, see where his body had lain only seconds ago. My cape lies empty—James is gone.

Father steps nearer. I can tell from the way Helena's hand trembles against my body that he's doing something to make her let go of me, but whatever it is, it isn't working.

"Stop, or I shall end her life." And then the agony begins.

My head feels as though it's being squeezed in a vice. I feel my eardrums pop, feel the warm rush of blood as it drips into my ear canal. And my head isn't the only part of me that feels compressed. It gets harder and harder to breathe until I'm only able to gasp out tiny breaths.

"Release her!" Father thrusts out his hand, sending Helena and I both flying off the dais. I land a few feet away from her, gasping and coughing, unable to even prop myself up on my elbows.

"Aw, a little daddy-daughter love. I didn't know you had it in you." Helena rises to her feet, but I close my eyes and concentrate on staying alive because right at this moment I'm not sure I can.

"You know nothing of love." Father's voice echoes in the room as his cloven hooves clomp down the stairs.

Helena laughs and the rocks around me skitter across the floor. "And you do?"

My chin jerks up, because that's what I want to know, too. *What does Father know of love?*

"I know everything about love." His face alight with truth and earnestness. "Everything I have done has been out of love for my people. I am the only one who truly loves them, *not* Odin. I am the only one who sought to ensure that everyone returned home. And now this world is mine and I will protect it. My chosen people deserve a home of their own—and you have not earned their love."

Helena's laughter rattles small rocks from the walls, forces my body to sag against the floor, crushed by the sheer pressure of her will. Predictably, Father's indignation has gotten the better of him and he lunges forward again. I feel, rather than see, the two of them fall to the ground some yards ahead of me.

I manage to get myself onto my knees and look around once more for James. The place has been demolished. Not a single chair still stands—except for Father's, which rises on the dais behind the dueling gods like some sort of sentinel or prize. I can't see James anywhere.

I hope he made it through the Door. Hope he knew to go home. He had to. Right? He had to have gone home. And that's exactly where I plan to go, too. I crawl my way to the wall and use it to help me get to my feet.

I slide along it, inching my way toward the Door. I'm almost there, I'm just stepping over the body of the dead zabaniyah when something slices down my back, making me arch away from the red-hot pain and stumble, falling onto the body at my feet.

Something drips onto my leg, causing my skin to sizzle with unbelievable agony. I scream and roll over, scrambling past the dead body. Above me, towers the other zabaniyah. *Where did he come from?* But there's no time for thought. I Become, thrusting the creature backward, and as soon as there's room between us, I whirl, slicing diagonally through it with the tip of my wing. The demonic dragon falls to the floor with two sickening plops.

Father stumbles into me, his wings beating forward, encapsulating us both for a moment. And in the second his eyes meet mine I see—I think I see—a glimpse of who he once was. I Remember when I loved him. When he loved me. Before the madness overtook him, causing him to deny Odin and steal away a third of Asgard. His Shadow recedes and I see behind him where Helena lies on the floor, her beautiful gown ripped and torn, blood splattered on it like raindrops.

"Are you all right?" Father's concern actually sounds sincere. I let my Halo fade and lean into him, allowing myself to believe, for just a second, that he's the person I remember, the one who was my friend. I'd always wanted this. More than anything, I wished for Father to choose me for a change, to think of me before himself, before his great disagreement with Odin.

Father stiffens in my arms, as if he's been frozen in time. I feel a sharp jab in my chest, right through my ribs. Father drops his arms and his eyes go wide with disbelief. Between us, I see the blade of a sword poking through my father and jabbed into my own chest. My breathing hitches, caught in my throat without actually delivering any lifesaving air to my lungs.

Over Father's shoulder, I watch as Helena pulls the sword from Father's back. He falls forward, crashing into me. We both go down, Father crumpled in my lap, blood gurgling out of his mouth and onto my legs. I gasp, gasp, gasp and stare wide eyed at Helena.

She drops the sword to the ground. Looks around for something to wipe her hands on, then leans forward to wipe them on Father's shirt. She smoothes her hair. Produces a golden mirror and tube of lipstick and fixes her lips.

"Wha—" I try to ask why she's killing us, what she's doing, but I can't frame the words. I can't seem to get anything past the junk that's filling up my throat faster than I can swallow it down.

Helena leans forward, her cleavage nearly equal with my eyes. "What's that darling? I can't hear you." She straightens with a sigh. "It's just as well. Bye now." She spins around and exits the throne room, leaving me lying there with my father by the Door, our life blood seeping away along with my hope.

TWENTY-TWO

DESI

Maybe this time I should just die. Death's come for me so many times—maybe I need to give in this time. I mean, it will keep coming for me, right? As it is, I can't fathom why I keep getting second chances. I am Loki's daughter—part Gardian. Shouldn't I be reincarnated? Or, as Mahria's daughter, couldn't I go to Vanaheim? Instead I just keep coming back to life.

Unless the right answer is that I should just stay here in Helheimer. I try to open my eyes, try to laugh at the irony. My body will die here in Hell—the perfect place for my soul to take up residence. I wonder if dying always feels like this—like a slow burn, like filling a bathtub, like waiting for the rain to stop before running outside.

You don't have to die, a voice, not my own, whispers inside my mind. Maybe a little craziness is part of death, of real death.

The voice is wrong, anyway. Michael, James and Miri—they'll be all right. Won't they?

Remember who you are.

That's a laugh. Because I know exactly who I am—that's the problem. I'm the girl who nothing works out for. I always screw things up. What's the point of being who I am if I never get it right?

Mahria and Odin were wrong to put their trust in me. To believe I was anything special.

But Michael believed. He'd always believed, even when everything about me shouted he was wrong. Screamed its ugly defiance of what he thought I was. When I was with him last—even I had believed.

Remember Michael.

I Remember his hand in mine. His kiss. The way it felt when he held me close, when we Become and gloried in all that we were. Together we were glorious.

Michael loves me for all that I was. All that I am. I know it. It's the one thing I know above all others. And he won't be happy if I don't come back. He's perhaps the only one, but the thought of his sorrow stirs something in me. Drives me to Remember.

Remember that I'd been created to protect Midgard. Remember all the sacrifices that had been made so I could fulfill my destiny. Remember how Michael said I was unlike anyone else, that I was glorious and fierce.

My chest and throat burn, but I struggle to sit up. Struggle to clear my mind, to think only of Michael, only of the time we'd spent together in our garden. I push away the thoughts that want to convince me I'm not worthy of his love. I'd listened to that voice my whole life and look where it had gotten me.

This time, I won't die alone. This time I will die with Michael's memory, his love, filling every part of me, every thought. I'll let his love consume me, let it warm my cold veins, let it fill my Halo, my Shadow, let it cleanse every part of me with its purity.

I reach for that love, try to be the person Michael says I am. Because if it's the last thing I do, if it's what takes my very last breath, I want to be the person he believes me to be. For him and for Aaron, for Lucy, for Miri and for James. For everyone who loved me, I owe this last act of Light.

When I Become, sparks of gold and silver shoot up my arms, through my wings and outward in ever-widening arcs. The throne room trembles around me, stones fall and the ground shakes. I scream with every ounce of strength I have left. I scream for love—for Michael, and his belief in me.

I face death, finally embracing all that I was, all that I am, because I am loved and finally, at the end of it all, that counts for something.

"Shh, baby, shh."

Lucy wrapped her arms around me, her hand on the back of my head, and held me to her, like a mother cradles her child. Lucy had always known how to make me feel safe. There was a time when she'd been the only one I let into my heart. Before Aaron, before James, before Miri, before Michael. Before I had Become. And I'd never been sorry.

"You're all right now, baby."

I'm all right.

I let the words sink deep into my consciousness. They filled every part of me like soft butter seeping into warm bread. I felt myself relax. Exhale. *I'm all right.*

And then I Remembered.

I jerked back from Lucy's arms, jumped to my feet and took three long steps away, my eyes searching wildly. I glanced at my chest, where blood darkened the crimson tunic. At Lucy whose white shift was marred by blood— my blood, and Father's.

Father.

But he was not here.

Lucy and I were in a garden, all green grass and fragrant blossoms. Lucy sat on a wooden bench, carved with flowers and woodland creatures. It struck me then, how this place suited her and how glorious she looked—even more beautiful than she'd been in life. Even more beautiful than in her Ascension.

"Where am I?" I said aloud, though I didn't exactly mean to.

Lucy laughed, a sound like low wind chimes in the breeze. "Come sit, baby. I'll tell ya all about it."

I crossed the grass and sat beside her, angling myself so I could face her. "I thought you were dead."

She shrugged. "So did I. And I think maybe I kind of was when Freyja found me and brought me here."

I let that name sink in, trying to find a home for it. I came up with nothing. "Freyja?"

Lucy smiled into her lap, her thick black lashes brushing her dark cheeks. "I know. It's crazy. I didn't know a thing about these people when I lived on Earth—what I did hear I thought was a fairy tale. Ya know?" She glanced at me and I smiled, but I didn't really know. To me, humans were the myth, the fairy tale.

"I guess we all have somethin' to learn though, ya know?" She smoothed the soft dress she wore and I noticed it was no longer stained with blood. "Take you, for instance. It took you a mighty long time to figure out who you are, baby. A mighty long time."

Lucy reached over and took my hand in hers. "But I knew you'd make it. And here you are."

I still didn't know where I was. I might have thought it was Asgard, but the trees here were not leaved in gold but in varying shades of green. It seemed like Earth but . . . not.

"No, baby. It isn't Earth. You're in Vanaheim, the home of the Vanir gods—the creators of all the worlds."

"So, am I dead? Fiahre told me the Valkyrie come here when they die. And Father? What about him?"

"Oh, you're not dead," she said with a laugh and small shake of her head that made my heart ache with how much I had missed her. "Though you aren't quite the same, either."

"I don't understand." My mind reeled with possibilities and the sudden and fervent need to see Michael. Right away. "I have to go." I jumped to my feet again and paced the garden. "How do I get outta here?"

"I know you have to go, baby. But first, you need you to do something for me. And there are people you need to meet before you leave."

"Anything." Anything for Lucy.

"Take a look at yourself."

"What?" I saw my hands, my clothes. "What do you mean?"

A standing mirror appeared before me, and Lucy stood behind me, her hands on my shoulders. "Take a look. A good look."

I stepped up to the mirror. "I look the same."

"Look closer."

I started at my knees and went up the left side of my body. When I got to my left hand, my breath caught in my throat. It no longer swirled with the black ice of my father's heritage, but was now streaked with silver. I hurried to look at my right arm, afraid I'd sacrificed my goodness, only to find it still traced with the gold of my mother's gift.

"Become, baby. I want you to see." She took a step back, giving me room to spread my wings.

It took me a minute to ground myself. I still wasn't used to Becoming on command, but I knew when Lucy got an idea in her head, there was no getting it out until she'd seen it through. Still, I twisted around. "And when I do, you'll tell me what's going on?" She nodded.

Facing myself again, I thought about how different everything was. From the clothes I wore, to this place, to all that had happened the past year. It hadn't been that long ago I'd refused to Become at all, certain it would mean submitting to Father's plans for me—or execution for harboring the golden spark. I feared it would be revealed if I Became, and Father would not tolerate its existence inside me.

Now though, it was as easy as thought. I was already dead—or something. And Father no longer owned me. I owned myself.

And so I Became.

I expected to see the yin-yang of black and gold I'd grown accustomed to—one golden wing, one dark. I expected to see the golden ribbon light up my right arm and upward onto my neck, never quite reaching the black swirls that darkened my left side.

I expected to see something ugly and freakish— because in my half-breed state I was neither truly lovely nor truly glorious, no matter what Michael said.

But I wasn't what I expected at all.

I wasn't ugly. I wasn't a bizarre freak show that should have never happened. I looked . . . glorious. Truly, honestly, glorious.

Ribbons of silver and gold snaked up both my arms, forming complicated knots that reminded me of Aaron's protections. And my wings—I gasped as I took them in.

They were Gardian wings and more. Beautiful feathers in gold with silver sprinkled throughout. My spirit radiated outward, gold and silver.

Lucy stepped in front of me and the mirror disappeared. "Now do you understand? Can you comprehend everything you were meant to Become?" I stared at her, dumbfounded, unable to find the words to express how little I knew and how much I hoped.

"Ah, baby." She pulled me to her and rocked a little while she held me. I let my— Halo? Shadow?— recede as

I sank into her arms. "You can call it whatever you like, though I think it's your Halo—don't you think? It's your spirit baby. Yours. Unlike any other in all the weavings of time. But—in many ways you are not so different from any of us."

She took my hand and walked with me back to the bench where we sat, my hand still in hers. Until Miri, Lucy had been the only one who'd ever touched me like this— the undemanding touch of friendship, a very specific kind of love. No expectations. Just the gentle exchange between two souls who cared for one another.

"None of us are perfect. And none of us are completely evil. There is good and bad in each of us—you should know this better than anyone."

I nodded, thinking of Father and what he'd said before Helena stabbed him—that he knew what love was, that everything he had done had been for love. It wasn't the kind of love I knew from Lucy and Michael, but to him, it was love. Didn't that mean something in the grand scheme of things?

"You know, it's precisely because of this disparity that Odin created Midgard and the quest for Ascension. Oh, don't look at me like that—I've learned a few big words since I've been hangin' around people a lot smarter than me."

She laughed then, and oh, she was beautiful. I leaned against her shoulder and we laughed and laughed and it felt so good. It felt perfect.

"Come on." She stood and pulled me to my feet. "Let's meet one of those smart people, okay sugar?"

We walked down a stone path with soft green moss growing in the cracks, and past a field of pale blue flowers where white unicorns grazed. While I watched, one raised its head, its gaze meeting mine. Its long silver mane fell into its eyes and it nickered. I felt a connection then, a greeting inside my soul. We passed through a copse of oak-like trees and stepped out onto a cobblestone street. To the right, a castle stood at the end of the road—a deserted castle with scorch marks at its windows and doors.

The castle grounds were well kept, but there were no doors in the doorframes or shutters on the glassless windows. "What happened?" It surprised me that such a beautiful world could house something so dark and dreary.

Lucy took the path to a cheery stone cottage adjacent to the castle grounds. "That is a story for Freyja to tell. This is her home." She smiled before knocking on the door, then stepped in without waiting for an invitation.

"Freyja?" she called, beckoning for me to follow.

Light streamed inside the cottage, adding to the bright and homey feel of the place. The smell of cinnamon and vanilla hung in the air, making me take a deep breath and sigh in response. Embarrassed, I glanced at Lucy, but she only smiled and gestured to a room with a fluffy couch and two armchairs flanking an imposing stone fireplace. A bouquet of hundreds of yellow and pink blossoms decorated the cold hearth. Tucked into the vases and scattered through the room, were the tiny nodding bells of Lily of the Valley. Seeing them caused a sense of peace to settle over me, a feeling of belonging.

"Coming!" a sing-song voice replied. A moment later a woman appeared in a shower of silver sparks. For a second, she wore her Halo around her like a glorious cape—the impression of silver wings shining behind her.

She let her Halo fade away as she stepped forward, reaching out for me. "Desolation." She took my hands in hers. "Granddaughter."

My throat dried up and words failed me.

"There is another." She kept a hand on my arm while she angled her body away, gesturing to someone who stood in the adjacent room.

A woman stepped into view. Tall, with golden skin and chestnut hair twisted into a knot at her neck. She wore a long, crimson dress and carried herself like a warrior. I couldn't help the gasp that escaped my lips.

"Come, come," Freyja said, pulling me toward the woman.

"Mahria?"

She stepped past my grandmother, who passed my hands to her, adding a gentle squeeze.

"Daughter," Mahria said. Her voice was low and musical like the winds rushing over hills of tall grass. She placed a hand on my cheek and leaned into me, resting her forehead on mine. "Well met, precious one."

And oh, my heart was full.

"Come, sit. We have much to talk about—so much to learn," Freyja said.

With Freyja to my left, and Mahria on my right, we sat on the couch that sank beneath my weight like a favorite blanket, like Lucy's comforter. Like home. Freyja tucked her feet beneath her and pulled her simple white-flecked-with-silver dress over her legs.

"I am so happy you have finally embraced your true nature, my dear. I can see it in your face, in your skin." She reached out and traced one of the swirls on my left arm that used to be dark but now shone silver—like the designs on her own arms.

"Yes," she said, holding out her hands and examining the patterns there. "They are very much the same, aren't they? And do you know why that is?" Her sky-blue eyes were edged with silver and I felt I could lose myself in them. I glanced at Lucy in the chair opposite us, but she was busy cooing to a large tabby cat that had invaded her lap.

To Freyja, I shook my head.

"It is a very long story, and a rather tragic one, I'm afraid. But the short of it is, you are my granddaughter—for Loki is my son."

"But he—but Odin . . ."

Freyja shook her head. "It was a very long time ago, and Odin only did what he thought was best—indeed, he did exactly as I hoped he might. It was Loki who did not . . . grow up . . . the way I wished.

"You see, the gods are not meant to have children of their own—our powers are too great to be unleashed in the universe. We tried once, long ago, but only found ourselves fraught with war and mutiny. We were able to come to a consensus of sorts with the Aesir gods, a precarious peace that, over time, grew into true brotherhood. To seal our commitment to one another, we created the nine worlds and appointed the gods who would rule them."

Freyja sighed, a musical sound to which the cat replied with a sorrowful meow.

"We intended for Thor to rule Midgard—but then I . . ." She glanced away and I thought perhaps she was crying; but when she turned back to me, though her eyes shone with tears, they did not fall. "It was our fault, you see. We fell in love and I bore a child—a child who had no place in the tapestry of this new life.

"My twin brother, Freyr, mighty and golden, was deeply angered at what I had done. At the child I had conceived. He convinced the Council that Thor should be punished, that he should be denied Midgard, claiming none of the gods could have favor, as surely I favored Thor since I loved him so. Then Freyr dictated that our child be cast out to the stars—a fate we could not accept.

"Thor fought for my honor, for the right to wed me, to raise our child here in Vanaheim or even Midgard if that would please the Council. But Freyr was beyond reason. On the night I gave birth to my son, in this very cottage, the tapestry changed forever.

"I could hear Thor and Freyr fighting through the castle windows. I fled with my child, believing I would find some friendly place where I could hide until Freyr could be reasoned with—but Heimdall barred my path and refused me access to the Bifrost." She reached out and patted my leg. "Oh, don't worry. He was very kind about it. After all, he was an old friend, a Vanir god we all agreed would guard the way—it would fall to him, forever, to mark the paths we trod, to keep order in the worlds.

"He knew a Vanir god could not remain hidden—especially with a child of unknown potential. Heimdall suggested an Aesir god, a guardian of one of the nine worlds, could perhaps find it in his heart to rear a child of mixed blood. He spoke with reason and care—the first time since my pregnancy began that anyone had looked upon the union with any amount of acceptance.

"And when he was done speaking I knew there was only one god who could be trusted with such a task. Only Odin loved as truly as Thor—and Thor is his son, so perhaps that says it all.

"I took my child, my son, to Odin, with Heimdall's blessing. I laid him in the arms of Odin's queen and returned to my castle—only to find Thor and Freyr still embattled. In a rage I lashed out at Freyr, my anguish over all that had happened, all I had lost, driving me to act beyond reason, beyond care.

"In the end, Freyr lay on the ground at my feet."

She bowed her head while silver teardrops dripped into her open palms. "The gods gathered and pronounced their judgments. Thor would be an emissary between the worlds, but could not claim a home of his own. He would never rule, never reveal himself to our son, never see me again. And I was to stay here, forever separated from the ones I loved. The castle had been all but destroyed and so I have lived here ever since, near my former home, to remind me of what fear and hatred can do. Of what prejudice can do."

I watched her face as she watched mine. Saw the freckles there—so much like my own. I had thought they were Mahria's, but now I knew they were Freyja's. My grandmother's.

Freyja leaned forward and took my hand. "Thank you for bringing my son home to me," she said. I shook my head, fumbling over the words in my mind.

"I'm so sorry," I finally said.

"Oh." Freyja's voice held laughter in it, which just seemed wrong considering Loki had died. "He is not dead, my dear. Loki is a god and as such, he is immortal—this was not his first time to die. It was, however, the first time he died with love in his heart—which is thanks to you, of course. Because of you I now have the chance I never had before, to meet my only child. It is a gift for which I will be forever grateful." She sat up straighter and patted my hand.

"Have you not wondered how it is your life has ended, only to resume again? You're here because I wanted you to see for yourself the source of your heritage, and to know the truth about your father. The truth about you." She gave me a pointed look, one that seemed to say, *Now listen up and listen good.* "The Aesir and Vanir gods were two sides of the same coin. Dark and light. Good and evil. Like Freyr and I—male and female, gold and silver. I won't go so far as to say he was good and I evil, or the other way around—though some will judge." She tried a shrug and found it didn't suit her. "I have to be at peace with that. I know what is true—what is in my heart." She placed her hand on her heart and stared at me, daring me to disagree.

281

"You are the best of us, you know. You hold our hope in your destiny. Be the woman you want to be—don't let yourself be shaped by the colors on your skin or in your Halo. You are exactly right, exactly perfect, just as you are."

She stood then, and walked to the mantle where she took down a small, golden box. She walked to the table, the box cradled in her hands. I joined her, sitting opposite her, my eyes practically glued to the box and the next mystery Freyja would reveal.

"Wait," I said. "What's going to happen to—?"

"To your father?" Freyja's eyes flicked over my shoulder to Lucy, then back to me. "Now that he has healed, Thor will come to collect him. It has been decided that Loki is too volatile to be allowed to return to Asgard or Midgard. Truly, he is too dangerous for any of the nine worlds. But, with the Aesir home world gone, and Vanaheim now home to the resting Valkyrie, the Svarts have offered up the northern reaches of their home to Thor and Loki. It is dark there, plagued by a rocky, unkind terrain and vicious cold, and barren of population. There, Thor will endeavor to have Loki atone for his sins against the gods. He will ensure Loki receives the punishment the gods have demanded of him."

"Punishment?"

"Yes. It pains me that my child has fallen so far from his potential glory, but even the gods are not immune to our laws. We decided long ago to hold ourselves accountable, to never abuse the power we hold over our people. And as my child—as Odin's great-grandson—Loki knew there would be consequences for his rebellion. He must answer to this higher law. You see how this must be?"

I nodded, my heart a weird mix of relief and sadness.

Freyja patted the box, bringing my attention back to her, back to this moment. "This was Thor's—your grandfather's. It is his most prized possession. He was stripped of it when he was sent away. I know he wished his son would wield it, but given Loki's choices, I am certain he would wish you to have it."

She ran her fingers over the gold inlay on the top of the box—a depiction of clouds and lightning. "Thor would be proud to claim you. As I am. I am told he has watched you and applauded your courage, your faith, your goodness."

I looked down, falling upon my usual reaction to discount her positive assessment of me. Freyja squeezed my hand. "Don't do that," she said. "You are the granddaughter of the gods. Remember what I said—be proud of who you are and the good choices you have made. Now," she said, taking a deep breath.

"Let me give to you this treasure. For it is a treasure beyond any in all the worlds."

She lifted the lid of the box and set it aside, revealing a multi-colored, swirling orb. It moved and shimmered like a living thing, astonishingly beautiful. Freyja reached in and plucked up the sphere by her fingertips and let it roll into her palm.

She held her palm out to me. "It belongs to you now," she said in a reverent whisper. "Take care of it. And remember who you are."

She let the sphere fall from her hand to mine, and I felt its warm touch on my skin, its familiarity. "It's alive!"

Freyja smiled. "I'd hoped it would speak to you. It is all that is left of the Aesir home planet—a piece Thor rescued himself. It is a thing of great power, and, if it speaks to you, can be a source of great knowledge and insight as well. I had hoped, and now I know, my choice was true—you are its rightful keeper. Use it to help you do what must be done."

I jerked my chin up, startled by her comment. "What's to be done?"

Freyja's sky blue eyes grew dark as though a storm approached. "Midgard needs a guardian. Odin has done his best all these long years, and he has done well. But Loki was relatively little threat to him—not divided as he has been. Helena on the other hand . . ." Freyja's mouth tugged downward and she swallowed against her strong emotions.

"Helena is a Vanir god and has always had her own devious plans for the universe. She was never happy with our choice to forbid having children and has long hated me for the birth of my son. I—I helped him overcome her at one time. I only wanted a home for my child and I thought Loki could do a better job managing Helheimer than she did.

"But I have paid my price for such an act, and I am forbidden from interfering again."

I shook my head, trying to make sense of her words. "I-I don't understand."

Freyja leaned forward and clasped my wrist. "Helena rules Helheimer now. And she hates you. You are my offspring—something she jealously desires and can never have herself. She will strive to undo you, if only to cause me pain. You must be ever ready, ever vigilant."

She stared at me with such intensity and she gripped my wrist until my fingers grew numb. I glanced at Lucy, but she only smiled, her empathy for Freyja painting her features with sadness. Mahria seemed content to observe in silence, her stoic demeanor offering no opinion.

"Come," Freyja said, standing up. "Our time is at an end—I must show you how to use the Genesis." I barely noted the name she used—I'd already begun to think of it as I did the spark. That this was a physical manifestation of the one I'd held secret my entire life.

"You must Become your spirit, embrace all your gifts," Freyja said, as she embraced her own. And oh, she was stunning. A silver being with feathered wings that undulated like a shining sea. "Come," she repeated.

I held the spark close to my chest and Became.

"Oh!" Freyja exclaimed. "You are even more glorious than I'd hoped." She reached out and trailed her fingers down the edge of my left wing, sending rivulets of happiness coursing through my body. "Yes, Thor must be so proud." She touched my arm, tenderness like warm honey seeping into my veins. "As I am."

"Press the Genesis to your heart and welcome its presence within your mind with your thoughts."

I did as she asked, feeling all the more that the Genesis was like the spark I already had. I wondered if it were possible that it was somehow related, that I somehow already had a piece of it with me. And then in a flash I understood—it was so much more than that.

This was life, true life—the power to give it and to take it away. This was omniscience, power and knowledge forged into one. I spread my arms wide as fire coursed through me, through my body, my mind, my wings. Into every thought came a deeper meaning, into every feeling came a deeper intensity. With the Genesis I Became so much more than I ever thought I could be. I opened my eyes and found the three women watching me, all wearing expressions of maternal pride.

Freyja stepped forward, somehow standing taller than before, more regal, her blue eyes and soft smile a benediction. "Desolation," she said. "You have Become a god."

TWENTY-THREE

DESI

With my Halo, I reached for Father—and found him resting in the cottage across the street. He was awake and he knew what Freyja had done.

The Genesis should have been mine, he said in my mind, but his words lacked heat.

You know you aren't worthy of such a gift, I replied, surprised by my confidence in this knowledge.

Father fell silent and didn't say anything else.

An object in my Halo beckoned me and I reached out for it—clasping my fingers around a solid handle. As I pulled it from my Halo, the object gained density and heft. It was a massive golden hammer with symbols in the Old Language carved into the handle and head.

Thor's hammer! Father said.

Mjölner, it whispered to me. Forged of the Genesis, it had a will of its own, and with it, I knew I would be invincible. I could rule worlds with the power of this weapon. I could defeat Helena.

Give it to me! Loki cried. He clawed against my mind, demanding that I relinquish the weapon to him.

With a start, I let go of Mjölner and tucked it away in my Halo.

I love you, Father.

It was the first time I'd ever said those words to him, and they startled me.

But I did. I always would—now more than ever. I knew there was good in Loki. Good that had been buried beneath a forever of hatred and jealousy. I wouldn't be like him—but neither would I take after my uncle Freyr and see the eternities with an unbendable eye. I would remember who I was—all of who I was.

Good and bad.

Dark and light.

Shadow and Halo.

And I would glory in my creation.

As Mahria, Lucy, Freyja and I walked back to the garden, Freyja took my left hand. "Your hand should be whole."

I glanced down, saw the ugly stub of my finger there, and jerked it out of her grasp. "I cut it off when—"

She took my hand again. "I know, dear. But you have only to wish it to be whole and it will be so."

We'd stopped walking and now stood, both of us looking at my hand in hers. I thought about how ugly my hand was with only four fingers. Of what a relief it would be to be free of the reminder of how far I'd once fallen.

And then, between one blink and the next, the ugly stump was gone and in its place was a healthy finger, my hand whole once more.

Freyja laughed and squeezed my hand. We resumed our walk; my grandmother on my left, and on my right, my first friend, Lucy while Mahria walked just behind. I breathed in their presence, the beauty of the place, the Genesis that had joined with the spark in my heart, and I knew what I needed to do, knew what my mission would be. Thor was meant to rule Midgard, but due to his transgression his weapon and his place in the nine worlds had been stripped from him. I would claim my grandfather's place and rule Midgard in his stead.

I would be so much more than a weapon against the dark. So much more than Desolation.

"It's time for you ta go, baby," Lucy said. She ran her hands up and down my arms like she'd done so many times before. Before, when I was a lost and broken girl, a puppet in the hands of my father.

But things were so very different now.

Now, I am a product of Lucy's love and of Aaron's. Of Miri's and Michael's and James's. Of Mahria's.

We stopped in the garden and Mahria stepped forward, pulling me into her arms. For the first time in my life I felt absolutely complete. She knew me, from the beginning of life, she'd known me. She gave everything for me, knew exactly what I was, and she accepted me.

"Daughter." She stroked my hair, while I listened to her breath, felt her heart beat. She pushed me back and examined me at arm's length, as I examined her. "You look so much like me." I nodded. "You are a great warrior, daughter, and I am so proud of you."

I fell into her arms again, mumbling my love for her, how much I had missed her, how I wished I could get to know her again. "I will always mourn what we could never have, daughter, the time together we have lost—but I will never regret giving you life. Your life will be extraordinary. Your life will be filled with power and goodness and with love." She held my face in her hands. "Always remember love. Remember Michael."

I beamed back at her, feeling, *knowing*, that I would never, ever forget.

A sensation of need tugged at my heart—the draw to Midgard, the draw to fight for it, to protect it.

"Even now, Midgard calls to you," Mahria said.

I looked at my mother, at Lucy and Freyja. "Yes."

"Then you must go. You must never lose sight of your duty."

"I won't. I promise. But what about you? All of you?"

"We are where we belong," Mahria said. "I am with my goddess, this is my eternal home."

"And I will stay here also." Lucy met Freyja's gaze and I saw the hope shining within them. "Freyja's been alone too long. We'll watch over you, baby." Lucy, glorious, perfect Lucy. It made me feel a million shades of wonderful to know she would be watching over me—she and my mother and grandmother.

"It seems we have much in common and I like sharing my home with a Valkyrie and an Ascended One. Lucy is as fierce and loyal as any of my warrior handmaidens. She certainly knows how to keep me in line!" Freyja laughed, even Mahria tucked her head, mirth shining in her eyes, and I laughed out loud.

In a moment of abandon I threw my arms around Lucy's neck. She rubbed my back and whispered, "I love you too, baby. I love you, too."

Freyja moved to Lucy's side. Reluctantly I stepped back, facing the three women before me; Mahria, beautiful and proud; Freyja, shimmering with silver light, power radiating from her like a force field; and Lucy—the one who taught me what it was to love, what it was to have a friend.

"You know how to travel, now?" Freyja asked.

And I did.

I knew it all. Knew everything. I felt the universe spreading outward from my mind as if it were an open book and all I had to do was focus on a single word to find it on the page. I felt Heimdall watching me. Knew Odin stood beside him, observing the progress of the battle which still raged on Midgard.

Knew Michael and the Gardians, and Fiahre and the Valkyrie fought a new wave of Svarts and Giants. Knew the war was not going well and they were all so very tired.

I pulled my awareness back to myself and smiled at Freyja. She knew what I knew—I could feel it in her.

She stepped forward and took my hands in hers. "Be a faithful guardian, granddaughter. Celebrate all that you are. Perhaps you will be able to do what we were not."

She pulled me into her embrace. I breathed in the scent of her—happiness and sunshine—and closed my eyes, letting myself be wholly there in that moment.

She leaned back and squeezed my hands.

"Perhaps Midgard can finally have the peace it deserves with you as its caretaker."

There was a time when I'd deny those words, deny that I could do anything close to taking care of anyone—let alone a whole world. But in my grandmother's warm and confident voice, I found a new hope. I wanted to make her proud. To make all of them proud.

"I will try," I said. And I knew that I would. For all my days, I would strive to bring peace to Earth.

Freyja let go of me and reached for Lucy. They stood side by side, Mahria with them, arms touching, a pillar of hope and strength created by three lives, three souls.

"Thank you," I said. "I love you." *Love you all.*

I pictured Earth, pictured the desert where my love fought for the world that was now my own.

"Wait," Freyja said, reaching out and taking my hand, drawing me back to Vaneheim. "Don't do it alone, Desolation. Don't make the same mistakes Freyr and I did."

I was already going. Already taking her advice. I didn't want to be alone another moment. I smiled, bigger than I'd maybe smiled my whole life, and nodded. And then I sent myself across time and space toward Michael. And once I found him, I would never, ever leave him.

TWENTY-FOUR

MICHAEL

Sweat stung my eyes but there was no use in wiping it away as I'd already done a million times—there was no rest in this battle, no time to catch my breath. By turns I was frozen to the core by the passing of a Svart-blade, all ice and shivers, and toasted by the breath of a Giant that singed my eyebrows. Cold and heat beat against me, wearying me, weakening me as surely as any steely blow.

I feared we would not prevail. I felt it in my warriors, saw it even in the way the shi'lil now flew lower in the sky, no longer shooting like falling stars, but stumbling across the heavens. The mounted Valkyries' arrows flew, first one

. . . and then another. Slow enough that I could see their pathway to Earth. Not like before, when we first came to this fight, when their arrows flew like lightning, so swift and deadly.

More of us lay on the hard-packed desert floor than our enemy. And the enemy kept coming. Even now I felt like I swung my blade in slow motion as I watched Svarts pour from the sky like a river of blue ice.

It was then that I saw her from across the field—she appeared in a shower of rainbow light. Our eyes met across the death that lay between us, and then she was gone.

TWENTY-FIVE

JAMES

Huddled on the gravel, out of the way of the sprawling crowd that crawls up and down the skeleton stairs, I press my forehead to my knees and wonder how it will all end. *Can I die if I'm already in Hell? Or am I already dead?*

Something tells me I'm not dead—not yet. I'm not like those empty-eyed people going up and down the stairs. And now that I'm free of Helena, my thoughts are finally my own. I wish it had been like drugs—wish I couldn't remember what had happened.

But I remember it all.

I feel deeply ashamed that I ever chose to go with the Ferryman—or woman. Helena had played me from the start and I didn't know what she got from it except the cheap thrills of making a guy into a total tool.

What will Miri think of me now? Of how far I've fallen? I'm nothing. Less than nothing. A stupid guy, a tiny piece of cloth covering the essentials and gravel poking into my butt while I cry into a river of blood. The damned have never been able to find a way out of Hell—what made me think I could?

Desi will come for me.

Right?

I mean, she found me once—won't she do it again?

Except I'd seen Helena's handiwork first hand. I'd seen the way she could order someone's death or, with a thought, bring death all on her own. She's way more powerful than anything I'd seen Lucifer or Desi do. That chick was a world apart. Maybe Desi hadn't even survived.

Maybe she's dead and Michael's dead and . . .

Maybe Miri's dead.

As her name crosses my mind, as I picture her lying on that desert ground, her blood spilling out of her, my own blood freezes. *Miri.* I taste her death, test it for truth.

It doesn't feel true.

Miri is alive. I know it. I can feel her—somewhere.

I force my foggy mind to think of her. To picture her face, her shining eyes. Feel her kiss on my lips, her body beneath my hands. I think of the way she crinkles her nose when I make her taste one of my culinary experiments and it isn't any good. And the way she closes her eyes and moans with pleasure when she tastes something especially delicious. Man, the girl makes me feel alive. Even though it kills me—killed me—that we can't be together in that way yet, I love her for it. Cherish the little glimpses of what making love to her will be like. I can wait for her.

I'd wait forever for her.

But I won't live another moment without her.

Without knowing what to do, I jump up, refusing to acknowledge the bite of gravel in the soles of my feet. I stand tall at the edge of the river. The damned river that ruined my life. To my left, the river extends through a tunnel that runs under the shiny black granite mountain where Desi used to live. The glossy surface rises as high as I can see, occasional windows and balconies jutting out from the smooth surface. It freaks me out to think of Desi living in that place her whole life. A life that lasted an eternity.

To my right, the river disappears into a dark and shadowy tunnel cut into a very ugly, rocky cliff face. It was that direction that Helena had taken me in her little glass boat. I try to remember where we'd gone, but once crossing beneath the mountain, my memory blinks out. The next thing I knew I was her little pet slave, cowering nearly-naked at her feet in the throne room.

Across the river from me, boulders lay strewn all across the beach. I remember taking tunnels and paths beyond that to find Desi. Not sure what else to do, I take a step forward. The water is freezing cold. Colder than the air, colder than Hell.

I bite back a cry and stand there like an idiot for a few seconds while I get up the guts to take another step.

The water feels . . . alive. For a second I think I see something shift out of it, like the fin of some blood red fish poking above the roiling surface. I swear I hear a voice in my mind shout *Jump!* I jump backward, stumbling onto the gravel beach.

I shut my eyes and try to think. How the hell can I get out of here? I crouch to the ground again, my head clutched in my hands. *Desi*, I think. *Desi!*

And then I start a constant chant, screaming at the top of my mental lungs, my body quivering with the energy, with the work of it.

Desi! Desi! Desi!

I feel like I'm going to blow a capillary but I keep screaming. I stand up, scream to the deathly-orange sky.

"Desi!"

I grab at a passing crazy fat man, who reaches out to me, hold him by the shoulders and scream, "Desi!" at him so loud it should rupture his eardrums. Of course he keeps moving, keeps petting me in that weird and creepy way the people do here.

"Desi!" I cry again.

Desi! Desi! Desi!

I scream until my voice is raw and I can't scream anymore. I scream with my mind until my brain feels like mush. I fall to the ground. Wrap my arms around my knees and rock like an idiot.

Desi!

Desi!

I fall sideways, stars popping behind my closed eyelids.

Desi!

A sudden, searing brightness of light flashes in my mind, followed by a crystal clear image of Miri laughing, the sunshine lighting her face, making her bright blue eyes sparkle like the fourth of July.

Desi.

TWENTY-SIX

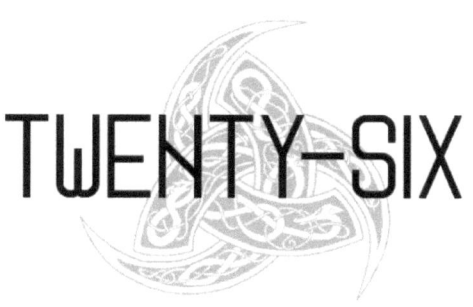

DESI

I heard the whisper while I travelled. *Desi.*

Felt the pull even before I appeared on the packed sand of the battlefield.

Still wearing the smile I'd shared with Lucy and Freyja, my eyes sought Michael's. I saw him—knew he saw me, too.

But the cry, my name, carrying the power of desperate need, could not go unanswered.

Desi!

And then I knew.

James.

James. It was James.

And so I had to leave before Michael, running now, could reach me. I'd promised to be with him forever, to never leave his side. But James cried for me again and I had no choice but to fly.

He feels so cold to my touch. As cold as the hard gravel he lies on. As cold as I had once been.

Colder.

I pull him into my arms. Feel the death that lies over him like a poorly made quilt.

I take him to the only person in all the worlds I know can heal him, if anyone ever can.

I take him to Miri.

I expected her to be in the desert, where I'd seen her last, but instead I found myself in the same one-room cottage where I'd discovered that demon Eleon and his vamp pet, forever ago. Yet here I was, the cottage repaired, Miri propped up by a dozen pillows on top of a wide, white-draped bed.

Miri scrambled back against the headboard, a cry of alarm on her lips that quickly changed to a different cry altogether.

"James!" She rushed forward, jumping from the bed, hurrying to touch him, find him all right.

But he wasn't all right.

I laid him on the bed and stepped back while Miri fussed over him. She looked at me then, her eyes pleading, so much need shining there I had to break eye contact. "Can you . . .?

"Please," she added in a near-whisper.

My heart jumped into my throat, choking me. "I ca—" but Helena's magic was at play here, things I still didn't understand. The truth felt like a sucker punch and made me wonder what all this power, what the Genesis, was for if I had to stand by and watch my friends die. I shook my head in shame.

"What happened?" A girl stepped through the front door of the cottage and for a moment I didn't recognize her. "I heard you screaming from the patio.

"Oh my gosh—Miri. Is he okay?"

Miri had thrown a blanket over James, but he remained perfectly still. Perfectly pale. I reached out with my Halo and I knew he still lived—but barely.

"We've gotta get him to the hospital," the girl said. She brushed past me as she made for the door, keeping her eyes down, avoiding touching me. I remembered her. Eleon's pet. I searched my memory. *Taige.* "I'll get the car."

Images of her flashed before my eyes. In bed with Eleon, baring her sharpened canines at me, kneeling on the ground in worship before me.

Judgment tempted my senses, tried to disarm me, but with a gulp I pushed it down, pushed it away. Things were different now. People change. People can be better. I knew that better than anyone.

A car drove up to the front door and Taige jumped out, opened the back door and ran in. "Um," she looked at James, then at me. "Can you, um . . . Excuse me, mistress?" She fell to her knees. "Forgive me, but can you—"

I grabbed her arm and pulled so she could stand. "I'm not your mistress. And I have much to apologize for. But right now, yes, I can move him." I picked James up while Miri tucked the blanket all around him. She climbed into the very tight barely-there backseat of Taige's silver sports car and I set James inside, his head in Miri's lap. She cradled him against her chest and soothed him, whispered to him. Begged him to wake up.

Not knowing what else to do, I took the passenger seat and Taige backed down the driveway with speed and precision. It felt strange, surreal, to be sitting in a car next to her. Like either this wasn't real or my time with Freyja hadn't been real. How could so much have changed— everything have changed—in what felt like a heartbeat? In what felt like an eternity?

I realized I was still dressed like a Valkyrie, and giving no thought to what Taige might think, I willed my silly clothes to morph into the jeans and shirt that made me feel like me. Taige didn't seem to notice. Not that it mattered, so many more important things had happened. I had died (again), met my mother, received a gift from a god, learned to travel and see the universe all at once—everything had changed.

See the universe . . .

An idea struck me. I reached out with my Halo and felt Taige's spirit—a generous soul who had seen and done so much evil in her short life, but who was doing everything in her power to set things right. She'd make it, too. I knew she would.

There was Miri—her spirit quivering with determination, hope, need, fear. I didn't want to let her down.

And there was James. Except he wasn't in his body; he stood on the rainbow Bridge, his hands in the pockets of his blue jeans, his hair mussed in that perfect style he loved, and a band shirt stretched across his chest. I stepped up beside him, appearing in my own jeans and black T, silver-penned Chucks on my feet.

"Hey," I said as I stood so close to him our arms brushed. I faced the direction he was facing—and watched as Miri's tears fell onto his lifeless face. "She'll never forgive you, you know."

A sad smile tugged at his lips. "No kidding. She seems all sweet and innocent, but the girl has balls. Once she decides she wants something, she pretty much doesn't stop until she gets it."

"She wants you to come back."

Out of the corner of my eye I saw James smile.

"I've never been able to say no to her."

"Will you say no this time?"

He faced me then, and the smile slipped from his face to be replaced with a sad expression I recognized. The expression of giving up. Of hopelessness. Of doubt.

"I don't know," he finally said. "I don't know if I can give her what she wants. Or even if I should." He dipped his chin and rocked back onto his heels.

"Cut it out, James," I said. "Quit messing around and go back to her already."

Questions filled his eyes along with his tears. "How?"

But he meant so much more than just, *How do I go back?*

He meant, *How do I go back to normal after everything I've seen and done?*

How can she love me when I threw myself at Helena?

How can I love her the way she deserves to be loved when I am who I am?

I thought of Taige then—of the sweet hope that radiated from her. I didn't know where she'd gotten it from or how she'd managed it, but it was a beautiful thing. I shared my thoughts with James, let them sink into his awareness for a moment.

"Everything's different, James," I said. "But not everything has changed."

He looked at me like I'd just spoken in a foreign language.

I took his hand, then pulled him into a hug. "I love you. I always have. Always will. But you and I? We're not the same anymore."

"I know." He choked and pressed his face against my shoulder.

"We're not the same. We're better."

He stilled and I knew he was processing what I said, trying to make sense of it.

"Now, you'd better get back there and give that girl what she wants or she's gonna kick your ass."

He held on to me a minute longer before giving me a squeeze and pulling back. "Can I?"

"You can."

"What about you?" And oh, James. He was as deep as an ocean. How had I ever missed how good he was?

"I've changed a little, too," I said. And I let him see. Let him see all of me, my Halo, my hope, my love.

"Damn, princess," he said, a wide smile spreading across his face. "Well, let's get to it, then." And he stepped off the Bridge.

"James!" Miri cried out, joy coloring the sound.

I smiled out the car window but didn't look back.

"What happened?" Taige cried, swerving the car a little in surprise at Miri's yell.

"He's gonna be okay! He's gonna be okay!"

James would be more than okay.

TWENTY-SEVEN

MICHAEL

Fiahre jumped into the air and swung her leg around as she did, her arms like helicopter blades whipping her sword and dagger as she spun. The Giant fell to the ground, its head rolling a few feet away. She landed near me and when our eyes met she smiled and tapped her fist to her heart. I didn't know how she still had the energy to fight the way she did, but I'd join with her in celebrating any small victory—and they were getting smaller and smaller by the moment.

She ran to my side, Longinus shadowing her. Our forces depleted, we huddled together, Valkyrie, Human and Gardian. I took comfort in their strong shoulders against mine, felt their breathing settle into my own rhythm, felt them adjust their grips on the hilts of their blades even as I did the same. We would stand together this last time, we would fight and die with honor.

"I saw her—your lady. But then she was gone," Longinus said to me while we paced our enemy.

"Yes," I said. "I saw her, too."

I felt his questions, knew them as my own, though he didn't give them voice and neither did I. *What happened? Where did she go? Will she come back?* I had no answers because I didn't want to say the words that weighed down my heart like an anchor.

I don't know.

Darkness shrouded the desert, the only light a pale wide moon, and the fire that danced in the Giants' hair. The enemy, both Giants and Svarts, had isolated us from our brethren and now closed in from all sides. I saw no break in their line, no opportunity to overcome this hopeless situation.

I thought I should say something, something to mark this moment when we would pass from life to death, to honor Fiahre and Longinus and the lives they had led. I had completed no quest, would gain no Ascension—my death on this battlefield would release my soul to reincarnation and I would forget Desi, forget all that I had learned in this life. Fiahre would be granted refuge in the paradise of Vanaheim, but I knew it wouldn't sit well with her. Not when Longinus would likely rise again on Earth.

None of these thoughts held me with such fierceness as thoughts of Desi. Of her touch, her kiss. Her smile. I had waited so long to see that smile. Yet she had only just come back and I hadn't said goodbye. I raised myself taller, thrust the sorrowful thoughts away—they were not becoming of me, or of Desi. She lived and in the brief glimpse I had, I saw that she was glorious. That was all I needed to know, all the peace I needed to accept my death.

I adjusted my grip on my sword one last and final time and braced myself for the fight. With Desi on my mind, her love in my heart, I ran toward the Svarts and their deadly, icy blades, determined to make them pay dearly for my life.

I fought like I had just begun, with strength and energy renewed. But as my enemy matched me blow for blow, I knew it could not last.

"For Desi!" I shouted at the faces of the Svarts who shoved their blades at me and bore their teeth in laughter. "For Midgard!"

I heard similar shouts from Fiahre and Longinus and my heart swelled to be in their company—true warriors to the end.

Three Svarts circled me, so close the hairs on my face froze in their icy breath. They laughed, swinging their blades in loose circles, as they played with me like a cat teases a mouse. And like the mouse knows there is no escape, I knew this was my last fight. All my senses narrowed down to this one moment.

The feel of my right hand, blistered and raw from a long day of fighting, scraping against the damp leather wrapped around the hilt of my sword. The song of my blade as wind skimmed off it, causing it to hum as if it were alive. I'd miss that sound. I felt the weight of my baldric as it pressed against my shoulders, the cold breath of the dark elves against my skin. The feel of my boots on the grit at my feet.

I felt it all in a moment that seemed to last forever.

I was ready when the taller of the three elves pounced forward, using his height to bring his curved blade downward. I knew their plan. Could sense it even before they moved. I would not survive it.

The blade plummeted and I had no choice but to raise my sword to block it. While I did, the other two Svarts dove toward my belly. I thrust my Halo outward, bringing it to my defense in a flash of golden light. My wings were useless now, wounded as they were, but I could cut through one of the evil things before his sword found my flesh.

But the other—the one who came at me from the left, ducking low, blade angled upward—his was the killing blow.

I filled my mind with thoughts of my love. Saw her lying on the green grass, her black hair spread around her like raven wings, glossy and radiant in the golden light of our garden. Her dark eyes, swimming with drops of sunlight as I stared into them. My soul was there, with her, not on this battlefield. Not falling to the ground, a blade protruding from beneath my left arm.

I didn't see the dark desert sky spread vast above me. I lay beside my love, with her curled against my side, while I watched the golden leaves flicker above me, watched the soft clouds skimming past. I'd die with her in my arms, in my heart.

"Michael!"

I'm here, love.

"Michael!"

And . . . *Oh, love.*

I'm here. Here.

TWENTY-EIGHT

DESI

My intent was to travel to the desert. That was my singular goal—to find Michael and fulfill my promise to never, ever leave him again. But what should have been a momentary flash, the time between one thought and the next, was interrupted as Heimdall stepped in front of me, the rainbow Bridge spread out behind him, an eternal path going wherever he commanded.

"There's no time to waste," I said, moving to angle past him, wishing I didn't still need his permission to Travel between worlds. "Why did you stop me? Did I do something wrong?" Maybe everything had been a dream. Maybe I'd only been deluding myself into thinking I could have this power, the gifts of a god.

He faced me and put his hand on my shoulder, its staggering weight making me check my balance. I searched his fierce face, but he was always so stern I found I couldn't read it, couldn't guess his intentions.

"Wait," he said. He raised his left hand, holding it out to his side, all the while maintaining eye contact with me.

"What—"

"I cannot allow you to go alone."

"You can't—" I shook my head. "What do you mean? What's going on?"

With a sound of thunder and light so piercing I had to close my eyes, scrunching my face as if that could protect me from the coming . . . something . . . another Path joined us. A light laugh, like bells ringing in a church spire, like wind through the pines on a mountainside, brought my eyes open once more.

Standing to my left stood a tall, slender man with eyes so light they shone like stars and skin the color of pearls. "My lady," he said in a musical voice. He reached for my hand before I could snatch it away. He brushed his warm, dry lips against my skin and took his time releasing my hand.

"Do you know who I am, lady?"

I started to shake my head, certain I'd never met this man, this creature. *Elf*, my mind provided. *Alfahr— a light elf.*

And then I realized, I did know. "You are . . . li'Morl? Of the Alfahr?"

He laughed, raising his chin and closing his eyes as if savoring the most delightful bit of news. "Indeed, lady. Indeed."

I still shook my head, unsure of this turn of events, anxious to get to Michael, to put an end to this battle over Midgard. Earth was mine now and it was time to let the other worlds know it.

"Indeed," li'Morl repeated. "It is yours. Shall we go?"

I knew my eyes couldn't hide my surprise—how did this creature know my mind?

"The light elves hold a piece of the Bifrost within them," Heimdall said, his voice a low rumble through my body. His expression shone with tenderness as he looked down on li'Morl. "In a way, they are my own children, and possess many gifts given by my power."

"Okay," I said. Being a god hadn't done anything for my eloquence. Words were obviously still not my strong suit. "Um . . ."

"Michael, yes. You are eager to reach him and . . ." li'Morl cast a glance up to Heimdall, concern flickering across his features before he replaced it with a tight smile. "It seems we should hurry." li'Morl took my hand and turned away from Heimdall.

"What's going on? What's wro—" We stepped into nothingness, the Bridge giving way to a path that plummeted us through space. Unsure what else to do, I filled my mind with Michael's face, willing myself to go wherever he was.

It surprised me to find my hand still clasped tightly by li'Morl when my feet hit the hard surface of the desert. But in a moment's glance I saw all I needed to know. I was too late. I'd taken too long.

I stood amidst the enemy, dark elves ready with deadly weapons, hisses upon their lips. In front of me, a Svart lay on the ground, his blue blood following the course of the incline like a river. Another stumbled backward, his sword arm clutched to his side, his blade fallen to the earth. As he fell toward me, I saw a golden wing spread low across the ground. Saw an elf with his arm tight against Michael. Saw him shift sideways and see me, a malicious grin on his face. He stepped back, and with him came his kukris, red to the hilt with Michael's blood.

"Michael!"

I'm here, love.

"Michael!"

I'm here. Here.

Nothing had prepared me for this. How could I have just found everything, only to lose it all?

"Michael!" His name tore from my throat without thought. Because my mind was a tumult of anguish, sorrow, loss.

And anger.

Pure and visceral, as dark as Father's granite mountain. It rose inside of me, its piercing peaks sending everything but hatred and revenge scurrying to the furthest parts of my mind. It left me with a singular need. A dreadful purpose.

I called upon my glory, Thor's hammer in my fist. I stepped in front of my love, death and destruction rising, awaiting only my command. I opened my mouth, raised Mjölner—

"Hold." A soft touch on my arm. A bell-like voice in my ears, my mind.

I struggled with Mjölner, finding it growing heavy in my arm as it dropped an inch.

"Hold, lady."

"li'Morl?" I blinked at him. Blinked and tried to focus. "Don't stop me! Let me go!"

His hand remained on my arm, his focus did not move from my face.

"This is my world," I hissed at him, trying to refuel the anger that would surely make him understand his foolishness in trying to restrain me. "I am a god. I am god of this world!" My voice rang across the battlefield, caused the mesas and mountains to tremble.

"Already the field is being cleansed, lady." li'Morl gestured with his free hand and I followed his gesture with my eyes to see his meaning. All around me light elves flowed across the battlefield, and like a flood of righteousness, they forced the Svarts and Giants back through the portals.

But I still had cause for revenge, still had need of my power, because my love lay on the ground. My love had lost his life and I hadn't said goodbye. I thought of the moment I'd returned, when I'd seen him across the desert. I thought of how I blinked away, even as he ran toward me. *What he must have thought?* He must have thought I'd left him. Chosen some purpose other than him. And I had! I'd chosen James! I'd chosen again—and again made the wrong damn choice.

Mjölner weighed a thousand pounds, drawing me to my knees. Down and down I sank until my forehead pressed against the blood-stained ground.

li'Morl crouched beside me, but I didn't look at Michael. Didn't acknowledge him. I couldn't

"He is not dead."

He's dead. I know he's dead.

I can't feel him.

Can't hear him.

He's dead.

A horrible sound filled my ears. A keening sorrow that crushed my spirit, stretched it thin, snapping it out of shape, distorting it, killing it. I rocked forward, my hands clapped to my ears, but still the high-pitched wail continued.

"Yes, take her," I heard through the siren song of pain.

"Forgive me, lady."

A dim part of my mind was aware that I knew the voice. Knew the arms that held me, carried me across the Bifrost. Longinus.

"Here, here." I was placed on a soft mat, but I didn't care. I curled and curled, making myself a tight ball, an armored, broken being. "Desi."

The keening, the crying, wouldn't stop.

Couldn't stop.

Make it stop.

"Desolation." Heimdall's voice rumbled through my consciousness as he gripped me. I thought the pain in my heart would rip me into a thousand pieces. Scatter my soul to the stars.

I felt Michael near, smelled his familiar oranges-and-honey skin, even through the gore and grime that covered him after the day's fighting. And then Heimdall pressed Michael's hand to the center of my chest.

My eyes flew open, the golden spark, fed by the Genesis, burst outward, filling all of me, seeking a way out, seeking Michael. I threw my head back, my arms and legs stretching wide as I Became like an erupting star, my light so bright it burned through my retinas, colored everything around me with blinding multicolored light.

The Genesis filled me, expanded beyond me and raced into Michael's body. I felt it, an extension of myself, filling his lungs, pumping blood through his heart, firing the electrons in his brain. He recoiled, flinching away from me, but I heard it, felt it, saw it.

"Desi!"

His first breath, his first thought—for me.

TWENTY-NINE

MICHAEL

I was told she was awake, but she hadn't come to see me. And so, I went to her. I knew where she was, could feel her presence, her spirit, as clearly as if she were a blinking light on a map in my mind. I stepped through the golden gates of Valhalla, ignoring protocol and taking advantage of the sisters' depleted numbers. I walked the long corridors toward the room that had once been Mahria's, but now was Desolation's.

Fiahre fell in step beside me. "You look well."

I glanced at her, but didn't answer. Ahead, I saw the door to Desi's room and my footsteps slowed. Her presence wrapped around me, I felt her everywhere now, and I knew she'd feel the same. Knew she'd know I was here. I waited for her door to open, for her to come running down the hall, to fly into my arms.

But I'd walked ten feet, twenty feet, her door an arm's reach away, and still it remained closed.

Fiahre placed a hand on my arm and we stopped. "She fears the evil that is part of her. Fears the curse of Loki's heritage," she said. "She holds herself to a higher degree— you know it has ever been thus."

I Remembered days, long, long past, when I'd watch her train with her sister Valkyries. When she failed to best Mahria, she'd stay on the practice field for hours afterward, working through her missed transition, opportunity or pattern. Even before I'd formally met her, I'd watched this stubborn, hard-headed girl push herself far harder than anyone else, demanding perfection and accepting nothing less.

I'd also seen her lend a hand to a less-talented fighter, give praise and learning, never judging another, never expecting anyone else to live up to her own standards for herself. It was perhaps the most frustrating thing about her.

And I loved her.

Loved her in spite of, or perhaps because of, her keen demands on herself, her love and patience with others, and her utter inability to grant herself such kindness.

I breathed in, squaring my shoulders, preparing myself for the fight of my life. Beside me, Fiahre laughed and returned the way we had come. Her fingertips brushed against my arm as she passed. "You two are well-suited."

I glanced over my shoulder, the question in my raised eyebrow, the slight upward turn of my lips.

"You are both as stubborn as mules."

I chuckled then, picturing Fiahre and Longinus—and I knew she did the same because her cheeks flushed a burnished red. She ducked her head, angling away from me.

"Still . . ." she said with a shrug as she strode away.

Still.

After all we'd been through, Desi had to know.

I was still hers.

And she was still mine.

THIRTY

DESI

Being a god, holding the Genesis in my soul, didn't make me a perfect person. I'd been willing to kill those people—to kill everyone. I knew now that if li'Morl hadn't stopped me, I might have used the Genesis to spread my pain and sorrow everywhere. Earth would have fallen. And who knows if it would have stopped there?

If I would have stopped.

Shame boiled inside me like an angry sea. I couldn't face anyone, couldn't bear to see the truth in their eyes. That I was crazy. A loose cannon. That I'd almost destroyed everything, undid all the sacrifices that had been made to save Midgard. All for myself. For a misplaced sense of retribution.

But life is life and there isn't any true retribution. There would always be winners and losers, the haves and have-nots. Always.

So when I felt Michael coming toward me, I hid in my room, hoping against every unreasonable hope that he wouldn't find me. But of course he found me. Of course he'd know where I was—he would always know where I was. And not just because a piece of me was in him now. A piece of the Genesis.

We were like two halves of a whole—something I think we'd always been, but the Genesis made official.

There would never be a me without him.

There'd never be a him without me.

And it was that part that had me hiding in Mahria's room.

He didn't knock. Before he'd even closed the door behind him the stupid, traitorous tears had already begun to flow down my cheeks. I sat on the corner of the bed, pressed against the wall, trying to hide from the one person in all the worlds I could never hide from.

He leaned against the door and folded his arms. I forced myself to concentrate on my hands, on the silver swirls on my arms. But of course I noticed how handsome he looked in his gleaming armor, the gauntlets over his arms that emphasized his corded forearms, his massive arms and the tunic that ended just above his knees. I suddenly wished he wore a T-shirt and jeans. A hoodie and jeans.

He didn't speak, and I was glad for it—I didn't trust my voice to not give my traitorous heart away and right now, I needed him to let me go.

The day grew long, casting deep shadows across the room. And still he didn't speak. He didn't move.

Nighttime fell over Asgard. Darkness draped over us like a blanket. And in the darkness, in its protective embrace, I finally broke the silence.

"I'm sorry."

The silence stretched away from my words, building upon itself, emphasizing all the in-between time in which Michael did not respond.

I thought of repeating my apology. I cleared my throat. But no matter how quietly I'd said them, I knew he heard my words, and so I said nothing.

And he said nothing.

I woke when the morning light laid a line of warmth against my cheek.

With a start I looked at the door, terrified he really had left me—but as I came to my senses and realized I could still feel him near, *here*, I saw him. He sat on the floor, his back against the door, his head tilted to the side. His eyes were closed, his lips slightly parted. I watched his chest rise and fall with the steady rhythm of sleep.

I stretched out on the bed, my head at the foot of it, my cheek on the back of my hands, and watched him. And thought of what to say. Of whether there was any way back from where we had gone. Where I had gone.

I must have drifted off again, because when I next woke, I found myself staring directly into Michael's soft lion eyes.

The light in the room lit them up until they seemed almost translucent. I could see into his soul through them. Could practically feel the golden flecks of his spirit that floated there, painting me with his love, with tenderness.

I jerked back, not wanting to go there, to let him love me.

"Don't," he said, and oh. He sounded so tired. So weary.

"Don't." He moved onto his knees and crawled the few feet between us. He put his hands on the edge of the bed, mere inches away from mine. I could feel his heat, smell his warmth, see myself reflected in his eyes.

I was just a girl. Same as always. But he had to know— I wasn't the same inside anymore. I'd never be the same. Never be able to forgive myself for the things I had done, the things I'd been willing to do.

He slowly reached out with his left hand, as if I were a wild bird that might fly away at a moment's notice—and in a very real way I was. I wanted to fly away. But his eyes held me to him and so I stayed. Gods help me, I stayed.

"Don't," he whispered.

Don't leave.

Don't push me away.

Don't.

Then his hand was on my cheek, soft at first, a barely-there touch. I closed my eyes, leaned into him. I didn't want to, but . . . oh, I had to. I had to.

And then his hand was in my hair and his breath was on my cheek and his words were whispered all over my face, words with kisses, words of love and forgiveness, kisses of hope, words of forever, kisses given and returned.

THIRTY-ONE

MICHAEL

We stood in the Wheelhouse, the Bridge to Midgard partially open before us, watching events unfold below. I held tightly to Desi's hand—I had barely let her go except when absolutely necessary, ever since this morning when we'd found each other again. I could never take her for granted, never give up my post by her side. Not that I thought she was too fragile and might go flying off into the stratosphere at any moment, but because love is precious. It's the rarest of things, and I had fought too long, too hard, to not cherish it and protect it every moment of the rest of my life.

On the grounds of St. Mary's beneath us, Fiahre shifted her weight. "Well," she said.

"Lady." Longinus stood utterly still, his face unreadable.

She'll ask him, Desi said in my mind. She could barely contain her excitement—it was all I could do to convince her to remain quiet so events could unfold without our influence. Though my money was on Longinus. I'd bet he would be the one to ask for Valhalla. We had all learned something about pride. That sometimes, in the name of love, one had to set it aside.

"I would ask, but I am tired of the answer." Fiahre kept her eyes on Longinus, as stoic and unreadable as he.

Desi's shoulders drooped. *Dang it, Fiahre!*

I fought to keep the smile from my lips, focusing on my boots until I regained control. I squeezed Desi's hand. Fiahre and Longinus couldn't have been better suited for one another, except that nothing would get said between them. Everything of worth hung in the spaces between the words.

Well, no one more suited than you and I. Even in my mind, Desi's own words were a whisper, like even now, after everything, she was afraid to suggest that I loved her as much as she loved me. I'd told her a thousand times—and planned to tell her forevermore—that I loved her more. I would always love her more and that was as it should be.

But then, something different happened. Something changed.

Longinus took a step toward Fiahre. "Ask," he said.

Oh Odin, I thought. *Let this be.*

Let there be love. Let there be hope.

"Valiant warrior," Fiahre said, her voice barely above a whisper.

Yes! Desi squeezed my hand, sent me images of her doing the crazy happy dance. I coughed and examined my boot laces again.

When I thought I'd managed my emotions well enough, I looked up. There stood Fiahre, this fierce Valkyrie, stone-faced and unmatched in her dedication to her calling, now trembling with hope, her eyes wide and shining. "Will you take your rest in the eternal halls of Valhalla?"

Longinus moved closer. Took Fiahre's hands in his own. Hands as calloused as his. As stained with blood as his.

"Noble lady," he said. "Will I only be resting?"

Desi and I faced each other, our foreheads resting on each other as we shared a chuckle. Everyone here knew how this would go—how it had to go. Desi had already promised she'd forgo free will if she had to and exercise her new power as a god to make them make the right choice.

For a long moment Fiahre didn't answer. I sensed her Valkyrie sisters and the Gardians who had gathered nearby, drawn by the hope that stretched from all our hearts to

Fiahre and Longinus—a hope that they could finally be free. Finally free to embrace love over duty.

Fiahre's mouth slowly stretched into a smile and her beauty shone. Her Halo rose out behind her, her golden light a radiant, living thing. It embraced Longinus as she stepped to him, so close that their bodies pressed together. She kissed him then, and I looked away and into the smiling eyes of the one whom I would die for—again— and the one I would live for, forever.

Desi's eyes told me everything I hoped for, everything I hoped for Fiahre and Longinus. Yes, even pride could be overcome, even duty would take its place behind love.

After a moment I turned back and watched while Fiahre whispered something into Longinus's ear and he nodded seriously. "Then I will go with you," he said.

Heimdall whipped his horn to his mouth, threw his head back and blew. The sound rang like a golden bell, radiating through my mind, my chest, over all of us assembled there. It called to all the worlds, to all the gods. It rang in our hearts with Heimdall's wish for them—for this valiant couple who had earned their eternal rest, who earned the love and adoration of the eternities. Fiahre took Longinus's hand and led him onto the Bridge. His cheeks flamed red when he saw us, but he didn't once let go of her.

All around us, Gardians and Valkyries celebrated. Longinus tolerated the hugs and congratulations that were poured out upon him, his eyes never leaving Fiahre. He seemed like a dying man who'd found his oasis—which I knew in a very real way, he had.

The couple was led to Asgard, but Desi and I stayed behind. When I looked away from the celebrants, I found Desi watching me.

"Hi," she said.

"Hi."

Before me stood my love, her skin a pearlescent glow, a smile on her lips that I'd dreamt about for eons. Her left hand clasped on and off the hilt of her sword as if she didn't quite know what to do with it. A beautiful glow lit her cheeks and strands of her black hair fluttered around her face.

But it was her eyes that drew me in. Her gold-flecked eyes that told me everything I needed to know.

She was here.

And she was mine.

I gathered her into my arms and for a long moment just held her. Just her and me, our arms wrapped around each other, our souls caught up in our intertwined spirits so there was no longer any separation, just us. We were one as we'd never been before, the Genesis within our souls uniting us. I didn't know how long we stood like that. How long she held me in her Halo, and I held her in mine. We were one. We were complete. And I knew—I *knew*—we would never be apart again.

Things were different. Things had changed.

And that was a good thing.

When our glory finally faded, when our kisses had slowed and we'd said *I love you* about a million times, I found we were standing in a hospital room. The lights were dim, but Desi had her own light which radiated outward with a pearly glow. James lay on the bed while Miri sat in a chair next to him.

My heart rejoiced to see them!

"Desi!" Miri hissed. "You gotta be careful, ya know. You can't keep popping in all magical and fairy godmother-like."

Desi smiled, a warm blush rising to her pale cheeks while she drew her radiance inward. "I knew you were alone," she said.

I squeezed her hand. I had so many questions about her new powers, but asking how she knew could wait.

"How is he?" She let go of my hand and I felt a tiny twinge of regret, which I ignored. I hadn't waited a hundred lifetimes to not be okay with waiting a few moments to touch her again.

"He's gonna be okay," Miri said, her voice ringing with happiness. "He could go home in a day or two if he'd just wake up. They said he was hypothermic and dehydrated, but his temperature regulated pretty quickly."

Desi placed her hand on James's forehead and he stirred. His eyes fluttered.

"James! James!" Miri leapt to her feet. She kissed his forehead and put her hand on his chest. "Wake up, James," she whispered.

Desi stepped back and reached for my hand.

"What did you do?" I whispered.

She shrugged as she smiled up at me. "I woke him up. He's always been a sleepyhead."

I yanked her to me and wrapped my arms around her waist. "You are full of surprises."

"You don't know the half of it." Her smile grew into a Cheshire cat-like grin, then she surprised me again by leaning upward and kissing me. It had been a long time since she'd done that. Just been free with me. Just loved me. With nothing but love between us.

No doubt.

No fear.

Just love.

The door to the room swung open and a pair of nurses hurried in. Desi and I stepped out of the way and squished ourselves into the corner of the room while the nurses bustled around James. Miri backed up until she stood against the window, but she watched the activity with joy on her face, her hands in the manner of prayer, pressed to her lips. I heard her whisper a prayer of gratitude and healing and smiled. It made me glad that she'd kept her faith through all of this, despite everything. A faith that still had a place in the world.

James cleared his throat and opened his eyes. Miri bounced on her toes, barely restraining herself from flying into his arms.

"How are you feeling Mr. Mason?"

"I'd feel a helluva lot better if you'd let my girlfriend kiss me," he said.

"Well, there'll be plenty of time for that real soon, I think," the nurse said. "Keep this up and you could go home as soon as tomorrow."

"Not now?" James pled.

"We'll see what the doc has to say." She jotted down some notes in the chart that hung on a hook outside his door, while the second nurse took his blood pressure.

"120 over 80," she said to the nurse with the chart. She took the cuff off James's arm and gave his hand a squeeze. She leaned down close to him. "You're gonna be just fine, baby."

I watched his eyes grow wide with surprise.

"Lucy?" he asked, his voice a hoarse whisper. Desi squeezed my hand, and the nurse with the warm brown skin and dancing eyes smiled and left the room, closing the door behind her.

"Did you see that? Did you hear her? What—? Was that—?" James half sat up, staring incredulously from Desi to the door.

For her part, Desi smiled and gave a half-shrug. She let go of my hand again and stepped forward, pulling one of James's hands out of Miri's grasp to hold it in her own. "It's good to see you, James."

"Good to see you too, princess." But he couldn't take his eyes off of Miri.

"Hey, we'll let you guys . . . you know." Desi barely concealed her laughter as she took my hand and I pulled open the door.

"Hey, princess," James called before we'd closed the door.

Desi leaned back into the room. "Yeah?"

"Thank you."

"You're welcome." She pulled the door shut and we walked out of the hospital the usual way—one step at a time.

THIRTY-TWO

DESI

After a mile of walking hand-in-hand, saying little, we realized it was a really long way back to St. Mary's. And an even longer walk to anywhere else we might want to go. Michael pulled me onto a bus stop bench and put his arm around me.

"Where are we going?" he asked.

I'd been mulling it over since leaving the hospital and still didn't have a good answer. "With Longinus gone and Cornelius . . ." I didn't know exactly what had happened, but I knew he no longer lived, could feel his absence in the world around me, could feel the hole he'd left behind.

"I know. That's what I was thinking, too."

We fell into silence for a while longer and watched a bus approach from down the street. When it pulled up in front of us, the doors opened. "You gettin' on?" asked the sour-faced driver.

"No," I said, shaking my head. She glowered at me, closed the door and drove off.

"Guess we can't really sit here all day," I said.

"Guess not."

"Michael, I—" I looked away. Down the street to the gas station at the next corner. At the auto parts store beside it. At the coffee shop across the street.

Michael said nothing, but he pulled his arm from around my shoulder and took my left hand in his. He didn't ask where my markings had gone, how I managed to conceal them. Didn't ask how my hand was whole.

"We can't go back to Asgard," he finally said and oh I loved him for saving me from saying it. "Desi," he pressed after I remained silent a beat too long.

"Yeah?"

Suddenly Michael stood and, with my hand in his, pulled me behind the abandoned store we'd been sitting in front of. When we reached the shadows of the building, he took me by the shoulders so I faced him.

"I want you to do something."

My mind flew a mile a minute trying to guess what he'd ask me. Trying to figure out what he had planned. "Okay."

"Close your eyes."

So I did.

He pulled me closer, so close our bodies pressed together. Our arms wrapped around each other and I pressed my cheek to his chest.

"I want you to think of home. Of the place you were the safest, the happiest. Of the place where you felt the most like you."

Asgard, I thought. I pictured the place, pictured our garden nestled in a stand of golden-leaved trees. But then another image took its place.

"Take us there," Michael whispered against my hair.

I took us to the one place in all the worlds I knew for sure I belonged.

I took us to Lucy's.

"I wish Cornelius was here." I lay in the crook of Michael's arm, snuggled as close as we could get on Lucy's white couch. As the sun set, pink hues softened the light in the room, warming it and making it seem like a romantic escape. Which, I guess, it was.

"So do I," Michael said. "But what are you thinking?"

I smiled against his chest. "Because then we could get married."

His chest stopped rising with his breath, but his heart beat out a loud staccato against my cheek. "You're kinda young for that, aren't you?" His words were strangled, like he was trying to speak without breathing, without disturbing the air around him with his words.

"Well, that's why I wish Cornelius was here—he'd know we are both a lot older than we seem. Plus, it would have made him happy."

"Our marriage."

"Yeah. Don't you think so?"

He chuckled, then let out his breath. The rise and fall of his chest resumed its natural rhythm. "It would have. But you know we are already married, so to speak. Odin bound us a very long time ago."

I leaned back so I could see his beautiful, handsome face. "I know," I said softly as I brushed back his unruly curls. "But on Earth we should be married if we're gonna live together."

"Oh, we're going to live together, are we?" He grinned wolfishly, but my eyes were soft and my expression serious.

"I don't ever want to live without you."

He squeezed me and kissed the corners of each of my eyes. "Married or not, I will never leave your side again." He spoke with such fervor, such intensity that tears sprang to my eyes and I didn't say anything.

What could I say? After so long I finally had what I wanted and the reality was at least a thousand times better than any of my dreams.

I must have drifted off, but was jerked awake by a strange rattling sound.

"What's that?" I bolted upward, my head turning this way and that, grappling for a sword that wasn't there.

The sound came again and my head whipped around, seeking the source.

Michael kept his arm firmly around me, probably so I wouldn't start karate-chopping shadows. "It's okay, love."

"Did you hear it?"

He laughed, a warm sleepy sound that filled the space between us like spun sugar. "It's a cell phone."

A cell phone. "Oh!" Michael shifted and I jumped to my feet and looked around—finally spotting the small black device on the kitchen counter. It had jiggled its way into the space between the coffee maker and the backsplash. I picked it up and swiped the front— discovering a picture of Miri and James, their faces squished together and their tongues sticking out.

Michael wrapped his arms around me. "So who was calling?"

The screen had gone dark so I swiped it again. Three missed calls, it said. I clicked through to the Recent Calls list and saw three messages, all from the same unknown number.

I pushed play on the last message, left one minute ago.

"I know you're a princess, savior of the world and all that—but do you think Her Majesty could manage to get off her high horse and come and pick me and Miri up? I'd call Taige, but after all you've put me through, I think it's only right that you come get us. I managed to convince the doc that he should let me go—you've gotta spring me before he changes his mind."

The line went dead and Michael chuckled. He stood behind me, his arms wrapped around my waist. His laughter resonated through my body and I closed my eyes and just lived in the moment.

"Well, you heard the guy. You've been summoned." He leaned down and kissed my neck, then my collarbone. I leaned into him. "Except I think you'd better change."

Change?

"I don't think Asgardian attire is the height of fashion here." He flicked my skirt as he backed up, easily ducking the fist I swung back at him. He lunged after me and I dove away and skittered down the hall, laughing all the while.

When I stepped into my room and closed the door behind me, I had to stop and take in the scene. I'd been gone a long time. It was August and I'd been imprisoned sometime toward the middle of November, I thought. But even though I'd been gone so long, my room was exactly the same and with Lucy's downy white comforter spread across my bed.

On my dresser were the pictures Lucy had displayed before I took over her room. There was a picture of me and Lucy, and a picture of me, Lucy and James. I picked each one up, remembering. When I set them down, I surveyed the room and saw a new photograph on the nightstand.

Framed with silver angel wings, the image inside it made my stomach flip. It was a picture of Michael and me. Our heads were together, foreheads and noses touching. Our eyes closed. Our arms around each other.

I sat on the bed, the photo in my hand. I had never seen a picture of Michael. Never seen one of the both of us. It reminded me how richly blessed I was. I closed my eyes and gave thanks to the universe, to Odin, to Freyja— to anyone who might be listening.

Thank you, I thought. *Thank you for friends who love me no matter what. For Aaron, Lucy, James and Miri.*

Thank you for letting me have this. This time with Michael. This love.

Thank you for giving me this chance.

Thank you for this life.

I kissed the picture and when I did I noticed my reflection in the glass—and I was smiling. The girl born of sorrow now lived in happiness. I never would have guessed.

Coming out of my room, I found Michael sitting on the big armchair Lucy loved, with a book in his hands. He must have borrowed the clothes from James because they were a little tight. Man, he looked delicious.

As for me, I wore my favorite black T-shirt and favorite dark wash jeans. Wore my favorite black Chucks with silver sharpie designs all over them. I was still pale, but I no longer looked like death. I looked like me—like a regular girl with long, wavy black hair. Michael glanced up when he heard me come in and the expression on his face made me stop, suddenly self-conscious.

"What?" I finally asked after a moment of embarrassment.

For two heartbeats Michael just looked. Then he stood, put the book on the table and walked toward me. He put his hands on my neck, and scooped my hair up into his hands. "You're beautiful." He stared intensely into my eyes. And then he kissed me. He kissed me so long, so deeply that I stretched onto my tip-toes and leaned into him.

James's phone buzzed in my back pocket. "He's summoning us again," I said, my lips against Michael's.

"Then I guess we'd better go."

He kissed me again.

About three more phone calls later, Michael and I strode into James's room, hand-in-hand, matching smiles, matching blushes on our faces.

"About bloody time!" James said from a wheelchair beside the bed.

"Ugh, thank you!" Miri jumped off the bed and grabbed their things. "He's driving me nuts." She pushed a button on a remote next to the bed. A moment later a male nurse stepped into the room.

"Finally ready to get sprung, huh?"

"I've been ready. It's little Miss Highness who took her own sweet time getting here."

The nurse smiled at me and rolled his eyes. "Well, you're on your way now. That's something, right? Got your paperwork?"

James waved it in his face and the nurse laughed. Then he pushed James out of the room, and when he passed me, James glowered.

A flicker of doubt swept across my mind. A whisper of the fear that had been the hallmark of my time on Earth.

Miri fell in step beside me and squeezed her arm around my waist. "He's just giving you a hard time," she said.

But it wasn't until we'd pulled the car up to the curb and the nurse had helped James into the backseat that I caught a glimpse of James's face again and saw the joy that shone there. He winked when he caught me staring. Sunlight burst in my chest and burned away all the old yucky feelings. Things had changed. Really changed. And they had changed for good.

It might take a while to get used to, but I was willing to keep trying, for forever if I had to, if it meant being with these people, meant having these friends. This love.

THIRTY-THREE

DESI

We ordered pizza and lounged around the apartment while James and Miri regaled us with everything that had happened over the past eight and a half months.

About how after the Attack of the Genies as they called it, Miri's mom got to have a funeral that was attended by a million people and that Miri hardly remembered at all. Her dad was still governor and she only saw him at social functions where he paraded her out like a prized pony.

She didn't have any bitterness in her voice when she said it, but I knew how she felt. Knew what it felt like to be on display, to be used. But Miri was a better person than me. She always had been.

"It's how it is with Dad," she said. "I've just decided to be happy with what I've got, with him even remembering I'm alive. It's what he can give me right now, so I'm okay with it. Besides," she elbowed James gently and leaned into him, "I've got James to pay attention to me as much as I want."

"I'll always pay attention to you, bright eyes." James kissed her and I thought I'd never seen him happier. And man, he deserved it. They both did.

"Oh! Remember that Shakespeare assignment Mrs. Park gave us?" Miri jumped up and smiled down on me.

"Uh, I guess. Kinda." Truth was it only barely tickled my memory, but I didn't want to admit I hardly remembered it at all.

"So you know how I said we should do an Ophelia scene from Hamlet? Well, I remembered what you told me about her—about the real Ophelia." James flinched at the mention of her name and Miri paused, a question lighting her eyes. I nodded, not sure where she was going.

"Well, I did this totally dark, perverted version of Ophelia's singing scene. Mrs. Park said she was surprised I had it in me and that it was the most disturbing interpretation of Ophelia she'd ever seen." She twirled around then dropped back onto the couch. "I got an A."

I laughed, marveling at how she could be so normal, so human after everything she knew. Everything she'd seen.

How she'd made friends with Taige, who after the Attack of the Genies, was so upset over all she'd witnessed that she'd gone to Cornelius for Confession.

"He asked us later what we thought of her joining The Hallowed, so he invited her. It's been good, I think," James said. "Miri kinda took her under her wing and, well. You saw her, right? She's come a long way." I closed my eyes and leaned against Michael, who sat behind me on the floor, his back against the TV cabinet. I knew exactly the power Miri's care had. *That's another thank you*, I thought. That Miri could help Taige. And that Taige would let her.

A heavy silence fell between us then and I knew we were all thinking the same thoughts. What would happen now? How could we go on without Cornelius? Without Longinus?

Michael cleared his throat. "So what are you guys going to do now?"

James and Miri gazed at each other for a moment before facing us. James focused on me. "I'm so happy you're home, Des. I can't tell you what it means to see you like this—you know, normal." His eyes flicked above me, to Michael. "Happy."

"We're all happy," Miri said quietly. I knew that look in her eyes. I knew she was going to say goodbye. That they both were.

"We still have a lease on our flat in Paris," James said. "I'll have to do a helluva lot of butt-kissing, but hopefully

I haven't lost my spot at Cordon Blue and Miri's been accepted at École des Beaux-Arts and—" Miri turned to James and he paused, reading something in her eyes. This time they both presented us with the same expression. Determination. Hope. Regret.

"You need to go," I said. Hoping to spare them the trouble of saying the words.

Miri nodded and tears gathered in her eyes. James looked down at their hands clasped together in his lap. "We'll stay, princess. If you need us to—we'll stay." But I'd already seen the future in their faces. Already recognized the hope in his voice.

"No," I said, shaking my head. "Go. It's good for you to go."

"What about you?" Tears made Miri's voice rough and croaky.

I felt Michael squeeze me, felt his strength behind me. Michael was with me. Wherever I went. Whatever we did. We'd do it together.

Forever.

"I don't know. But," I added, a smile spreading across my face, "we'll be okay."

"The Hallowed has an empty watchtower," Michael said. "The new recruits will need training—and this time I think they ought to be taught to fight as well."

"What's a watchtower?" Miri asked, a little too eagerly. Anxious to find a happy ending for me, I figured.

"It's what we call each pocket of our brotherhood, of The Hallowed. Taige is here—and there are others. And I am here."

His arms tightened around me again.

"So am I," I said. *I am here.* Exactly where I wanted to be.

Early Sunday morning, Miri snuck into my room. She didn't knock, just crept inside and climbed onto the bed. I was already awake, watching the sunlight peeking through the blinds, painting lovely patterns across the carpet. I'd been considering getting up and going onto the balcony, of trying yoga again like I used to do. Before. But Michael slept on the couch and I didn't want to wake him.

"Hey," she said. "The boys are still sleeping." I laughed, and rolled onto my back, stretching and enjoying the feeling of life. I'd never known I could be so comfortable.

"Come on," she said, rolling off the bed and pulling the covers off of me.

"Where?"

"Just come on. I've got a special day planned for us and I want you to look your best." She pulled on my wrist until I slid out of bed and followed her into the bathroom. She stood me in front of the mirror and examined me critically from over my shoulder. "Okay," she announced. "Have a shower."

"Okay," I said as she backed out of the room. She gave me a pointed look that took any argument right out of me.

"And shave!"

Shave. Got it.

Twenty minutes later, I sat on the toilet seat, a towel wrapped around me while Miri ordered me around, "Look this way. Now up." She proceeded to fuss over me; she made up my face—which was good because I didn't think I remembered the few things Lucy had taught me—and tsked over my hair as she dried it. I didn't bother to tell her that with my new abilities I could probably take care of all of this with nothing more than a thought. I didn't want her to leave. To stop showering me with her love.

"Done." She stepped back and considered me, like I was a work of art or something.

"It's about time," I said, standing and turning toward the mirror.

"No!" She practically shoved me out of the way so I couldn't see my reflection. She forced me to side step out of the bathroom. "Here, put this on." She pointed to a white sundress she'd laid out on the bed.

"I'd rather wear jeans. I'm not much of a dress girl." I eyed the dress dubiously.

"Put it on." Miri skewered me with a glare that brooked no argument. Then she smiled brightly. "Come on, the boys are up."

"What's the hurry?" I searched my dresser for under things, trying to hide the blush I felt creeping up my cheeks. Miri leaned in and snatched up a pair of panties with tiny blue flowers on them and a matching bra.

"Wear these."

"You're gonna dictate what kind of underwear I put on?"

"Trust me."

She put a mock-serious expression on her face until I said, "Fine," and slipped on the blue-flowered undies.

Miri threw herself onto my bed and covered her eyes with her arm, but she couldn't hide the smirk on her lips or the blush that made her cheeks as pink as a sunrise.

"So?" I prompted, slipping the dress over my head.

"So I want it to be perfect. Is that a crime?" I'd have thought she was mad if it hadn't been for the light laughter that followed. "Finish getting dressed. Put everything here on, okay?" She got off the bed and walked to the door. "Everything."

"Jeez, okay. Get out already." I opened the door and shooed her out. On the bed she'd left me a white lacy shawl, a pair of delicate, dangly earrings with stacked pearls and a necklace I'd seen Lucy wear. I knew it was her grandma's—a delicate piece of antique silver filigree and pearls. I held it in my hand for a minute, remembering how beautiful Lucy had been in it. How her hands had caressed the pearls as she told me how her mama had shared so many sweet stories of her gram's strength. How her mama thought Lucy was as strong as her gram.

I put it around my neck and worked the clasp, trailing my fingers over the pearls as they draped over my collar bone. I knew Lucy was strong—and now I knew I was strong, too.

Finally I slipped on the flat, strappy sandals I knew had never belonged to Lucy—they weren't nearly sexy enough for her. But they were perfect for me. You know, if I were ever to dress up, which I never had until now. Everything on, all ready, I stepped to the door.

On the other side of the bedroom, beside the dresser, stood a mirror draped with boas and gaudy necklaces that had been fabulous on Lucy and I'd been too sentimental to get rid of. I had to peel some of them back in order to see my whole self in the mirror, but when I did, tears sprang to my eyes.

I didn't recognize the girl there.

She was beautiful.

Lovely.

Happy.

"Aren't you ready yet?" Miri asked, poking her head into the room. "Oh," she said. She came in and closed the door behind her. "Oh."

I fell into her arms and cried onto her shoulder.

"Hey now, you'll ruin your makeup." She patted my back but made no move to push me away. "You're beautiful," she finally said.

I stepped back and tried to pat at the tears under my eyes without smearing my mascara too much. "So are you." She wore a strapless sundress the color of buttercups.

"Well," she said, spinning around so her skirt twirled around her, "we've got a hot date with a couple of very handsome men."

"Oh, we do?"

"We do." She looped her arm through mine and together we walked out into the living room.

James and Michael stood at the sliding glass door to the balcony, talking in low tones.

"Ahem," Miri said, and the boys were quick to spin around.

Oh, my love, Michael said.

I smiled. *You, too.*

"Well don't just stand there not saying anything," Miri said, pushing me forward. "Go give the guy a hug."

I stumbled forward, not bothering to correct her. Not bothering to tell her that what Michael and I shared was so much better than words. Words could never mean as much as the thoughts and feelings he filled me with. Thoughts of love. Of joy.

Thoughts of forever.

When he took me in his arms, he whispered, loud enough for Miri to hear, "I love you."

I squeezed him tighter, and said, "I will love you forever."

Miri sighed, which made me laugh.

"Happy now?" I asked.

"Yes." She and James, holding hands, headed for the door. "Okay, let's go."

"Where are we going?"

Michael took my hand and walked me to the door. "Somewhere special," he said.

"Ohhkay." I purposely dragged behind him, but inside, my heart was dancing a wild mamba of joy.

We drove to St. Mary's, which was not at all what I had in mind since we were all dressed up. I had pictured brunch at a fancy restaurant somewhere. Michael got out of the car and came around to open the door for me, while James did the same for Miri.

"What are we doing here?" Confusion dropped into my stomach, cutting off the happy flips it had been doing.

"You'll see, princess," James and Michael shared a secret smile that had me narrowing my eyes at her.

When Michael took my hand, his palm was damp and I thought I could feel him trembling. I stole little glances at him as we walked into the cemetery, trying to figure him out, but he kept his emotions closed to me. My mind flicked to the crypt, fear making a sudden appearance in my heart.

Don't worry, love. Think of something else—this is a day for happiness.

I took a deep breath, forcing myself to focus on his words, on his hand in mine. *You look very handsome,* I told him, sending a little smile along with the thought, trying to tease him out of his silence. He really was handsome in heather gray slacks and a white linen shirt open at the collar. I noticed he wore silver cufflinks that sparkled in the sunlight and the whale-tale charm I'd given him— Thor's hammer, I now knew it was called. Everything came full circle, it seemed. He glanced at me then and smiled, making my knees quiver. My stomach resumed its flips and for a second I thought I might be sick—but in a totally good way.

"Here we are!" Miri proclaimed when we came to a stop in front of the little stone angel that had long been a safe haven for Michael and me.

"Okay," I said for the millionth time that morning.

"Just wait," Miri said, bouncing on her heals and jiggling all over.

"What is it with you guys?" But James refused to meet my eyes, smiling at Miri instead, who was this constant excited mess. I waited for Michael's answer, but he only took my hands in his. I thought he'd look away, thought he'd be coy like the others, like he had been the whole way over here.

Instead he stepped nearer. "I love you, Desolation." His eyes were so warm, gold flecks swimming in sweet chocolate. "I have loved you always, from the moment I laid eyes on you so very long ago.

"I loved you when you were sent on your mission.

"I loved you when your path took you away from me and all I had was your memory.

"I loved you from the moment I saw you again in that classroom. From the moment I heard your voice, saw your eyes.

"I have loved you always. And I will love you always.

"You are the love of my heart, of my eternal soul.

"If you will have me, I will love you for as long as my heart beats, and I will do everything in my power to see that it never, ever stops."

He hadn't taken his eyes off mine and so I'd seen the truth there; felt it reflected in every possible way in my own heart. With his eyes still on me, he began to shine. Brighter and brighter he grew, the golden warmth of his Halo spreading through me, around me, embracing me, drawing me nearer, laying bare every emotion, every thought, every hope.

"Will you be mine?" he whispered against my lips.

How do you tell someone you love them as much as they love you? How do you tell them you would gladly give up your life today if it meant you wouldn't have to live an eternity without them?

I didn't know how, so I answered in the only way that felt right.

I filled my own Halo with all that I was—the old and the new, all the darkness, all the light—the rainbow of colors that was the good and the bad, every regret, every hope, and all my love. I closed my eyes and leaned into him, welcomed his lips on mine, gave myself to every sensation, the taste of him, the feel of him, the smell of him.

"Desi," he said in the softest whisper. *Open your eyes, my love.*

I didn't want to, but I did as he asked—and discovered a new scene entirely.

Color of every shade filtered through my vision, golden buildings rising in the distance. On the Bifrost, all around me, I found the faces of my friends, my loved ones. James and Miri, who looked a little stunned at the sudden change of scenery, Freyja, Lucy and Mahria, Fiahre and Longinus, Heimdall and Odin. Even li'Morl, Horonius and Helonius were there.

Odin stepped forward, reaching out for us. He took my hand, and Michael's. "My children." His voice resonated like a deep, golden song. "I believe we are waiting for your answer, daughter."

For a moment I panicked, suddenly unsure of the question.

Will you be mine? Michael repeated in my mind.

"Yes," I breathed. "Yes!"

"Of course it is yes." Odin's eyes sparkled. "Now at last, let it be as on Asgard, so also on Midgard.

"Desolation, you have accepted a calling to be guardian of Midgard. To stand at its defense against the forces that would seek to misuse it."

He paused and I nodded, unsure of his question.

"Michael, you have promised your eternal life to Desolation. Indeed, you made that choice so long ago I can scarcely remember." Some chuckled around us because everyone knew Odin didn't forget.

"Yes, my lord," Michael said, his voice hoarse with emotion.

"She has changed from the girl you once knew."

"Yes, Lord."

"Yet you would still renew your pledge to her?"

"Always."

"Of course," Odin said. Michael caressed the back of my hand with his thumb for a moment before Odin continued. "Are you willing to stand with her, to guard her and protect her while she serves my children on Midgard?"

Michael faced me, and I felt his smile before I saw it on his face.

"I gladly submit my life, my heart, my soul to her protection."

His mind lay bare before me, and mine to his. There were no words, but the emotion we shared—no words would ever suffice. Tears streamed down my face and his. Love shone from us like a star.

"Desolation." Odin waited until I pulled my eyes away from Michael's and looked at him. "You are a young god, with much to learn. At times the responsibility will seem too great to bear. You must remember, always, that Michael is your companion, your help-meet. Turn to him. Share your burden with him, and you will find yourself more capable of greatness than you ever could achieve alone. Do you understand?"

"Yes, Odin." I squeezed Michael's hand as I returned my gaze to his. As I felt myself swallowed up again in the power of his love. "We will rule Midgard together." Michael beamed at me, his image growing watery beyond the tears in my eyes.

"Then be one," Odin said. He placed my hand in Michael's and stepped back. "Be one."

Heimdall pressed his golden horn to his lips, announcing our union to the universe, to all the worlds. A sound filled my ears, a note of pure happiness, ringing across the Bridge, resonating through the space all around us. Rainbow sparks fell like rain while Michael pulled me into his arms and kissed me.

THIRTY-FOUR

DESI

M iri hugged me so tightly I wondered how she had ever grown so strong.

James pulled on the strap of her carry-on bag. "Come on bright eyes, we've gotta go." He tugged again, making Miri jerk back a little, but still she didn't let go of me. "You'll see her at Christmas."

I looked over Miri's head and smiled at James. *Come and get her*, I tried to tell him. He couldn't hear my thoughts, but he seemed to understand. He stepped forward and wrapped his arms around her waist and gently pulled her against him.

"Take care of her," he said to Michael who stepped up beside me and put his arm over my shoulders. "and don't forget to mail in that marriage certificate."

"You know I will," Michael said.

"See you soon, princess."

"See you soon, James."

He and Miri took a couple steps backwards, Miri waving like a crazy person, before James smiled one last time, pulled Miri after him, and with his arm around her, walked through the expedited security line.

We watched until we couldn't see them anymore. We left the building without saying any of the things in our hearts. We didn't need to.

Instead of driving to the apartment, Michael took us up the mountain, past St. Mary's, past Daniel's old estate. Up to the cliff overlooking Desert Peak where he stopped the car and we got out. I hadn't been back here since that night almost a year ago. The night all my nightmares were made of. I'd been afraid, I think. But now, with Michael's hand in mine, it seemed like nothing at all. The past was the past—what mattered was right now and all that lay before us.

We climbed over the railing and sat on the edge of the cliff, the sparkling lights of the city brightening the valley below.

"Look." Michael pointed to the lights of a plane flashing in the dark sky.

There they go, I thought, sending my wishes for love and happiness winging across the distance.

And then I returned my attention to this world whose future I now held in my hands. Michael bumped his shoulder against mine.

In our hands, he corrected.

Yes, I thought. *In our hands.*

THE END

Thank you for reading the Desolation trilogy.
I hope you loved it as much as I do.
An honest review on Amazon or Goodreads
would mean so much.

If you loved James & Miri,
check out
Desolation Diaries, vol 1-4

Also, if you haven't yet subscribed to my newsletter,
it's not too late! Join now and get
Sacrifice, a 30k word prequel to *Become* for free
alicross.kit.com/aliarchernl

ALSO BY
ALI ARCHER

DESOLATION
Sacrifice
Become (book 1)
Desolate (book 2)
Destined (book 3)
Desolation Diaries v. 1-3

MINNIE KIM: VAMPIRE GIRL
First Kisses Suck (Book 1)
Deadly Sweethearts (book 2)
Seoul Demon (book 3)
Blood Moon (book 4)
Den of Death (book 5)

THE EDEN PROJECT
Dragon Protocol

ACKNOWLEDGMENTS

This time, my readers really made a difference in how I wrote this book, how I felt about writing it, and how I felt about the story itself. I'll admit that for a long while I doubted the value of Desi's story because it was "too dark" or "too emotional" or too . . . whatever. But now I know that you get it. You get Desi. And for that there are not enough "thank you's" in the whole wide world.

Some amazing people have been involved in the nitty gritty of my writing life, and I'd like to thank them too . . .

My husband, David, for his unfailing support.

My critique group—Christine Bryant, Elana Johnson, Sara Oldes and Stacy Henrie.

My new (and holy-freakin'-cow-amazing) editor, Jen Hendricks.

Every member of the Indelibles, my amazing support group of indie authors who have cheered and encouraged me along the way (often pointing me in the right direction!).

And finally, a huge shout out to Dustin Hansen who gave Desi a face and is responsible for the beauty of *Destined's* stunning, original, artwork.

ABOUT THE AUTHOR

Ali Archer is the USA Today bestselling author of young adult fantasy and science fiction, including the Desolation series and the Minnie Kim: Vampire Girl series.

Ali's always loved science fiction and fantasy, as the first books she read were by such greats as Isaac Asimov, Ray Bradbury, and Lloyd Alexander. But when she discovered *Dragonriders of Pern* by Anne McCaffrey—a perfect blend of fantasy and science fiction—her own imagination was set aflame.

At eleven, Ali met Ms. McCaffrey in one of the single most illuminating moments of her life. When she told the eminent writer she wanted to be an author when she grew up, Ms. McCaffrey said, "Never let anything stand in the way of your dreams." Ali's been following that advice ever since.

Let's Connect!
www.aliarcher.com
www.Facebook.com/aliarcherbooks
www.Facebook.com/groups/AliCats
www.Instagram.com/aliarcherbooks

Subscribe to Ali's Newsletter & Get a Free Book!
alicross.kit.com/thiscreativelife